MW01134072

MONSTERESS

BOOK 1

C.K. FRANZISKA

Cover art and design by Getcovers

Imprint: Independently published

First Edition October 2023

MORE FROM C.K. FRANZISKA

A Speck of Darkness
A Speck of Dawn

Monsteress
Hunteress

TRIGGERS/CONTENT WARNINGS

Monsteress is a dark high fantasy with gothic vibes and dark world-building. The female lead in this series is cruel, domineering, and manipulative. She goes beyond my typical morally gray antihero and is, in my opinion, an actual villain who has a very disturbing past.

Triggers include:

- graphic violence

- rough and explicit sexual content

- forced proximity

- brutal injures

- betrayal

- graphic language

- trauma

- death

- murder

- intense violence

- graphic depiction of blood

- physical harm inflicted upon the main characters

- & more

Readers who may be sensitive to these elements, please take note, and prepare to enter Monsteress' world...

OCERIS

STARSTRAND

CRYMZON

TERMINUS

ESCELA

ETERNITIE

TENACORO

CONFINES

To all the readers who are done being the good girl; who are done doing what they are told; who are done waiting for someone else to save the day.

Be the villain of your story and own that shit!

GUIDE

Gods
Zorus
King of the Gods
Lunra
Goddess of the Moon and Love
Otyx
God of the Underworld
Aqion
God of the Ocean and Strength
Emara
Goddess of Vitality
Nelion
God of Destiny
Odione
Goddess of Wonders

Places
Crymzon

Queen Soulin SinClaret/Lunra
Terminus
King Keres/Otyx
Oceris
King Usiel/Aqion
Tenacoro
Queen Synadena/Emara
Starstrand
Queen Caecilia/Nelion
Eternitie
King Citeus/Odione
The Confines
Godless

<u>Names</u>
Soulin SinClaret
Queen of Crymzon
Father: King <u>Obsidian</u> (†)
Mother: Queen <u>Ria</u> (†)
Brother: Crown Prince <u>Felix</u> (†)
Moths: <u>Adira,</u> <u>Velda,</u> <u>Storm,</u> <u>Barin</u>
King Keres
King of Terminus
King Citeus Matrus
King of Eternitie
Sons: Prince <u>Cyrus</u> and Prince <u>Cyprian</u>
Daughter: Crown Princess <u>Catalina</u>
Queen Synadena Roja
Queen of Tenacoro
Daughter: Crown Princess <u>Opaline</u>

Son: Prince <u>Crystol</u>
King Usiel Oarus
King of Oceris
Queen: <u>Cleolia</u>
Queen Caecilia
Queen of Starstrand
Myra Eslene
Adviser of Queen Soulin
Wife: <u>Elia</u> (†)
Khaos Zedohr
Grand General of Crymzonian Army
Aemilius Vosdon
Outlaw
Liza
Outlaw
Devana
Outlaw
Father: <u>Wayne</u> (Blacksmith)
Jeremia
Trusted soldier of Crymzonian Army
Remy Cengor
Trusted soldier of Crymzonian Army
Conrad
King Obsidian's trustee
Lady of Fate
Destiny Forgeress. Oracle.
Blake, Kasen, Charli, Rene
Soldiers of Crymzonian Army

PROLOGUE

In a vast and empty void, a God named Zorus was floating aimlessly, feeling bored and unfulfilled. Gazing out over the vast expanse of the universe, he felt a sense of boredom creeping over him. For eons, he had ruled over all of creation, watching as the stars and planets came into being and witnessing the birth of countless civilizations.

But now, he felt a sense of ennui, as if the thrill of creation had faded and all that was left was the dullness of routine.

In a moment of inspiration, Zorus created six new Gods to rule over different aspects of an uninhabited planet. He reached out with his divine power, conjuring six glowing orbs of energy that swirled and danced before him. With a thought, he imbued each orb with a portion of his own power, crafting six new Gods from his own essence.

First, he created a God of the Ocean and Strength, Aqion, a mighty being whose realm was the vast waters that covered the surface of the planet.

Next, he created a God of the Underworld, Otyx, a dark and mysterious figure who ruled over the realms of the dead, and with the ability to wreak havoc on those who crossed him.

Then, he created a Goddess of Wonders, Odione, an intelligent deity with a vast and insatiable curiosity who would guide mortals on their path to create miracles with their bare hands.

After that, he created a God of Destiny, Nelion, a radiant being with the power to rule over the sky who would bring starlight and wishes to the world.

Then, he created a Goddess of Vitality, Emara, a playful and lively Goddess, with a fondness for all things beautiful and delightful.

Finally, he created a Goddess of the Moon and Love, Lunra, a graceful and mysterious figure who would watch over the night sky and embody the power of love.

With the creation of these six new Gods, Zorus felt his boredom dissipate, replaced by a sense of excitement and anticipation.

The new Gods quickly set to work, each taking up their mantle and beginning to shape the planet according to their will. The God watched with interest, knowing Escela would never be the same. And for the first time in a long while, Zorus, the King of the Gods, felt truly alive and engaged in the great cosmic game of Godhood.

ONE

AEMILIUS

Screams rip the air, and the metallic smell of blood rises into my nose.

I listen fearfully to the sounds of the soldiers outside, their metal armor pounding into the ground with each step. The shouts and screams, the gut-wrenching sound of swords cutting through flesh, and the crash of buildings being destroyed make me want to throw up.

My heart pounds in my chest the longer I stand there.

I know we have to stay hidden if we want to avoid being caught, but it's unbearable not to jump to action.

I look over at my beloved, who shakes with fear. I reach out and take her hand, giving it a reassuring squeeze.

"It's okay," I whisper. "We're safe here. As long as we stay quiet, they won't find us."

But Liza's eyes are filled with disbelief.

The sound of the soldiers getting closer makes me tremble. We're running out of time.

"What are we going to do?" she asks, her voice trembling. "They're going to find us. I know it."

I press my hands to my ears and shake my head to drive the pain-distorted faces of our neighbors out of my thoughts. We need a plan, but the commotion outside makes it hard to concentrate.

The moment is finally here.

I expected an attack from Monsteress, but now that the presumption becomes reality, I just want to jump on my horse and flee.

"Aemilius?" her petite voice penetrates into my consciousness and brings me back to reality. "We gotta get out of here."

I think for a moment, trying to clear my head, and then remember the plan that has been set in stone for months. "We don't have time to run. Hide as we practiced, and I will hold back the soldiers!" A slight push is enough to lead Liza toward our bed.

Our one-room hut is cramped, but it's the only shelter we have in the hot, arid climate. The walls are made of rough-hewn logs, and the roof is thatched with straw to keep out the sun.

Inside, the hut is stiflingly hot, and the air is thick with the smell of sweat and dust. There's a small bed in one corner, covered with a thin, threadbare blanket. In the center of the room, there's a small table and two chairs, and a few pots and pans are stacked in the corner.

I had been forced to flee my home because of family circumstances. I wandered the desert for weeks, searching for a safe place to settle. On the brink of collapsing, I had almost given up hope when I stumbled upon this small hut and a girl who offered me a place to stay. I had gratefully taken refuge inside. That girl was Liza, and since then, a year has passed.

Yet I know I can't stay here forever. But for now, it's a welcome respite from the scorching heat and the dangers of the outside world.

Liza grabs my hand and tries to pull me with her to get away from the bloodshed right outside our door. She struggles because I'm twice her size, and it feels like a child trying to move a boulder.

"I'll follow. I promise!" I pull her into my arms and press her delicate body against my chest.

Leaning down, my lips touch her forehead softly. As we part, I look down at her. Her eyes are still closed, hiding her shimmering blue irises as her blond, short hair tickles my face.

"Don't make a promise you can't keep," she warns, driving her hand over my stomach to my hip, where a sword belt rests with two scabbards with a short sword and a dagger. "May no God stand with you."

My gaze follows her as she moves across the room, and as much as I long to embrace her and hide with her, there's no time.

I take a deep breath to prepare myself for what's coming next while Liza crawls under our bed and disappears under a clay-covered trapdoor I had installed for this exact moment.

Down there in our camp, she can survive for days, if not months. I made sure of that. The rations of food, water, and candles are enough for both of us to last about two full moons.

Queen Soulin, also known as Monsteress, is one reason I set up camps under the huts of our village. Our rural community lies on the edge of Crymzon—Monsteress' kingdom—and has been attacked several times by her forces on their way to or from Crymzon. But no one has ever been killed—until today.

This bloodbath can only mean one thing: she's finally here to take us prisoner.

Queen Soulin exterminates entire villages and keeps some residents at her palace as trophies, just to dispose of them later and watch them die in agony. Or she uses them as servants until there's no more enjoyment left in seeing them wither under her power, and they choose to end their lives themselves.

Monsteress, that's what the inhabitants of my village call her, is a matchless name for her cruel nature.

I look again through the room, from the small, cluttered kitchen to the homemade wooden furniture and then to our small bed, to make sure Liza is safe and didn't sneak out to help me.

To my surprise, I'm alone.

Liza is no woman to cower from a threat and retreat, but no one with a sane mind is foolish enough to step in Monsteress' way.

The wooden latch creaks under pressure when I turn it to the side to open the door a hand's breadth to look out. The bright sunlight burns on my cornea as I lean in closer to take a glimpse of the carnage.

Just as my eyes get used to the light, I watch in horror as a soldier drags a woman through the village, her feet stumbling and scraping along the ground. She cries out in pain and fear, but the soldier pays no attention to her cries. He's on a mission, and he won't be deterred.

The woman he drags behind him, I know her. Her name is Anna, and she's the baker's wife.

Of course, I had heard the rumors of what the soldiers do with the inhabitants of other villages. That woman is in grave danger.

Anna begs and pleads with the soldier, trying to reason with him. But he's deaf to her words, and he only tightens his grip on her hair.

With a burst of strength, I wrench myself free from being frozen in place and am about to leap forward when a sword pierces into the wooden leaf just inches from my face.

Within the next breath, the door jolts open, slamming into my chest, forcing me to stumble back and almost lose my footing.

My instincts set in.

I grab the dagger and pull it out of the sheath instead of the sword.

I instantly regret my choice.

I point the little fighting knife at the attacker, knowing it's no match for the long sword he's holding.

The sun bounces off his metallic arm tiles and helmet, and under the silver chest piece, I recognize the dark red fabric—Crymzon.

Monsteress is really here.

Her entire kingdom is painted crimson. From the sandstone each house is carved from, over the trees that grow there, to her lush curls. Even the moon they pray to shines in crimson, and Lunra, their Goddess.

My body stiffens as I prepare for my first blow, but a blood-soaked blade penetrates the soldier's throat before I could move. His eyes widen in horror, and with a gurgling sound, he falls to the ground.

Behind him Devana appears, my neighbor's daughter.

Wayne, her father, works as a blacksmith in a small forge near the center of the village. The forge is made of stone and has an enormous fireplace where he heats the metal to be worked. He's a strong and skilled man, his muscles rippling as he pounds on the hot metal with his hammer, shaping it into the desired form. I'm used to the sound of the hammer striking the metal, filling the air, along with the occasional hissing sound as he plunges the red-hot metal into a bucket of water to cool it down.

Devana's father works tirelessly, his dedication to his craft is evident in the quality of his work. The villagers rely on him for all of their metalworking needs, and he takes great pride in being able to help them.

But his greatest accomplishment is his daughter, Devana.

As skilled as he is with metal and hammers, his daughter is with his swords and her footwork.

But before her father decided to pick up a hammer, he had been the best swordsman known to the village, and that might be the reason Devana is unstoppable with a blade. Plus, he's the only one who escaped Monsteress' deadly hands and still had a tongue to tell the tale.

Devana never went into detail about how he managed to get into the crossfire of the Queen, but she loves telling the story of how he escaped Crymzon without a scratch. Knowing that Devana and her father came from Tenacoro, the Kingdom of Warriors, I always wondered how he ended up in Crymzon but never had the courage to ask.

During my first week in the village, Devana tried to teach me sword fighting in return for completing the hiding place under their hut. It was a bitter lesson.

I wasn't born to bear a sword, and that was another reason I had to leave my home.

Devana, on the other hand, had been playing with blades before she took her first step, and it shows. Her leather pants and white shirt are soaked with blood from defending our village.

"Thank you," I choke out, my eyes still on the lifeless body in front of me.

"Where is Liza?" Devana asks, climbing over the soldier into our hut.

"She's in hiding."

I look over at our bed again.

"It's even worse than we imagined," Devana says, wiping the blood off the blade on her trouser leg. "There are not only Crymzonian soldiers out there, but also soldiers of King Keres. It looks like we're in the crossfire of the kingdoms."

"What are Keres' soldiers doing here in—"

But before I'm able to finish my question, a figure blocks the light in the doorway.

Another soldier dressed in red steps on the back of the Crymzonian soldier on the ground, forcing goosebumps over my body when the dead man's ribs cracked under the heavy weight of his armor. His face is splattered with blood, almost covering a deep scar on his left cheek, and his teeth make a crunching sound as he clenches them together, followed by a devilish smile.

"You must be the last," he grumbles, raising a hand, and everything around me turns dark.

TWO

QUEEN SOULIN

"**M**onsteress! Monsteress!"

The sound of people shouting carries through the windows into my ears. It sounds like the melody of a sweet lullaby.

People have given me dozens of names—Blood Queen, Crimson Queen, Unforgivable Ruler—over the last decade, but this word seems to have stuck with them.

At this point, I'm not sure if people remember my real name.

Queen Soulin SinClaret, Ruler of Crymzon, Protector of Lunra.

My father, King Obsidian, had named me the second he saw my burgundy hair.

He said I was sent by Lunra herself, born under a lunar eclipse followed by a blood moon. It's said that my silver freckles are tears of joy Lunra cried when she laid eyes on me for the first time.

A maiden stands nervously beside me, her hands shaking as she tries to brush out the wavy, long hair. I sit rigidly in my chair, my eyes staring straight ahead as I wait for the maiden to finish.

"Be careful, girl," I say, my voice filled with ice. "You don't want to mess up my hair. I have a very important meeting later and need to look my best."

The maiden nods, and I hear her heart pounding in her chest. She takes a deep breath and tries to steady her hands as she continues to brush my hair.

Every time she pulls the brush through, I wince and let out a sharp gasp.

"Ouch! You're pulling too hard," I snap. "Can't you be more gentle?"

The maiden's face flushes with embarrassment, and she quickly apologizes. "I'm sorry, Your Majesty," she says. "I'll try to be more careful."

A gasp forces me to raise my head, and I look into the reflection of the maiden's wide eyes resting on my head.

Quickly, I drive my hand through my thick curls, undoing the work she tirelessly tried to perfect.

Her slim fingers uncovered my *only* imperfection—a snow-white strand of hair—which is usually covered deep beneath my curls.

I hear her sigh again and glare at her through the reflection.

"What was that?" I ask through clenched teeth.

She immediately lowers her eyes to the ground, sinking into herself like a sack of potatoes, mumbling another inaudible apology.

I shake my head. "This is ridiculous. I can't believe I have to put up with this. You're dismissed, girl. I'll have one of the other maidens finish."

The girl nods, bowing her head in defeat as she backs away from me. She quickly gathers her things, tears streaming down her face.

I pick up a metal bell, the coldness cutting into my hand, and shake it until the ringing stings my ears.

The door bursts open, and a woman walks in, her face tense. "What do you want, you old crow?" she asks, coming to a halt beside me.

The maiden flinches at the way the new arrival addresses me, their Queen.

Her once short, dark hair is now long and streaked with white and gray, pulled back into a sleek bun, making it impossible to guess the original color.

Despite the signs of aging, the gray hair only adds to her charm, giving her a distinguished and elegant appearance.

I look up, and our eyes meet, a warm smile spreading across her face.

I can't help but notice the wrinkles etched around her eyes and mouth, the proof of the many years of laughter and joy she experienced before I was born.

I notice the way her dress hangs on her slim frame, the fabric draping elegantly over her body.

"Don't forget that you are older than me," I say, fixated on Myra, my closest advisor, deciding if I should punish her for those words. "This new maid is as useless as the last one. Go fetch me a new one and lock this one in the dungeon with the rest."

I wave my hand in the air as if I'm trying to strike a pasty bug out of my face and don't even dare to look at the girl again, who stands shaking behind me.

That's when she begs for her life like every other maiden before her. "No, please, Your Majesty. You got it wrong. I wanted to—"

I cut her off. "You think I'm stupid? That I'm unable to recognize frustration when I hear it?"

My eyes burn into the girl's face, but she dares not take her eyes off her feet, tears rolling from her cheeks to the floor.

"And stop damaging my floors. It takes an eternity to get these drops out of the stone."

I sigh and run through my hair again, the attached metal clips falling out which previously pinned my hair in place. The heavy strands now fall over my shoulders to my chest just the way I always wear my hair.

The girl starts to scream and fight back.

What else did I expect?

It would've been too nice if at least one of those poor souls would stop fighting me.

With a nimble hand movement in her direction, the sounds of her efforts to escape Myra's rough grip fall silent, and I comfortably devote myself back to my reflection.

The spell I used to silence her is so small that it doesn't need much of my energy.

Crymzon is imbued with magic. Every inhabitant born within the Crymzon Wall prays to Lunra, the Goddess of the Moon and Love, and can use magic.

But the magic isn't as breathtaking as everyone thinks.

It's enough to carry out everyday activities, to heal small wounds, or summon protective spells, but not enough to protect us from the attacks of other kingdoms and their armies.

Until the moment my subjects claimed I was the 'chosen one'—the child with red hair Lunra chose herself to lead and possess the lost magic of my ancestors and return the magic to Crymzon.

Such bullshit.

A sultry breeze blown in by the wind carries the sound of my name with it—Monsteress.

"Why do you have to be so... hateful in the morning?" Myra asks grumpily, standing in the doorway.

"I'm supposed to be sleeping right now. Daytime might be the time other kingdoms run their parts of the realm, but Crymzon is designed for nighttime when the moon shines upon us, and the stars grant us wishes," I mumble under my breath.

"You are the only one who can be bad-tempered on a day like this. You have another victory under your belt," she says, grabbing the bell. "Sadly, your army couldn't wait until nightfall to arrive. Your beauty sleep has to wait."

"*Victory?*" I laugh mockingly. "We only counter-attacked Keres before he could annihilate the village and take the inhabitants as prisoners. Now his warriors are free to find the next village, and we have more prisoners. I wouldn't call that a victory. And I certainly don't need beauty sleep."

"Well..." Myra's eyes study me. "You can't play this game with him forever. You have to attack him straight on."

"And I didn't ask you for your advice," I snarl, spinning around to meet her gaze. "Where's my new maid?"

Myra shrugs her shoulders. "I handed her over to a guard to take her to the dungeon. I asked him to fetch a new one, but I'm sure Khaos won't be very pleased to hear about another dismissal."

My jaw twitches when Myra says his name.

Khaos was raised inside the palace. Through pure determination, he worked his way up from a stable boy to a soldier and is now one of my closest advisors and my Grand General.

I get up, moving my shoulders to release the tension building up inside me. "I should hang you both. You starting to forget who you serve."

"I serve no one but Lunra," Myra laughs, stepping towards me, opening the first drawer of my vanity, and taking out a bronze clasp decorated with a red moth. She pulls some of my hair back and attaches the clasp.

I focus on the red moth and when I close my eyes, the face of a young man with a breathtaking smile and dancing freckles flashes before my inner eyes. His red, curly hair bounces frantically as he throws back his head to laugh.

Oh, Felix.

I blink a few times and gaze at my reflection, my eyes catching on the dark red silk stretched from my olive-colored shoulder over my chest to my right thigh. The corset on top of the fabric gives my curves the perfect squeeze.

King Obsidian, my father, would turn in his grave if he could see what has become of his daughter.

Queen Ria, my mother, and my father were on the Crymzon Throne for 432 years, and our subjects adored them. Every day, they showed their love publicly and had no fear of sharing it with everyone around them.

Felix SinClaret, the Crown Prince of Crymzon, was my older brother... and my soul.

Our lives were perfect...

Until I became their downfall.

Their executioner.

During the childbirth of the newest SinClaret member, my mother lost too much blood before she could even push the baby out.

My little brother never opened his eyes or took his first breath.

When my father called me to the throne room and told me I would never see my mother again, a magical impulse surged through me, killing both my father and older brother and every soul inside the hall.

And that's when my name, Monsteress, was born.

The same year, at thirteen, I was crowned Queen after I vaporized the entire throne room, leaving me the sole heir to the Crymzon Throne.

And with that, a new age began.

It's our tradition to reset time the moment a new heir claims the throne, and so King Obsidian 432 ended, and the age of Queen Soulin 1 began.

Besides Crymzon, there are four other kingdoms: Oceris, Tenacoro, Starstrand, and Eternitie, each wielding a specific element.

Thus, there was a balance between the elements and Kingdoms until, at sixteen, Keres entered the picture, forming his own kingdom in the north of our land with the lost souls of Ordinaries to do his bidding.

Most Ordinaries live in small villages between our territories after they rejected their elements and left their kingdoms.

It's rumored that Keres came into existence to bring the elements together to build a new empire under his command.

I'm not sure what to believe anymore. He already has more power than any of us. So why bother getting more?

In times when all our kingdoms should have come together to take him down, something drove a wedge between our kingdoms—fear. It drifts us further apart by the day.

But Keres isn't to blame for my family's death.

It was me.

After the magical impulse, I closed my vulnerable heart and swore that I would never love someone again. Erasing every weakness I have and putting my faith in myself instead of a Goddess who allowed my family to die, I changed the way my father used to run Crymzon.

I also vowed I would never call Keres a *king*, no matter what.

There can only be one lethal ruler, and that's me.

Myra was the one who found me amid what remained of my brother and father. She was my mother's maid and has been mine ever since the day my father died.

Meanwhile, we have arrived in Soulin 14.

"Soulin, did you hear me?" Myra asks softly.

I turn to her, and my facial muscles harden. "It's still 'Your Majesty' for you," I bark and walk towards the sandstone door.

She sighs. "General Khaos should be back any minute from the attack on the village. We must hurry to receive him in the throne room."

"If he's already back, that means Keres is moving his army closer and closer to our limits." The thought that he's only a half day's ride away from Crymzon constricts my chest.

I exhausted my army by countering his attacks. I had to pull them all back so they can rest in case he makes it to the Crymzon Wall.

"I already called a meeting with the council. The Council members will arrive after you receive our soldiers."

"How many times do I have to tell you I'm giving the orders?"

"And how often do I have to tell you that *you* don't have to do everything alone?"

I roll my eyes and stroll past her into the hallway.

The palace is made entirely of red sandstone, making it the most majestic and imposing sight of Crymzon. The red-tiled roof adds to the overall reddish hue of the palace, and the interior is equally grand, with high ceilings, intricate frescoes on the walls, and sandstone floors. Arched windows framed by intricately carved stone and elaborate stone doors are spread throughout the building.

My glass slippers click under my weight with each step as I head to the throne room.

As I walk through the palace' halls, the guards stand at attention, watching my every move.

My long, revealing, burgundy dress cascades behind me and I hold my head high, and my shoulders squared, just as my mother taught me.

I know what my subjects think of me.

The Blood Queen. The Unforgivable Ruler. Monsteress.

And even though I should be outraged over the whispers behind my back, deep inside, I dwell on the thought that people hate me.

That they fear me.

I'm not the Queen everyone expects me to be. I'm not loving and naïve, letting everyone walk all over me like my parents did.

I'm a force of nature no one wants to reckon with. And I'm the last royal member Crymzon will ever have once I'm done with my plan.

I will break the chain once and for all!

The guards, dressed in their finest armor, heel behind me, filling the halls with clanking metal and footsteps in unison, their swords at the ready.

I stride confidently towards the throne room, and as I enter, I feel the weight of responsibility on my shoulders.

The throne room is grand, the red hues of the walls glowing in the light from the high, red-tinted windows.

Fourteen years ago, another layer of sandstone was added to cover the blackened swirls my magic left behind after claiming its victims. It would have been wiser to leave the deadly trails of my family's dismay for everyone to see, but the reminder was too painful.

As I reach the dias of the throne, I turn around and pause for a moment, looking at the assembled nobles and courtiers.

Every single one of these fools before me has no clue what I'm planning.

Each of them cowers before me, their foreheads pressing against the warm stone, praying to Lunra that I won't harm them next.

I wonder what the word in the streets is that so many of my subjects decided to stay awake while the sun is still in the sky. Apparently, the entire kingdom is sleepless, from the citizens screaming my name through the closed windows to the ones I'm staring at.

Then, with a sense of determination, I climb the steps and take my seat on the throne.

The throne itself is a work of art, carved from a single block of red sandstone and decorated with images of moths.

As I sit, the stone melts against my thighs like warm wax, reminding me how it feels to be in charge.

But the feeling quickly subsides as the doors are pushed open, and the room fills with murmuring voices, footsteps, and metallic noises.

The man leading the new arrivals is tall and muscular, with black curly hair and piercing dark eyes. His face is tan from the burning heat of the desert surrounding Crymzon. A scar runs down the left side of his face, a testament to his bravery. Despite the scar, he's handsome with chiseled features and a strong jawline.

He carries himself with the confidence and bearing of a seasoned general, his posture straight and his gaze steady.

Even though his armor must have been polished after the battle, it's dented and scratched in places, but he wears it with pride, a badge of honor for the battles he fought for me and the enemies he defeated.

He looks around the room, his eyes taking in the assembled courtiers and nobles.

He's a man of action—I know Khaos all too well—and even though he grew up beside me, he's still not used to the pomp and ceremony of court life. But Khaos knows his duty as he stands before me, ready to present me with the spoils of his victory.

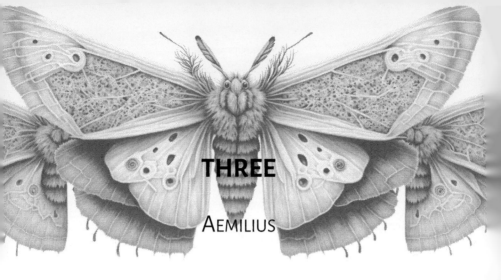

THREE

AEMILIUS

I groggily come back to my senses, my head throbbing from something that feels like a blow to my head. As my vision slowly comes back into focus, I find myself in an opulent hall, the walls and floors carved of rich red sandstone. Sunlight streams in through tall windows, illuminating the space with a warm, golden glow.

At first, I'm disoriented and confused, unsure of how I ended up in this luxurious setting.

But as my mind clears, I remember the soldier who had broken into our hut and had used a single-hand movement to take me out.

Bile rises in my throat as I realize he had brought me *here* against my will. The only place I tried to avoid, like the incurable sickness that had claimed countless lives just two years ago.

The Crymzon Palace!

I look around the hall, taking in the countless details. The ceiling is high and vaulted, with ancient carvings of moths and scenes of the lunar calendar held in place by stone pillars. The walls are lined with images depicting battles and royal courts.

My hands and feet are bound with ropes as I try to get up. I struggle against the restraints, but they're too tight to break free. I look around, hoping to find someone who can help me.

That's when I see her lying unconscious at my feet.

"Devana," I whisper, my gaze washing over two dozen bodies sprawled around us. "Devana! Please, wake up!"

She doesn't move.

Footsteps ring in my ears as a group of soldiers enter the hall. They're dressed in gleaming armor, their swords and spears glinting in the sunlight.

They march towards us, their faces hard and cold. Their boots thud against the stone floor before coming to a hard stop at the first body on the ground.

One guard reaches down and roughly grabs the shoulder of the prisoner who lay before him, shaking him awake. The prisoner groans and stirs, his eyes fluttering open when he's pulled to his feet.

My heart pounds as I recognize him.

It's our blacksmith, Devana's father.

The other guards hurry down the aisle, waking up prisoners in the same manner.

As I watch the guards, searching for any weaknesses, I see the fear and confusion in the eyes of my fellow prisoners as they're rudely awakened.

"Line up in a single file!" The guards bark at us.

It doesn't take them long to realize that we're unable to move with tied legs.

An icy shiver runs down my spine when a guard approaches me, holding a knife in my direction.

My heartbeat echoes in my ears.

I don't want to die.

Not here and not in front of Devana.

But instead of harming me, he lowers the blade, wedging it between my legs and the rope, and releases me with one cut.

"Get up, you lazy shit!" another guard yells.

The prisoners, my friends, obey, their movements sluggish as they shake off the effects of being knocked out and tied up.

My eyes search the hall.

There has to be a way to escape this madness.

Then, my eyes lock with Devana's, and I freeze.

She's nothing like Liza.

Devana is a vision of beauty, with long, flowing brown hair and golden brown skin. A slim face frames her delicate features, with full lips and radiant amber eyes. She has a slender, athletic build, with muscles from sword fighting in all the right places.

Looking at her now, Devana is in a sorry state.

She's dressed in tattered, dirty clothes, her hands bound tightly behind her back with ropes, and her face is bruised and battered from the ordeal.

But despite our situation, she holds her head high, her eyes blazing with determination.

She looks like a warrior, even in captivity, and even though she would never acknowledge it, she radiates a fierce strength that I fell in love with. She's not a woman to be trifled with, and I know she won't go down without a fight.

That's the moment I change my mind.

I can't leave her here.

And what if the guards found Liza? Or maybe they already did. Is she also here?

I need to find out.

Shakily, I stand up, making my way in her direction, but a guard stops me and pushes me into the line before I can reach her.

Once we're all lined up, the guards march, heading to a massive set of sandstone door panels.

The doors are pushed open, and I watch as the head of the line disappears from view, knowing that we're being taken to an unknown fate once we step over the threshold.

As we're pushed into the throne room, I'm overwhelmed by the vastness of the space.

The high ceiling is supported by massive columns, and the floor is made of polished sandstone.

I'm one of many prisoners being brought in, huddled together like scared sheep pressed against each other, escorted by an imposing army of guards.

When I finally tilt my head up at the Queen, I'm struck by her beauty.

Red, lush curls cascade down her shoulders, and her olive skin glows in the red light of the tinted windows. Green eyes pierce in my direction, her face covered with silver glowing freckles. She wears a thin red dress that hugs her curves in all the right places, leaving not much of her body to the imagination.

She looks like a Goddess, making it hard to rip my gaze off her.

I shake my head vigorously.

There's no way I will let this monster inside my head. She's heartless and the last person I want to look at.

The silence in the throne room is deafening, and the only sound is the distant metallic noises of the guards' armor.

The Queen sits upon her throne, surveying us with a cold, haughty expression.

Despite her beauty, I sense the cruelty within her. She is the Crymzon Queen, a ruler known for her ruthless tactics and bloodshed.

As one of many male prisoners standing before her, fear begins to creep into my heart.

I've heard what she does to male prisoners.

Public execution.

I'm not sure what happens to the women and children. But I've been told that they're never spotted again after being presented to her. So while she might not portray their deaths in front of an audience, I'm certain of their fate.

As I continue to look at her, I see a flicker of something else in her eyes. Something I can't put my finger on. It's only there for a moment, but it's enough to make me hold my breath.

The sound of an army behind us, their armor clinking as they stand at attention, makes me lower my head. I breathe through my mouth to remain calm, but it's difficult.

Without warning, a guard rams his elbow into my side, forcing me to my knees along with the other prisoners.

My body trembles as I watch Monsteress, awaiting her command.

She stares at us, her eyes sweeping over the group of prisoners as if we're nothing more than a pest.

"My Queen, I bring you news of victory," the man standing between us and Monsteress says, his voice loud and confident. "I've defeated our enemy on the battlefield and have brought you these prisoners as a sign of our triumph."

Suddenly, the Queen speaks, her voice cold and harsh. "These prisoners are weak and unworthy," she sneers. "I expected more from you, Grand General. You have disappointed me."

The general bows his head, his pride visibly deflated as he lowers his shoulders. "I apologize, my Queen. I'll do better next time."

The Queen waves her hand dismissively. "Take these prisoners away. You know what to do with them," she says coldly. "I want to see results from you, Grand General. Do *not* disappoint me again."

He nods, and someone violently pulls me to my feet, leading me away, our fate sealed.

The throne room falls silent as the guards open the doors again, ushering the pleading and crying men, women, and children away.

This can't be true!

I wrench my arm away to pull myself free, but a guard strengthens his grip around my arm, breaking my skin with his nails. "Stop it! If you escape, we're both dead!" he hisses into my ear.

But I can't stop.

There's no way I will let Monsteress win!

I need to get out of here!

I struggle with the guard, trying to wrench myself free.

The guard lets out a grunting sound when my elbow collides with his nose. He hunches over, splattering my arm with blood rushing from his nostrils.

"Seize him!" someone yells behind me as I break through the fearful crowd of my villager friends.

I will come back for Devana!

I will come back for all of them!

No one will die under my watch.

But first, I need to get out of here alive to save them. I need to get back to Liza to make sure she's okay.

A glimpse of light at the end of a grand hall gives me hope. My legs burn as I take off running, darting, and weaving through the columns and pillars that dot the hall.

I'm so close.

Boots hammer on the ground behind me.

A guard must have seen me and given chase.

He shouts for me to stop but I continue to run, my heart pounding in my chest.

I hear the guard's footsteps drawing closer with each passing moment.

Just as I reach the exit, the guard grabs me from behind, throwing me to the ground, before he kneels down on my chest.

"It's for your own good," he growls, pressing all his weight on me.

I push my tied-up hands against his face with all my strength, shifting my body beneath him, but before I can wiggle my way out underneath him, a sword handle comes flying down on me.

The last thing I remember is the ugly scar crossing the left side of his face before my surroundings blur and fade away.

FOUR

KHAOS

Summoned by Soulin, I return to the throne room after disposing of the new prisoners.

I carefully split the enormous size of captives into two categories: the most violent ones will spend their misery in the dungeon below the palace, surrounded by enclosed cells and guards, while I sent the others off to the prison outside the Crymzon Wall, slightly less guarded but yet secure.

They cannot outrun the guards' arrows in the leveled, outstretched desert landscapes if they attempt to break free.

So far, no one has tried to leave the prison, which means I'm good at picking the bad seeds from the crowd.

As I approach the throne room, Remy and Jeremia, my two most trustworthy guards, open the doors, and I give them a slight head bow in return to thank them.

"She's in an extra bad mood today," Jeremia whispers when I pass by.

"I got it from here," I growl back and walk through the open doors into the room.

I halt, waiting for the doors to shut quietly behind me before continuing.

My eyes wander over the dais up to the Crymzon Throne where Soulin sits leaning against the backrest. I scan her crimson dress clinging onto her like a second skin, the long slit drawing up so high that her thick thigh is visible, nearly to her hip, and then to the glass shoes discarded beside her on the ground.

If she took her shoes off, that could only mean one thing—things were about to get heated.

Slowly, she rises off the sandstone-carved throne and glides down the steps without taking her gaze off me.

My Queen doesn't need a crown to underline who she is. Her posture alone is enough to pick her out of a crowd as a royal, and her hair...only a SinClaret is blessed enough to resemble the most potent moon known to our kingdom—the Blood Moon.

"You took your sweet time," she teases as she reaches the last step, her figure silhouetted against the faint glow of light falling through the red-stained window behind her.

My heart pounds so loud in my ears that I can barely make out her words. Instead of answering, my eyes are glued to the shiny freckles on her face that get more visible with each step she comes closer.

"How can I be of service, my Queen?" I say, bowing my head.

The heavy armor prevents me from doing anything more.

If I had been given a chance to change into my palace attire, a blood-red leather armor, I would be more flexible and in less agony, sweating my butt off.

But instead, I didn't even have time to take a piss between the arrival and separation of the new prisoners.

"You know why I called you here," she drawls, sending goosebumps over my entire body.

I close my eyes, trying to swallow down the desire to touch her.

Like always, she's teasing me. But I make it too easy for her.

I force my eyes open, determined to stop her from playing with me, as a glint of metal catches in the light in the corner of my eye.

My reflexes take over, and I'm fast enough to shield my face with my arm, resulting in the sharp chain links to curl around the armor instead of my face. Then, without another thought, I press my other hand on the deadly weapon and pull on it.

Soulin fastens her stance as I yank on her metal whip. But I'm more robust, forcing her to stumble forward.

"I should've known you're armed," I hiss at her, releasing the chain, and Soulin whips her weapon back. "Why use that puny whip when you can destroy me with your magic?"

I scanned her wrists for the shimmering silver bracelet that usually coils tightly around her forearm, almost up to the elbow joint, like a serpent.

It wasn't there. I'm one hundred percent certain.

So how did I miss the delicate chains and sparkling jewels that catch everyone's eye without raising suspicion? Even though it looks like a seemingly harmless piece of jewelry, it's, in fact, a whip disguised as an accessory. Its slender form is embellished with intricate designs, adding to the illusion of a decorative piece rather than a weapon.

Her nose wrinkles when she smiles at me, showing off her white teeth. "What would be the fun in that?" she asks, her eyes flickering with fire. "I must ensure that my Grand General is always on his toes."

While Soulin is the most powerful sorceress in our Kingdom because of her link to Crymzon itself, she loves being armed. She's fascinated with whips in all shapes and sizes, and it slowly became her trademark known throughout the palace.

That's when I notice that the weapon she holds in her hand is longer and thicker than her go-to one.

But where did she hide it if not around her arm?

As if Soulin can read my mind, she pulls on the slit of her dress, revealing even more skin. "The new blacksmith is a genius. He made me a few new toys to test, and this beauty..." She lets the chain links slither behind her over the ground and drops the dress. "It fits perfectly under my dresses around my thigh."

Heat flashes into my cheeks.

I should have known she was hiding something in plain sight, but her bare skin made it almost impossible to keep my head straight.

Instead of falling for her tease, I step back to distance myself more. "I think you could use a little more training to better yourself. You missed my face."

Soulin huffs, and I expect her to attack again.

Instead, she drops the rounded metal handle and steps closer to me, leaving her new whip behind. "This is just a prototype I needed to test. I can't wait for you to experience the actual masterpiece."

The threat in her words is palpable, but I know Soulin.

She won't harm me.

I'm her first in command for a reason. And our history goes way further back than Queen and Grand General.

"I can't wait to test it with you," I smile back, and her eyes flicker at the challenge.

We have been playing this cat-and-mouse game since we were kids.

It started as harmless dares, like jumping into the courtyard fountain without getting caught or stealing a horse to ride through the desert for hours. With each year, the dares grew more extensive, and so did her beauty.

I would be a fool to think she doesn't know how I feel about her. I would jump through a circle of fire if she asked me to, and she knows it.

But that's where I draw a line.

As much as I want her to return my feelings, I know it will never happen.

Not because I'm the son of Crymzon's former stableman. Those social standings mean nothing in our kingdom. But Soulin promised me after her family's death that she would never be as weak as her parents. In her eyes, nothing makes you more vulnerable than love.

Soulin stops before me, and I feel her warm breath caressing my skin. "I need you to recheck the kingdom for any dead bodies."

My mind snaps back into place. "I sent my guards to search the kingdom just a moon ago. There wasn't a single trace of bad blood anywhere."

Her eyebrows draw together. "There has to be. I can feel it."

It's impossible. Not only did I send most of my soldiers to search the kingdom from top to bottom, but I also helped. I would know about it.

"I'll see to it, my Queen," I answer, knowing it's not my place to argue with her.

Something tells me there's more she isn't telling me.

Everyone knows the tale that a corpus on the ground of Crymzon can corrupt the magic seeping through the ground into its citizens.

However, no one wants to test that theory.

Therefore, every person dying inside the Crymzon Wall is carried outside and burned in the pits. Only then can the soul be released from their body and reclaim their freedom to be reborn.

So why is Soulin so fixated on finding the source of the fading magic when the cause is simple?

Since the death of the royal family, Soulin hasn't worshiped Lunra once. And without the Goddess's favor, Crymzon is just a piece of land, like the rest of Escela.

Soulin steps back, and her golden-green eyes search my face. "What are you waiting for?"

I straighten my shoulders. "It's not my place to advise you, my Queen, but when will you lead a ceremony again in the cathedral? Your subjects haven't seen you in years, and with the fading magic, I think it would be a good time to make amends with Lunra and regain her mercy."

She bends down to pick up her whip. "You're right. It's not your place," she snarls back.

"Please consider," I whisper before bowing my head to leave. "You're father would be proud to see you take over his position before Lunra."

Her scoff brings me to a halt. "I'm nothing like King Obsidian," Soulin says, curling the metal links around her bare thigh, and it takes everything out of me not to stare. "His reign might have been peaceful and filled with strong sorcery, but my father was foolish. He made the whole Soulmate scheme up to chain my mother to his side to produce heirs while he played around with his whores. And because of his misguidance, he put the image into my mother's head that it was acceptable to have a Starstrandian lover, knowing that the child would mean her death. Now tell me, where was Lunra to guide her away from the path she was taking? When did Lunra intervene with my father's delusion that *love* means sharing intimacy with everyone freely? Neither my father nor Lunra deserve the respect everyone gives them."

I turn her words over in my head again and again. I understand her fury toward her father and why she feels Lunra has forsaken her.

Yet, no one suffered under King Obsidian.

There was plenty of magic for everyone to go around, and his subjects adored the ground he walked on.

"If you do nothing, Crymzon's magic will be the least of your worries," I answer truthfully.

I didn't come here to upset her.

On the contrary, I couldn't wait to be in the same room as her again just to see her lips curl into a vicious smile.

But as her Grand General and advisor, it's my duty to make her aware of the whispers going around in her kingdom.

A few months ago, I encountered a mother with her newborn on the street while searching the grounds for any sign of a decomposing body. She approached me wearily and told me her magic was drained from giving birth, which never happened before while delivering her other three children. She cradled her baby against her chest while she held onto my arm, begging me to help her find her magic.

But how could I?

She wasn't the first to initiate a conversation about the weakening magic, but her encounter stuck with me the most.

"What are you implying?"

I take a deep breath. "Your subjects are losing the ability to use magic." I pause for a moment, trying to find the right words. "More and more citizens seek the guards' help to find the cause. It's just a matter of time until they stop searching for the fault in themselves and start pointing their fingers at others."

The silence brewing between us is more potent than any words. Soulin is either building up an intelligent response to debunk my statement, or she's about to rip my head off.

"How many?" she asks, catching me off guard.

"Pardon me?"

"How many people have approached you already?"

I press my lips together, contemplating if I should tell her the truth.

She grabs my arm, her nails scratching over the shiny metal, forcing me to speak up. "About a dozen."

Soulin releases me, spins on her heels, and marches toward the throne. "I'll take care of it," she says, her voice as confident as ever.

Wordless, I bow my head again, knowing she won't see my dismissal.

The other guards think I'm a fool for trusting the Queen, especially since more and more soldiers started questioning her capability to run a kingdom after their magic disappeared.

However, I can't leave her.

Besides Myra, I'm the only person who knows the real Soulin, and I will fight until the bitter end to gain that version of her back.

Until that day comes, it's my job to guide her in the right direction and serve as her good conscience.

In addition, I have the responsibility of voicing the citizens' concerns.

Despite being raised in the palace under my father's eagle eyes, I was born a subject under King Obsidian. I stand with one foot in the royal world, the court, while my other is positioned in Crymzon, a small two-story sandstone building where my mother birthed me and my father still resides.

"You're still here," Soulin growls from the throne, snapping me out of my thoughts.

My gaze falls on her one last time, and my eyes fall on her lips, curled into a teasing smile before I spin around to gather my soldiers for the search.

That smile.

That woman.

She will be the death of me.

FIVE

Queen Soulin

"Your Majesty. The Council is waiting for you in the mirror room," Myra says, standing behind me as I come to a halt in front of a door.

I glance over my shoulder at her and rest my palm on the warm rock doorknob. "Did everyone come?"

"Of course! They're waiting for you to take your seat first before entering. I sent out word two nights ago. What a coincidence that Khaos returned on the same day."

What a coincidence indeed.

I shrug my shoulders and push the doors open, disregarding the attempt of the guards to open them for me.

The mirror room is a spacious chamber with walls entirely covered in broad, red mirrors.

Everyone thinks I equipped this room with mirrors to stare at myself, but that's not the case. In the reflections, it's easy to spot any threat. If a Council member just shifts his weight, I can check the mirrors for weapons.

I walk confidently, my heels clicking against the polished floor. As I move deeper into the room, the mirrors reflect my every angle.

At the center of the chamber stands a vast, round stone slab table surrounded by shiny silk-covered chairs.

I take my seat on the biggest chair, and the Council members file into the room, taking their seats around me. The room is filled with the indistinct murmur of conversation as they greet each other and prepare for today's agenda.

I wait patiently, my hands resting on the smooth surface of the table.

As the last Council member takes his seat, I raise my palm to silence the room. They fall quiet, their eyes focused on me as I speak.

"My dear Council members," I say with a clear voice. "We have much to discuss today. Let us begin."

A chair scrapes loudly over the ground, and all eyes are on the man with a mustache as he rises to address me. He's dressed in a leather suit, with a vest and pocket watch, and a pair of goggles sit on his forehead. His mustache is neatly trimmed and well-groomed, giving him the vibe fitting to his kingdom.

As he stands up, he adjusts the goggles on his forehead and clears his throat. I look at him with a mixture of curiosity and interest, wondering what he has to say this time.

I don't have to wait long until his confident voice fills the room. "I expected to find you alone, Queen Soulin, to address the matter of the Connection Ceremony."

The other members of the Council listen attentively, and my eyes flicker to Myra, then back to the man.

"I must apologize, King Citeus, for the misunderstanding. I assumed I made myself perfectly clear in the response letter that I would never settle for the second best," I say, trying to push down the disgust of his offer.

"My son, Prince Cyprian, is far more than my third born. Since the tragic death of his brother, Goddess Odione blesses his soul—" He raises his head to the sky, closing his eyes for a brief moment before continuing. "Since Cyrus' death, Cyprian will be next in line for succession after his sister Crown Princess Catalina."

"My condolences. I remember like it was yesterday when you offered me the hand of your oldest son. What a shame he died. But I would rather have your daughter as my Soulmate than one of your boys," I respond with a firmer voice, watching his eyes widen with my implication.

"But, Your Majesty, he's already completed his first wonder of a new invention to become a man just as our Goddess expects of him," King Citeus says, puffing up his chest.

King Citeus is part inventor, part engineer, and part mad scientist.

Our land, Escela, is divided into six sections with five kingdoms.

While Crymzon, my kingdom, is in the far southern part of the land and led by Lunra, the Goddess of the Moon and Love, King Citeus rules over Eternitie, the Kingdom of Gadgeteers and Tinkerers who worship Odione, the Goddess of Wonders. His land is rich in natural resources, as the kingdom sits upon a small mountain range. And they need it for their inventions.

My kingdom is flat, dry, and hot, carved into a bowl of red sandstone. Crymzon isn't unresourceful, but our biggest trading item is the silk we spin from our moths.

I scoff. "That might make him a man in your kingdom, but I have no desire to bed a man half my age, which makes him, in my eyes, a boy."

I'm exaggerating, but who cares? All his children are older than me, yet I couldn't resist firing another shot at King Citeus.

He swallows, narrowing his eyes at me. "I can't offer you my firstborn. It's unheard of for two rulers to accept a Connection Ceremony. And she's a...girl. I'm not going against tradition."

"And I never asked you to break one on my behalf. Goddess Lunra will not accept a Connection Ceremony if the person is not my Soulmate. And finding a Soulmate as a ruler while we're facing a war against an unknown entity is quite impossible. Once our kingdoms are safe, I will begin my preparations to find my Soulmate. Until then, I will reconsider your proposal."

"If there are any individuals left after your bloodshed," a firm female voice says, and I avert my eyes to meet Queen Synadena's.

My eyes scan the beautiful woman, the Queen of Tenacoro, as she fills the room with her presence. A green beaded, form-fitting dress brings out the dark skin tone of her kingdom. She wears a crown made of green beads on her head, and her long and lustrous hair curls down her back in a stunning display.

"Excuse me?"

"I said, if there are any people left after your bloodshed," Queen Synadena repeats, holding my stare.

King Citeus bows hastily and scrambles to his seat to get out of the crossfire.

Queen Synadena is the ruler of Tenacoro, the part of the land with fruitful trees and rich plants to make medicine. Freshwater surrounds her kingdom through rivers blessed by Emara, Goddess of Vitality.

She's also the only ruler who can—and will—stand up against me. Queen Synadena is fierce and the most loyal trading partner to Crymzon.

She raises from her chair, facing me straight on. "Queen Soulin, I don't think it's a secret that you have been attacking harmless villages of the Confines. Those Ordinaries shouldn't be your target."

"Did I find your soft spot? Lawless and godless people who fled from our kingdoms to outrun their duties. I didn't know you cared so much about them."

"I don't. But—"

"Queen Soulin is doing us a favor. If my spies are correct, the man who calls himself King Keres is a necromancer," says a woman with white wings protruding out of her shoulder blades.

If there's a person to portray the complete opposite of me, it's Caecilia, Queen of Starstrand.

She's beautiful and radiant, with a gentle demeanor. She has long, flowing blond hair and piercing gray eyes. Instead of a dress, she wears a battle chest piece with a flowing white skirt. Soft, ethereal light surrounds her, and a serene expression covers her face.

Nelion, the God of Destiny, shines upon her, making Starstrandians the luckiest people in the land.

"That's an outraged accusation, Queen Caecilia," King Citeus says, throwing his hands into the air.

"The same rumors are spreading through my kingdom like seaweed," another man says, flexing his brown, muscular chest.

My eyes rest on the last of the rulers at the table, Usiel, King of Oceris.

The underwater kingdom, just below Starstrand, is the only one I've never been to. Aqion, God of the Ocean and Strength, gives them the ability to exchange their fins for legs once on land. And strength is exactly the right word you think of when you look at Usiel.

I press my lips together, trying to come up with a new plan. "Is that so?"

My animalistic spies also offered the information that King Keres could be a necromancer.

But that was weeks ago and now old news to me.

"Keres isn't strong enough to attack any of the kingdoms. Not yet. That's why he is feasting on the villages to raise an army. We can't let that happen," I say, rising from my chair to look into the concerned faces of the council members.

"Upset that he is playing with your toys?" Queen Synadena asks, smirking at me.

I raise my eyebrows. "Actually, I have the pleasure of playing hide and seek with his army to counter him before he can claim a village. Did your spies not inform you of that?"

The room falls silent for a moment, but I see the flicker of amusement washing over Queen Synadena's face before it disappears.

King Usiel taps with his fingers on the table. "So, what's our next move?"

"Our next move?" I tilt my head in his direction to meet his deep brown eyes. "I have seen none of your kingdoms move against the north yet, while my dungeon fills up with Ordinaries waiting for their end."

Queen Caecilia shrugs her shoulders. "But why should we act? After all, you are the most powerful ruler. Can't you say a spell, sending him and his army back where they came from?"

King Citeus leans closer to Queen Caecilia, but his attempt to whisper fails. "You know Queen Soulin is powerless until she completes the Connection Ceremony. Until she fulfills Lunra's request to find her Soulmate, her powers are slim to none. That's why I offered her my son."

My hand hurts as I bang it on the table, sending a throbbing pain rushing through my arm. "And I told you that the son of yours will never be my Soulmate. Just because you decide it will work doesn't mean he's the one! And you, Queen Caecilia, not everyone is able to rid themselves of their husband if they feel like it."

The Council members lower their heads.

This is even a new low for me. Queen Caecilia lost her husband and her daughter within a day and acted like nothing happened.

While my loss turned into hatred, hers turned into ignorance, and I can't tell which is worse.

Rubbing my forehead, I continue. "Keres is a threat to every single one of us, not just Crymzon. Or do you think he builds an army just for fun? What is he planning? And where in all seven Gods' names did he come from? Aren't you a bit concerned?"

I watch as the other rulers cringed under my words. Their reaction doesn't surprise me.

I watched the Kings and Queens rule over their territories for years and until now, I haven't given them the satisfaction of muddling in my business. As long as I keep the trading going and don't attack their citizens, they turn a blind eye to whatever I'm doing behind my crimson-red sandstone walls.

The old Crymzon used to be the most powerful kingdom in the land thousands of moons ago. I didn't need a reminder of how weak I am against my ancestors. The magic surrounding my land is getting weaker and weaker with each moon.

But Eternitie offers weapons and inventions the other kingdoms can only dream of.

The citizens of Starstrand are born with wings and are the only airborne army in Escela.

Tenacoro is the home of the most fierce and lethal warriors on foot, and Oceris soldiers can walk on land and fight underwater with the help of their fins and sea creatures.

I have never seen the kingdoms with their full potential.

At only twenty-seven years of age, I'm the youngest ruler by three centuries. Queen Caecilia is the closest to my age, while Queen Synadena is the oldest by another four centuries.

"What do you want us to do? There hasn't been a conflict in over a thousand tides. And now you expect us to send our untrained armies into a battle against a mad necromancer?" King Usiel asks, continuing to tap his fingers against the warm, stony surface.

"How about we all take a moon or two to think about the matter and return with suggestions?" Myra cuts in, who had been standing by the door silently.

"Why is she allowed in here?" King Citeus snarls, looking her up and down, shifting in his seat.

"I suggest Starstrand for the next Council meeting," Queen Caecilia says, wiping sweat off her forehead with her fragile-looking hand.

"If there is something worse than burning to death in Crymzon, it's floating thousands of feet above the ocean," King Citeus mumbles.

"Starstrand, it is," I agree, just to see the King squirm for one more time before his departure.

As the meeting draws to an end with my last words, the Council members rise from their seats, bowing to each other before filing out of the mirror room.

I remain seated, my eyes lingering on the sandstone table before me.

The room clears of shuffling feet and flapping fabric. But when I look up, I notice emerald green eyes piercing at me.

"Your parents were my dearest friends, and that's the only reason I feel the need to speak up. Whatever you plan on doing with the prisoners, rethink it. Crymzon used to be filled with laughter and the sound of love every time I visited it. Now, it's a shadow of what it used to be. I'm truly sorry about what happened to your mother and how…the way your father's and brother's lives ended. But it wasn't your fault. You—"

"I killed them. How can it not be my fault?" I interrupt Queen Synadena.

"You were a child with uncontrolled magic. It was a tragedy. Something no child should ever go through." She cups my face, stroking her thumb over my cheek, searching my eyes. "Your subjects need you. They need you to be the Queen your kingdom deserves, the one you're meant to be. Not the cruel façade you want everyone to see."

The thought of my brother burns another deep hole in my heart.

I'm nothing like him.

I was only supposed to be the spare.

The second born.

The princess that doesn't deserve to sit on the Crymzon Throne.

I curl my fingers around her hand and pull it away. "You know nothing about me. My parents were weak. My father trusted everyone blindly, and that's why my mother had to die. He should have never let her have a Starstrandian lover. He knew her body wasn't created to bear a winged child. If my father had an ounce of pride, he would have ended his own life, knowing that it was all his fault," I growl, stepping back. "While I truly appreciate your loyal support, you're stepping out of line. I'm not a child anymore."

"In my eyes, you'll always be little Princess Soulin SinClaret," Queen Synadena says with soft eyes before she turns on her heels and strolls out of the room, leaving me behind.

Something catches my attention in the corner of my eye, and I turn around to face Myra.

She rushes over to me. "Well, the meeting didn't go as well as expected, but at least it's a start."

"Not now, Myra," I whisper, building myself up to my full height, my eyes fixed on my loyal subject and advisor.

She stands before me, her face etched with concern and sadness.

"My Queen," she says, her voice low and urgent. "I must speak with you about the situation at hand. The kingdom is on the brink of collapse, and we must do something to turn the tide."

I exhale sharply. "What do you suggest?"

Myra hesitates, her eyes troubled. "I fear that there's only one course of action that will save the kingdom," she says, her voice measured. "Find a Soulmate to gain your powers, and then we must go to war. It will be a difficult and dangerous path, but it's the only way to protect our people and our land."

"I can't. You know, I can't," I mutter, flaring my nostrils.

"At least, try. I'm surprised the Council hasn't noticed your hair yet. Or maybe they did and don't know what it means. If you keep going down the path you're on right now, you won't make it to the battlefield." Myra's face is distorted in pain, her eyes washing over my hair.

I look around the room, taking in the countless reflections of myself that fill the space.

As I approach the mirrors, my curls bouncing with each step, I notice a small white patch of hair among my lush red curls. I frown and reach up my hand to touch the spot.

She's right.

The appearance of this white patch is a troubling development.

I lean in closer, examining the white hair more closely. It's small and inconspicuous, but it's definitely there and has gotten bigger since this morning.

A wave of concern washes over me.

Maybe I don't have as much time left as I thought to execute my plan.

My mind races as I turn away from the mirror.

I cannot allow anything to mar my perfect appearance. I have to get rid of the white before it becomes more noticeable.

As I walk, I consider my options, my mind working quickly. "Bring me a bowl of red sand and water. And no one, I mean *no one*, can know about this," I demand, coming to a standstill before Myra.

"But Soulin—"

My ice-cold stare is enough to shut Myra up. "And let the guards know I want a selection of male prisoners sent to my room. Don't disappoint me! Oh, and one more thing," I add before storming out of the mirror-covered room to get to my chambers. "If you bring up Soulmates one more time, I will execute you publicly."

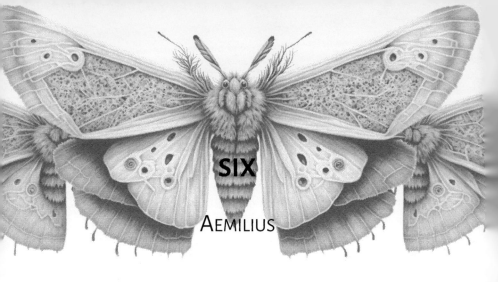

SIX

AEMILIUS

I find myself in a dimly lit dungeon made of sandstone, huddling in the corner of a damp and musty cell. The air is thick with the stench of mold and mildew, and the sound of dripping water echoes off the rough-hewn walls.

My wrists and ankles are shackled with heavy chains, and I'm clad only in my long bloodstained clothes that provide little ease against the heat of the underground chamber.

As I look around my cell, I see other captives in nearby cells, all of them emaciated and wearied by their captivity. Some of them are asleep on the blazing stone floors, while others sit quietly in their chains, staring off into the darkness.

I try to move, but the shackles restrict my movement, and I fall back against the wall with a clank of metal on stone. A wave of despair washes over me, knowing that I'm trapped in this horrid place with no hope of escape.

Suddenly, the rambling sound of boots thundering through the dungeon catches my attention, followed by a scraping noise of a heavy iron bolt sliding back. The door creaks open, and a guard enters, holding a torch in one hand and a whip in the other. He's a tall, muscular figure dressed in armor.

I peer at the whip, contemplating if I can snatch it from him and use it as a weapon, and choke when I see blood dripping off of it.

The guard sneers at me, his face distorted with disgust. "Get up, you filth! It's your time to shine."

My mouth is too dry to get a word out, my lips cracking from heat and dehydration.

I have no choice but to obey.

He leans down to my feet, driving his hand over my chain, and with a clicking sound, they fall to the ground before he drags me out of my cell and down a narrow, winding passageway.

Is it already my turn to die?

As I'm led through the sandstone corridors of the palace, the smooth walls shining in the dim light, the guard holds a tight grip on my arm.

We pass various servants and guards, who cast curious glances at me, and I lower my head to escape their stares. The sound of the guard's armor squeaking with each step echo off the walls, and the smell of incense fills the air.

My heart pounds in my chest, and I can't help but feel a sense of fear and anticipation.

Trying to lift the mood, I speak. "Is it custom in your kingdom to incarcerate helpless people who want to live in peace?"

"Be quiet," the guard snarls back, rounding a corner.

"I just want to understand," I mumble, trying to coax some information out of him. "We're useless to the Queen, and don't bother anyone."

The mountainous man pulls on my shirt, lifting my feet off the ground. "If you have to live in the Confines, some dirt must be sticking to you."

He uncurls his hand, and I drop to the ground, shaking.

Monsteress' guards are smarter than they look, I have to give her that, but it also shows me I have to be more careful.

Abandoning the idea to get more out of this hateful man, I'm relieved when he finally stops in front of a pair of ornately carved stone doors and knocks loudly. A voice from within commands him to enter, and the guard opens it, leading me into a chamber.

This isn't the place I imagined finding myself.

The room is filled with the soft glow of candlelight, and the *monster* sits in a chair at the far end of the room, surrounded by two maids. She regards them coolly, her eyes scanning me from head to toe before she turns back around, her back facing me.

The guard bows low and releases my arm, leaving me to stand before the Blood Queen herself.

Whatever tales the villagers have spun about her, Monsteress is a beautiful woman with long, red flowing hair and a regal bearing.

I clench my fists to stop myself from staring longer at her bare skin and lower my head to look at my feet.

Another knock sounds at the door, followed by more footsteps entering the room.

"Get on your knees!" a man snarls behind me, pressing all his weight onto my shoulders until my knees buckle and I collide with the hard surface beneath me.

My body aches, making it almost unbearable to stay in that position.

More prisoners are lined up beside me, forced to their knees by the guards, and I find myself, shoulder against shoulder, awaiting Monsteress' command—again.

My stomach turns when I hear the scraping noise of a chair. I don't dare to raise my head to meet her gaze. Seeing her feet entering my view is enough to send a cold shiver down my spine.

The prisoner to my right trembles when Monsteress speaks, her voice cold and emotionless. "Which one of you has done a Connection Ceremony before?"

A mumbling sound escapes the throat of the man to my left.

"Take him," the Crymzon Queen says, and the man lets out a gut-wrenching scream when a guard grabs him by the shoulders, dragging him out of the room.

The trembling beside me intensifies, and the smell of urine creeps into my nose.

"And that one, too."

I close my eyes and press my lips together as I ignore the screams of the man on my other side being taken away.

"Does anyone else want to leave the room before we get started?" She asks, moving in and out of my view before she comes to a standstill before me. "Look at me!"

Her voice cuts through me like a knife through flesh. I feel her eyes burning into my skin, and slowly, I lift mine to meet her gaze.

Her irises are golden-green and sharp like broken glass. Her lips curl into a tight smile before she moves on to the next prisoner, leaving me staring at the tall ceiling.

What does she want from us?

It takes a few moments before she stands before me again, and my heart stops as she points her finger at me. "This one," Monsteress says before she directs her finger to another man. "And that one over there."

My limbs tingle as I listen to the guards removing the unwanted prisoners.

She picked me.

Me!

But for what?

Monsteress builds herself up to her entire height in front of me. "Stand."

I hesitate, my heart pounding so hard that it feels like it's about to jump out of my chest.

I know I must obey, but anger coils inside of me, making me shiver.

Reluctantly, I rise off the ground and take a step forward. It takes all my willpower to force myself to look at her. I'm immediately struck by the Monsteress' cold, hard stare, and I sense the malice and hatred emanating from her body.

I'm in great danger, but I have no choice but to continue.

The Queen smiles wickedly and raises her hand, preparing to strike me. It's more of a reflex than intention when I grab her by the wrist, stepping closer to her to remind her who I am.

But to her, I'm nothing. I'm no one.

I'm a slave, just like the man cowering on the floor beside me. I'm filth under her bare feet, a thorn in her eye.

My life flashes before my eyes as I tighten my grip around her.

Meeting her gaze is already a violation, punishable by death—if the villagers are right. But that's nothing compared to what I've done.

My fingers burn, sending an unbearable pain rushing through my veins, and I stumble backward, releasing her wrist.

She will kill me.

I blink a few times to ensure I'm seeing right. Instead of using her magic to instantly kill me, her ruby-colored lips curl into a smile, showing white impeccable teeth. "What do they call you?"

I cock my head.

A faint smile lingers in her eyes as she reaches for the wrist I just touched. "Are you mute, or do you have a name?"

"Aemilius Vosdon," I counter.

"*Your Majesty,*" Monsteress says, and I blink. "For you, it's *Your Majesty* or *Queen Soulin.* I know you might not believe in rulers and Gods, Aemilius Vosdon, but I will fix that. So why would a man flee from Eternitie?"

"Why would you think I'm from Eternitie, *Monsteress?*" I spit out the last word like it's venom.

She doesn't even flinch.

Instead, her smile deepens as she walks around me, studying me like a pig for slaughter.

"You have a lot of nerves, I give you that," she whispers over my shoulder, sending ice down my spine before she comes back into view. "You don't have wings, clearly, so you can't be from Starstrand. Your skin is too light to belong to Tenacoro or Oceris, which leaves me to believe that Eternitie is your home. Am I right?"

My breath quickens. "Actually, Crymzon is my home," I say, holding her stare.

She shakes her head so faintly it's hard to notice.

But I do.

She looks me up and down again and then releases me from her invisible shackles by looking over at the other slave. "And you?"

A man I have never seen before still presses his forehead to the ground. He's not from my village, that's for sure.

"Eternitie, Your Majesty," he says with a muffled voice.

"Get up and look at me when I talk to you!" Monsteress shouts, and the man jumps straight into the air. His body shakes violently, and his knees buckle the second he lays eyes on the Queen.

Her nostrils flaring, she steps closer to him. "Why did you flee?"

"I...I wasn't meant to be a gadgeteer. I wasn't able to discover a new invention after trying it for over one hundred years, so I left. I swear, I had no other choice, Queen Soulin!" He crawls over the red ground to her feet and begins kissing them.

I can't take my eyes off him.

It's like watching a storm unfold right in front of me, and instead of running, I just stand there, waiting for the blast to hit me.

It didn't come as a surprise when Monsteress lifts her foot to kick him right in the face. But the blood splattering over the ground is.

She kicked the poor man hard enough to bust his lip.

She looks at her foot in distaste as if she's looking for any blood residue on her skin.

Then, with a boom in her voice, she says, "If you touch me again, I will make sure there is nothing left of you to send back to Eternitie."

My blood chills.

She wants to send us back to where we came from?

I can't go back to my home.

"Why are you doing this to us?" I ask, kneeling beside the man to check his injury.

"*Your Majesty,*" she barks, and I rise to my full height.

"*Monsteress.*"

Her eyes turn into slits.

"Guards!" she yells, and the door flies open immediately. "Take those prisoners away from here, but keep them separate from the others. You know what to do with the rest."

She flings her hair over her shoulder, turns on her heels, and walks away from us.

I take a step forward, but a guard blocks my way, shielding the Queen. "What are you going to do to the others?"

"Why does it concern you? You get the chance to see another night. Isn't that enough?"

Another night.

I totally forgot that Crymzon bustles with citizens at night and looks like a ghost town during the day. Everyone tries to hide from the blazing heat whenever they can.

"I have friends down there. You can't harm them."

"And you can't tell me what to do."

I ring with myself for the moment and say the words I thought I would never use toward the Crymzon Queen. "Please. I'm begging you."

She turns to me, fire rippling in her eyes. "Bring them out of my sight," she says towards the guards, and a firm hand grips me under my arm to pull me away from her.

"You can't harm them! That's not fair! They did nothing! They don't deserve it. You're a monster! You're—"

The door shuts right in front of my face before I can finish my last sentence.

SEVEN

QUEEN SOULIN

T he night slowly ends.

After the confrontation with the prisoners, it was my time to head to one of Crymzon's towers to guard my kingdom. From up here, I can oversee most of it, and I gaze out at the city stretched out before me.

I lift my head to gaze up at the twinkling stars and the waning gibbous moon above one last time. The stars seem to go on forever, filling the vast expanse of the sky with their radiance, while the moon steals the show with its beauty.

As the night wears on, I watch as the stars slowly fade, giving way to the soft light of dawn. The sky transforms from a deep, inky black to a beautiful shade of pink and red, casting a warm glow over the buildings below me and making my kingdom seem to glow.

Crymzon is a beautiful sight to behold, with its red sandstone buildings and winding streets.

As I look down upon it, I see the bustling crowds below, moving about their nightly business. The streets are filled with vendors selling their wares, and the smell of salt and children's laughter filled the air.

My eyes wander over the market square, where people are gathered to buy and sell goods, and the grand temple, its golden dome glinting in the morning rays of the sun.

The city is surrounded by a circular wall and filled with guards atop to keep watch over my subjects.

I have seen Crymzon from above when I visited Starstrand for the first time. From the sky, the Crymzon Wall is a perfect circle, filled with thousands of houses, the palace, the grand temple, and the market square.

But because Crymzon is embedded inside a bowl of sandstone, there's no way of expanding it. Every request for a new house, a new temple for Lunra, or even a new trading store has been denied.

Beyond the Crymzon Wall, the sandstone turns into a desert landscape until it reaches the river that divides Crymzon from Eternitie and Tenacoro.

Outside the Wall, attached to the smallest bridge known to man, stands the prison.

The narrow slits for windows and a heavy iron gate are heavily guarded by armed soldiers, their armor and weapons shining in the emerging light. Yet, to warn any unwelcome visitors, the warning "Abandon all hope, ye who enter here" is carved into the stone.

The walls are made of thick, blood-red sandstone blocks that were quarried from deeper layers of the desert to resemble the pain and torture the inhabitants endure for their crimes.

As the sun begins to rise, the prison walls glow an eerie burgundy color, casting long shadows across the barren landscape. The only sounds that can be heard are the howling winds and the occasional cries of the prisoners locked inside, paired with the hoove clacking of the horses waiting inside the stables beneath the prison for release.

I sit in silence, lost in thought, as I watch the sky continue to change and evolve.

In just a few minutes, my subjects will return to their homes, where they will get a day's sleep to escape the torturing sun.

My eyes drive over the stone buildings.

There was another reason I come up here often. It makes me feel closer to my brother.

Felix had his own chambers in the palace, in the West Wing, close to our parents. But nothing could stop him from coming up here to the East Tower.

This tower was his sanctuary, his quiet place to wait out the centuries for our father to die peacefully of old age until he could claim the throne.

One night, he had taken me up here, leaning over my shoulder as I took in Crymzon from above. I started to understand why he liked the East Wing tower. It showed us a world we didn't belong to and yet only centered on us.

Felix said that he needed to learn more about the citizens to be a righteous king. He hoped to live among them for some time to understand them better, their worries, their needs, their daily struggles, but also their blessings, happiness, and their view of life.

I took that from him.

Felix would have made the finest king Crymzon has ever seen...

But instead, they have me.

Monsteress; the Blood Queen; Death's Shadow.

No one prepared me for this role I never wanted.

I've tried to right my wrongs. To be a version of my brother's dream. A generous ruler with compassion for my subjects and love.

But my name—Monsteress—is burned deeply into the minds of my people, and my nature is so deeply anchored inside me, making it impossible to break free from the vicious cycle.

And there is something stronger than love—hate.

Being hated is something I am good at. I love the feeling of ruffling someone else's feathers. I love the feeling of control and power.

Looking over Crymzon again, I notice it only took a few minutes for the streets to clear out.

As I stand there, lost in thought, I suddenly hear a noise behind me. Metal clanking on stone.

"What are you doing here, Khaos? You're supposed to take care of the prisoners," I say, knowing it's my Grand General because he and Myra are the only people who know where I hide.

I whirl around to watch him approach, his face hidden in the shadows of his helmet. In his hand, he holds a knife; the blade glinting in the bright morning light.

My heart races as he draws closer, the knife held out in front of him. I can see the determination in his eyes behind the visor and that he means to harm me.

This armored tall man isn't Khaos. It can't be.

Even though he comes closer and closer, I can't move.

I study him.

His movements are smooth, although he's wearing full armor. My eyes move to his helmet again, and I watch as a red curl bounces out of the helmet onto his shoulder.

No.

He can't be here.

My stomach hollows.

He's only two feet away from me, and I still can't move.

The man lunges at me; the knife slashing through the air.

I finally return to my senses and dodge to the side, narrowly avoiding the blade.

"Felix!" I yell in disbelief, and the man halts for a moment, staring with his black eyes right into my soul.

Fear grips me by the throat.

"You're not real. You can't be here. I...you...this can't be true," I say, trying to make sense of what I'm seeing.

I watched my brother burn right in front of my eyes. I still smell the stench of burning hair and charcoal skin. His screams echo through my head, haunting me day and night.

But the red curl beneath his helmet, the vibrant color of it...it can only belong to a family member. I've never seen another person with the same red as mine—besides my brothers.

The man curls his black-gloved fingers around the visor and slowly tilts it up to reveal his face.

The second my eyes wander over the freckled face, my knees buckle.

"Hello, sis. I knew you would recognize me," he snarls, his deep, haunting voice sending ice through my veins like poison.

My throat is so tight, I can't talk. My mind throws images of Felix at me when we were younger to compare it to the armed man standing before me.

His face is fallen in and colorless. The deep blue eyes are replaced by total darkness. His kind smile has turned into a vicious one.

The only indicator that he's the same person I once knew and loved is the blood-red freckles sprinkled over his pale face.

I always hoped that my brother is still alive, that I only imagined him turning into ashes right before my eyes. Yet, I never expected to see him again. And now that he towers above me, I don't know how to react.

"I-I don't understand," I stammer. "I thought you were dead."

My brother chuckles, but there's no warmth in it. "I was, in a way. But I found a new purpose. A new path. It's time for you to come home."

I can't believe what I'm hearing.

What happened to him? How did he come back from the dead? How was he able to bypass the guards on the walls?

And what does he mean by *home?*

"I don't understand," I say again, tears welling up in my eyes. "What happened to you? How are you here?"

My brother's expression turns into something sinister.

My stomach flutters to see Felix again—alive. But at the same time, I'm terrified of the person he has become.

"You're not my brother," I whisper to myself, remembering the fear on his face when his cloak caught fire from the blast of magic radiating from me in the throne room fourteen years ago. "You're not my brother!"

I jump to my feet, locking eyes with the stranger before me.

"How can you say that to me, Soul?" he barks, raising the hand with the knife into the air, and instinctively, I lift my arm to deflect his blade with the whip curled around my forearm.

But it's not there.

I replaced my familiar weapon with the whip strapped around my thigh.

Before I can move to reach for it, the blade finds its way into my raised arm.

The pain of the metal slicing through my flesh is brutal, and nausea creeps up my throat.

"Get away from me!" I scream, trying to summon the bit of magic I have left inside of me. But the pain pulls on my strength.

I stumble back, sending blood gushing from my wound. I cover the slash with my other hand to stop the bleeding, not leaving him out of my sight.

"And you call yourself Monsteress? You're even weaker than the Soulin I knew!"

His words cut deep.

I did give myself that name. I earned it by killing him, my father, and every living soul inside the throne room the moment we got the news of my mother's passing.

"I'm not weak!" I hiss through my teeth, pull my hand away from my injury, and point it at him. "But it doesn't have to end this way! I can help you."

"You've done enough. It's time for Keres to reign and end the suffering. With his help, you will never feel pain again. You'll never die. Accept his offer!"

I shake my head slowly, trying to process what he just said.

Keres.

Keres sent my brother. But how?

"Never!" a voice screams behind him, and I watch as a blade drives through Felix's neck, slicing his head clean off.

Before his head hits the ground, it turns into black smoke, just like his body, and a tear escapes my eye when the wind takes the reminder of him away.

A figure rushes in my direction, and I lift my other hand to defend myself.

"Soulin! Are you okay?" the same voice asks, and I blink a few times to clear my tearful vision.

Khaos.

He's here.

"What have you done?" I scream, my lungs hurting with every word. "That was my brother!"

My arm gets heavier, and I feel my mind drifting off slowly. I'm losing too much blood.

Khaos rushes to me, securing me with firm hands from falling. "That thing wasn't your brother! It was a cruel trick King Keres sent to rid himself of you!"

My chest heaves with each breath. The urge to pull his sword out to do the same he has done to my brother befalls me, but my arm doesn't cooperate.

"We need a healer!" Khaos screams over his shoulder into the spiraling staircase behind him, and those are the last words I hear before darkness claims me.

EIGHT

KHAOS

My stomach turns when Soulin goes limp in my arms. Her head falls back, and her breathing immediately slows as she collapses into me.

I wedge my arm under her legs, scoop her up, and press her against my chest.

The long years of training finally paid off. The weight of my armor and sword is already enough to take a grown man down, and adding the extra weight of a person to it is pure agony.

But holding her in my arms sends a surge of fresh energy through my body.

"Wake up," I whisper to her as I wind down the spiral staircase into the East Wing corridor. "Healer! I need a healer!" I scream, and my voice echoes through the halls.

A rumbling sound shakes the palace, and before I can steady myself, my shoulder crashes against the wall from an aftershock.

What is going on?

Just as I reach the first corridor, a door flies open. The head of a maid pops into my view.

"Fetch a healer!" I order, staring the woman down. "Send her to the Queen's chambers!"

Fear crosses the maid's face, but without hesitation, she sprints through the corridor in her nightgown and disappears around the corner.

I look down at Soulin's beautiful face as I rush through the corridors, occasionally looking up to ensure I was still on the right path.

"You can't die! You need to fight! It's just a minor cut," I whisper to her, but her unmoving body gains weight with each step.

The sounds of shuffling steps rise into my ears, and Myra rushes around a corner dressed in a blue robe. "What in the seven Gods' names happened?" Her eyes blaze with fury as she takes us in.

Another quake shakes the walls, sending sand sprinkling down from the ceiling. This time I'm prepared and widen my stance to balance out the seismic wave.

I feel Soulin's blood dripping onto my boots as I scurry past Myra when the quake stops. "King Keres sent his first messenger. I'm not sure how he got into the palace, but Felix was here."

Myra's eyes widen as she tries to keep up with me. Her eyes scan over Soulin's body. "How is that possible? He's—"

Her voice cuts off.

It takes a few seconds for her to connect the dots. "Keres is a necromancer," she whispers to herself, but loud enough for me to hear.

"Why did I not know about this? And why is her magic not healing her?" I press out through clenched teeth, each step getting heavier.

Myra winces under the last question. "Because it was just speculation about Keres. Well... until now. Queen Soulin sent a handful of moths to

Terminus a couple of moons ago. Only one returned—in awful shape. Its memories showed images of an army that looked... soulless."

Of course, the Queen's moths.

Crymzon is known for the purest silk in the land.

Soulin has a whole palace wing dedicated to her moths. Between the thousands of palm-sized silk moths which die between three to ten days due to not having working mouthparts, she also breeds Fighter Moths that can be as big as a man and live up to...well, she's still figuring that part out.

I slow down for a moment to look at Myra. "What do you mean, *soulless*?"

"It's just as it sounds. The soldiers had black eyes, and they stood on a platform before a fortress like statues. I don't have to tell you how harsh the weather in Terminus is. No one with a soul can stand in formation for such a long time under those conditions."

Ice runs down my spine as I remember my time in Terminus, and the scar on my face itches.

King Obsidian sent me there to retrieve a rare type of rock for him. That was over twenty years ago when I was still a young boy. The icy wind rushing through the mountainous landscape cut straight through my clothes and settled into my bones for days, even after my return.

At that time, the mountains were uninhabited because of their brutal nature.

That was until King Keres claimed the mountains to build a fortress hidden deep inside the merciless region, and no one knows exactly how long he has been hiding there.

Ten years ago, the soldiers Soulin sent to keep searching for the rare mineral didn't return. She sent a second wave out to retrieve it. None of them were ever seen again.

"As your Grand General, I have a right to know about this! It's unacceptable!" I growl, laying eyes on the Queen's chambers.

"She said to keep it between us until she had proof," Myra says, turning her gaze to Soulin.

I scoff loudly. "He sent her brother. *Her brother!*"

All color leaves Myra's face as she helps me lower Soulin's body onto her bed. Her face is paler than usual, and the sheets beneath her arc soaked with blood. "Where is he now?"

I lock eyes with her, and she lowers her head as she understands my reaction without words.

"Who did it? Was it you or her?"

"Me," I whisper, moving a strand of her red hair out of her face, leaving a weird red residue on my fingers. I wipe it away hesitantly. "And I'm not sure if she can ever forgive me for that."

My heart hammers in my chest.

I swore to protect her with my life. So it was a simple decision to kill her brother—again—to save her. I would do anything for her. If provoked, I would kill him a third time if that means she was safe.

But the memory of Felix was the only thing that kept Soulin from completely turning into the monster everyone thinks she is.

And he was my friend, my training buddy, my Crown Prince since the day my father brought me to the palace to work at the stables.

The three of us were inseparable until the day of Soulin's magical overflow. King Obsidian sent me to the stables just minutes before Soulin's outburst to tend to the messenger's horse.

Besides Myra, I'm the only one Soulin accepted back into her life after climbing the throne.

"I hope you can forgive me someday," I whisper, and Myra's sad eyes and wrinkled eyebrows are enough to tell me that the day may never come.

NINE

AEMILIUS

Panicked screams rip me out of my sleep, and my mind brings me immediately back to my hut. I search the room for the familiar sight of Liza standing in the kitchen, mixing ground oats with water for breakfast.

My heart stops when I find red walls surrounding me.

I'm not sure what time it is because the room has no windows, and the only evidence that I'm not dead yet is a flickering candle on the opposite side of the room.

Instead of returning to the dungeon, I was led to a personal prisoner cell in the palace. The cell is bigger than the one in the dungeon but smaller than my hut. The walls are made of the same sandstone I start to hate more than the Queen ruling it, and there is a single door without a handle covering a wall.

Warmth seeps into my feet through the hard floor, and I feel a draft coming from underneath the door.

I spent hours listening to people pass my door until sleep claimed me. What I was waiting for? I don't know. Maybe for someone to open the door and release me.

I try to stand up, but my head spins, and I feel disoriented. I look around and see the room is empty except for the candle and a bed in the corner I refused to sleep on.

My bones crack when I walk over to the door and try to open it. Pressing my entire weight against it, but the stone slab doesn't budge. Panic sets in as I realize that this is my only way out.

I bang on the door and shout for help, but no one answers.

Desperation washes over me.

Devana needs me. I can feel it deep inside my heart.

And then there is Liza. Did she manage to stay hidden?

I have to get out of here and find Devana.

Only with her help, I have a fighting chance to make it out of Crymzon alive. Devana is the best sword fighter I know, and that means a lot. I had watched her beat a dozen villagers in an unfair fight during my training with her.

As a plan forms in my head, I let myself sink to the ground, my back against the warm, smooth wall, and I sit there, waiting for someone to come and open the door to unlock my freedom.

The voice of a woman creeps through underneath the door. "Fast! We need a prisoner to save her."

Save who?

I lean closer to the threshold and put my face against the door. My eardrums hurt when a set of heavy armored boots march past it.

I sit upright when they come to a standstill on the other side. Within a second, I'm on my feet, pressing my back against the wall.

This is it. My way out.

"Not that one! He's reserved as the sacrifice," a male voice yells through the hall, and my blood freezes.

He's reserved as the sacrifice, echoes through my head as I listen to the footsteps leading away from my door.

Monsteress indeed has marked me to die.

I turn the words over in my head again and again, but the outcome is the same.

I knew she would eventually kill me. After all, no prisoner gets out of Crymzon alive. But hearing it aloud, without any emotion, filled me with fear and... anger.

I pace through the room, trying to come up with a plan to escape, but I'm interrupted by the screams of a woman. The screams intensify, and my fists throb when I hammer against the stone door to get the guard's attention.

"Devana!" I scream, and my voice reverberates back to me.

"Shut up," a man yells, and I hear skin colliding with skin and the screams behind the stone slab die.

The cries for help ring in my ears, and I try to decipher if it was Devana or not.

But does it really matter who it was? I can't just stand here and let Monsteress claim another innocent life, Devana or not.

The noises in the hall clear and I stop my attempt to break through the door.

There's no point in draining my energy when no one is around to hear my screams.

Suddenly, the world around me shakes. I press my hands against the wall to steady myself.

As fast as the quake rippled through the room, it disappears.

Something big is happening. I can feel it in my bones. Why else would the guards rush through the halls searching for a prisoner to heal someone? And why is the world shaking?

Is Monsteress dying? Did someone finally have the guts to ram a blade through her charcoal heart?

The image of her lying on the floor with blood pooling from her chest sends a quiet cheer through my body, but I know better than to rely on my wishes. Those unheard wishes are the reason I'm here, locked away in a small room, waiting to become a sacrifice.

I let out a long breath.

I'm a dead man walking, so I might as well enjoy the last few hours before Monsteress disposes of me.

Once that door opens again, I'm going to do whatever it takes to get rid of that monster once and for all.

TEN

KHAOS

I t's unbearably hot in the gleaming armor, and I feel the sweat run down between my shoulder blades.

"She will be fine. I know it," Myra whispers to me as I pace through the room.

Another shock wave rolls through the palace.

"Where is that damn healer?" I growl, holding on to the bedpost, and rage ripples through me like fire.

The door jumps open, and a guard steps into the room, followed by a delicate female dressed in white silk on quiet feet as if she's trying not to disturb Soulin's rest.

My eyes fall on Soulin, her chest rising and falling gently as she sleeps on her oversized bed, hidden behind see-through fabric falling off the ceiling to the ground.

The room is bright and quiet, save for the soft sound of the Queen's breathing.

The healer approaches the bedside and gently lifts Soulin's arm, exposing the knife wound. The skin around the wound is red and swollen, and a small trickle of blood seeped through the fabric wrapped around it.

My stomach turns when I see how deep the cut is.

Her brother did this to her.

No, not her brother.

It was an undead version of him.

With a gentle touch, the healer washes the wound, using a mixture of water and herbs to cleanse it. The room is filled with the smell of chamomile, cloves, and valerian root.

As she works, Soulin stirs and opens her eyes, groggy from sleep. "What are you doing?" she asks, her voice barely above a whisper.

"I'm tending to your wound, Your Majesty," the silk-dressed woman replies, her voice soothing and calm. "You were injured in an attack, and the wound needs stitches. But don't worry, I'm here to help."

Soulin nods shakily, her eyes closing as she drifts off to sleep again.

My breath quickens as I watch the healer pull a needle and some thread out of her satchel. I step closer, squaring my shoulders. "Can't you use magic?"

"I don't have the power to heal such a deep wound without closing it first. Plus, this wound was caused by a Thallium sword, which is toxic. I will need a substantial amount of magic to withdraw it," the woman whispers, and I hear the fear in her voice.

Thallium? That's impossible.

I've heard of a blacksmith using Thallium to create incredibly lethal weapons, but he died from its toxicity before the first sword was even ready to cool down.

Myra grabs me by the arm and pulls me back. "If you can't be here for Soulin, wait outside."

My nostrils flare as I take in her words. Leaving isn't an option. Not yet.

There isn't much time left until Soulin awakens and remembers what I have done.

Until then, I'm going to stay by her side.

The woman reaches into her satchel and pulls out a small jar of ointment. It took her seconds to skillfully close the wound with stitches, almost so fast that I didn't notice. She carefully applies the ointment to the wound, taking her time to cover it completely.

Soulin moves slightly at the touch but doesn't wake.

The healer then wraps her fingers around Soulin's arm and presses against the irritated wound. Closing her eyes, she lifts her head up to the sky. A faint flow streams through her fingers, touching Soulin's skin, and I feel the energy radiating from her.

It's been years since I've seen another person use magic. Every person in Crymzon has a limited amount of it left, so they use it wisely.

I ran out of magic in my teenage years when I used it all to save the person I love. Since then, there wasn't a moment I regretted my decision. I would do it again.

Still, I beat myself up for not being able to heal her.

When the healer is finished, she stands back and admires her work.

Even magic isn't enough to prevent scarring, but this woman's power was strong enough to leave the faintest line behind.

"I've done what you asked me. May I return to the temple?" the healer asks, her head lowered to the ground.

My heart throbs as I think about what we asked of her. I expected her to arrive with the prisoner she needed to use to gain the power to heal Soulin. Because the magic of Crymzon is slowly dying, the healer needed to take the energy from something or someone else.

I nod to a guard. He marches over and grabs the woman by the arm to pull her out of the room.

As she leaves, she whispers a prayer for the Queen's speedy recovery, and I'm not sure if she means it sincerely or if she is praying because if something happens to the Queen, it would be her head rolling.

"The prisoner?" I ask, whirling around to meet Myra's eyes.

"She's alive but needs a few days to recover from the energy taken from her," Myra says, walking over to the bed to inspect the fresh scar. "How could you let this happen? Where were you?"

Her stony gaze meets mine.

I clench my teeth. "I'm not her personal guard anymore. She removed me from that position months ago. Do you think I did this on purpose?"

"Of course not. But how did the..." She holds her breath for a moment. "How did the attacker get into the palace? Don't you have guards spread through the entire palace and the Wall?"

My gaze shifts out of the window. "If this was a breach of my security, I will stand trial for my mistake. But I promise you, this wasn't the guards' fault. I'm not sure how someone could make his way unnoticed past hundreds of armed men, especially if he looks like the lost Crown Prince. Everyone knows him."

"Khaos, we're only days away from another Council meeting. We need the other kingdoms' help to stand beside us against Keres. Soulin is weakened as it is, and if this comes out... I'm not sure if they will support a dying Queen."

I shake my head and feel the wrinkles forming between my eyebrows. "Dying Queen?"

Myra's eyes widen, and I look down at Soulin, who is still sleeping peacefully.

"Get the fuck out!" I scream, and the guards clear out of the room, leaving Myra and me behind. "What are you talking about?" My voice is deep and shaky.

"I always forget how young you are," Myra says quietly, rubbing her temple. "I've served her parents for two centuries before Soulin appointed me as her advisor. A long time ago, I started as a young maid and quickly became Queen Ria's favorite. Back then, magic pulsated through Crymzon, filling the streets with wonders. But by the time Soulin was born, something had changed. It felt like something was cutting off the magic stream, draining the kingdom day by day. Soulin hasn't celebrated a single Blood Moon since she became Queen, and without a Soulmate to share her burden to keep this kingdom alive, she will die and Crymzon with it."

My heart stops. "That can't be true."

"Can't you feel it? How the magic disappears right before our eyes? I've never seen you use a single spell from your own magic. That means you depleted yours, just like I did."

It never crossed my mind that someone could pay attention to me and find out that I borrow my magic from dead soldiers. I did it during our last fight. By stepping on the dead soldier's body, I was able to catch the last glimpse of magic escaping his body and used it to knock the two people inside the hut out cold with a little snap of my fingers.

I look down at my hands and curl them into fists. "How long have you known?"

"That the magic is dying?"

"That Soulin is dying?"

The silence in the room is palpable as Myra takes me in. "I had my suspicions for a while, but this—" She turns to Soulin and reaches over her face to a strand of her hair.

"Don't touch her," I growl, jumping forward, but before I reach her hand to pull it away, I freeze.

Myra pulls on a piece of Soulin's hair, and the red color comes right off, leaving a strand of white hair behind.

"What did you do?"

"She uses red sand and water to dye her hair. I'm pretty sure this is a sign that the kingdom is consuming her until there is nothing left of her," Myra whispers, wiping the color off on her nightgown. "If Soulin doesn't start praying to Lunra and finds a Soulmate to strengthen the connection between the crown and Crymzon, she will die."

Hearing those words from the only person who loves Soulin more than I do feels like a spike through the chest. Myra has been at her side since her birth. She watched Soulin and I grow up, and become the grown-ups we are now.

My knees shake, and I almost fall to my knees. "You need to talk to her!"

I can't lose her, too.

It's already unbearable without my mother. And if Soulin dies, it would give me the rest.

"You think I haven't tried that? Soulin is as stubborn as you. There is no talking to her."

"You need to try again."

"To fail?"

"Myra! She doesn't understand!"

"Doesn't understand what?" a third shaky voice asks, and my heart stops as I meet Soulin's green eyes.

I just stand there, my mouth open, as I figure out my next move.

How long will it take Soulin to recollect her last memories before passing out? Maybe she has forgotten about it since the wound on her arm is practically gone and isn't there to remind her.

"Felix," she whispers, her eyes darting between Myra and me. "My brother. He's back."

"You should leave," Myra says, jumping to her feet and pushing me to the door.

"I can't leave her," I growl, pushing back while fear ripples through me.

"If you're not gone by the time her full memories return, we're both dead," Myra hisses, leaning against me to stop me in my tracks. "Just give me a moment with her to figure out how she's doing."

"But—"

Myra clenched her fists, her face turning into a stony grimace. "Get out!"

ELEVEN

QUEEN SOULIN

How can an almost invisible scar hurt so much?

I rub the spot on my arm, the reminder of my brother coming back to life and dying again.

There's no way I can erase the black, empty eyes from my mind.

All these years, I thought that watching him burn to death was the worst, but seeing him back from the dead, his body used as a vessel for Keres to reach me, is more haunting than seeing his flesh peel off his bones.

A knock on the door forces me to cover my hair with the loose dress fabric hanging off my shoulder, hiding the undyed white curl beneath it.

"Come in."

The door opens, and Myra steps into the room. "Are you sure you want to do this?"

Am I sure? No.

But it needs to be done.

I nod silently and turn back to my vanity, mixing red sand in water to create a thick paste. Myra watches me as I push the fabric off my head and cover my curl with the mixture, dyeing it from white to red. The color isn't an exact match, but it's enough not to raise suspicion.

I turn to meet her gaze. "Where are the prisoners?"

Myra inhales sharply. "One is waiting outside, ready to fulfill your request. The other one is getting prepared for the ceremony."

Myra's eyes search for mine, but I'm not giving her the satisfaction of looking at her and instead focus on the door behind her.

"You don't have to do it," Myra whispers, lowering her head.

My teeth send a sharp pain through my jaw from clenching them too hard. "That bastard used my brother. I'm going to kill him even if it's the last thing I'll do," I spit out, rage rippling through me in tide waves. "Bring him in."

Myra doesn't move. Her eyebrows are drawn together, forming wrinkles between them.

When our eyes meet, she flinches, turns on her heels, and storms out of the room.

My lungs hurt when I release the breath I was holding. I tilt my head to the ceiling, closing my eyes.

Please, Lunra. Please help me forget what is about to happen and give me the strength to kill Keres.

TWELVE

KHAOS

"Khaos, you really don't want to go in there," Myra whispers, putting her hand against my chest plate to stop me.

I draw up short. "I can't take it any longer. I need to talk to her and accept my punishment." My voice is thick but steady.

After I returned to my chamber this morning, it was impossible to find sleep, knowing Soulin is healed but upset about what I did.

My eyes burn from sleep deprivation, but I don't care. I need to see her and explain myself. I need her to know that I did it because of her.

Myra presses her weight against my armor to turn me around. I don't budge.

"Seriously. Don't go in there," she repeats, and my body tenses.

"I need to talk to her. It can't wait!" I spit out, pushing myself past her.

That's when I hear it.

The slapping sound of meat on meat.

Over and over again.

My heart races when I realize what I'm hearing.

The impact of my fist colliding with the stone door sends a sharp pain through my body and straight into my shattered heart.

"Don't," Myra screams behind me, but the door jumps open, revealing a naked man thrusting his hips into Soulin, who's standing pressed against a wall, holding up her dress on both sides to reveal her long, thick legs.

With three enormous steps, I'm across the room behind the man, still pounding into her, grunting, and I rip him away from her, throwing him to the ground.

"What the—" Soulin yells, whirling around and dropping the fabric between her fingers to the ground.

Jealousy rushes through me, and my mind goes blank.

I hear her gasp as I grab the man by the shoulder and pound my fist into his face, again and again.

"Get off him," Soulin demands in an icy voice, her fingernails biting into my neck.

I swing my fist back into the air to get a better distance between his face to gain more momentum when Myra rushes into the room.

"No," she screams behind me and rams her shoulder into my side to get me off of him.

I clutch my hands tightly into fists, my knuckles turning white from the force of my grip. My breath is ragged, and my cock hard as I think back to the decision that led to this moment. I replay the scene of the man thrusting into her, wishing I could go back and change what I did.

No, I wouldn't change beating him almost to death. I would go back to make sure he never laid hands on her to begin with.

Numb, I scramble to my feet, stumbling backward, taking in the scene.

Myra's arm is wrapped tightly around Soulin's shoulder before she shrugs it off, stepping closer to the victim.

My gaze wanders over to the man sprawled out on the ground, his erection still pointing at the ceiling and his face bashed in.

This man will never touch her again if he survives. The last thing he will remember before ever thinking of pulling down his pants again is my fist crashing into his face. I'm sure of it.

Myra's whispering voice in Soulin's direction snaps me out of a trance, and panic settles inside my stomach.

"Are you okay?" I mumble, staggering forward to touch Soulin, but Myra's eyes whip in my direction, and my body freezes.

"Guards," Myra yells, her eyes filled with hatred I've never seen before.

Soulin's face is unreadable. I stare at her, searching her eyes for gratitude or relief.

Then it hits me.

This man didn't rape her. That's why Myra tried to hold me back because she knew what was going on.

Soulin invited this man into her chambers, a stranger.

I blink a few times, trying to understand what's going on.

She never had a lover before. At least I've never seen one leave her room when I was her personal guard standing watch outside her door.

My stomach forms into a ball, forcing bile up my throat, and I swallow it back down.

Metal footsteps ring in my ears. The guards, *my guards*, are coming for *me*, their Grand General.

My mind finally snaps into place.

Soulin won't watch them take me away. I won't let that happen.

Straightening my shoulders, I take a low bow, turn on my heels and greet the armed soldiers outside the door before they can storm the room.

THIRTEEN

AEMILIUS

The door opens quietly, and I'm taken aback when two petite females rush into the room, closing it behind them.

I expected a soldier to drag me out of here and was ready to take him down once I hear him approach.

But these females? I can't harm them, can I? They look barely old enough to bear a child.

Their lowered heads and wrinkled one-layered fabric gowns reveal they're even less than maids. Maybe they're also prisoners being forced to do chores even too obscure for a maid.

"What are your names?" I ask, still trying to determine if they are friends or foes.

The black-haired female looks over at the brunette, who shakes her head before dropping it back to the ground.

They scurry in my direction, grabbing my torn shirt to lift it, and I recoil.

My eyes widen when they step closer again, cornering me.

That's when I notice a bundle of clothing under the black-haired girl's arm and stop retaliating.

The brunette pulls on the fabric again and exhales when I let her lift it over my shoulders and head. The other takes a deep breath, her eyes lingering on my bare skin. She throws the folded clothes onto the floor, picks up a crimson-colored shirt with embroidery, and unfolds it in front of her face to cover her red cheeks.

Forcefully, she pulls the shirt over my head, and the fabric drapes over my chest and stomach.

I run my hand over the smooth fabric, feeling the softness and coolness of the silk as it glides over my skin.

I have to lie if I say I don't miss the touch of silk and its gentle rustling sound when I move in it. However, I've gotten used to wearing stiff leather and scratchy cotton over the last year and never expected to feel that luxurious touch on my body again.

There's total stillness in the room for a moment, and I know what's coming next.

Silently, I turn around and pull my pants down, feeling their gazes burn on my buttcheeks.

Unfazed, I drop my blood-stained leather pants to the ground and reach my hand back for the new pants. The smooth red fabric handed to me almost slips through my fingers, and I tighten my grip to hold on to it.

After stepping into the holes, I pull it up and fasten the strings around my hips to lock it in place.

Mesmerized by the texture rubbing against my skin, I didn' notice the girls grabbing my old clothes and leaving the room without a sound.

Alone again, my mind races.

There's only one explanation for why Monsteress sent them to dress me.

My time has come to an end.

Those girls marked me for death by dressing me in expensive fabric for one last time.

"No, I'm not dying today," I whisper to myself, marching back to the spot beside the door to wait for the next person to enter the room.

I will find Devana, and together, we will slay the Blood Queen and escape.

FOURTEEN

QUEEN SOULIN

I can't remember the last time I set foot on the uneven roads outside the palace.

My glass heels click on the ground beneath me, and my long, flowing dress drags behind me, occasionally getting stuck on the rough sandstone. A swift breeze tangles my hair, and I close my eyes for a moment to take in the warmth of it.

High in the sky, the moon casts a soft glow over the city, reflecting off the small building windows as I make my way through the quiet streets.

The citizens, about to wake up from their daytime slumber to escape the heat of Crymzon's sun during the day, have no idea I'm among them.

Not yet.

As I continue my journey, I come across a group of children playing on the street. They stop and stare in awe as I approach, having never seen me outside of the palace walls.

I don't pay any attention to them as I stroll past, but hear their excited chattering behind me, followed by doors flying open to find the culprit of the commotion.

"Queen Soulin!" someone yells behind me, but I keep my eyes focused on the grand temple coming into view as I near my destination.

Behind me, my subjects fall in line, their footsteps filling the streets. Some bow and curtsy as I pass, showing their reverence and loyalty to me before following me.

Effortlessly, I climb the steps and enter the dimly lit temple, my eyes immediately drawn to the center of the room, where a large tree stands.

The wing-shaped tree is made of red wooden branches, and it burns brightly in the center of the room, casting flickering shadows on the walls. A pool of water forms a circle around it, and small candles are spread throughout the hall, adding to the ethereal ambiance of the sacred place.

The eternal fire burning inside the Heiligbaum is dimmer than I remember when I watched my father lead his last ceremony. Shortly before, he showed me how to enchant a rare gem and offer it to the tree in return for the everlasting flame until it eventually dissolves, needing a new rock to take its place.

The air is thick with the scent of burning wood and incense, and the temple is silent except for the occasional crackle of the fire and the sound of flowing water.

I approach the tree, the heat of the blazing fire burning my face, and kneel before it, bowing my head in reverence.

My attendants' footsteps echo behind me as they follow me into the temple, but I remain focused on the fire, concentrating on the next step.

I've seen my father do the ceremony countless times.

I lift my eyes to look out the window with ornamental silver borders that catch the moonlight falling in. The lead cast lines that hold the pieces of glass together as one are thin and precise, adding to the overall symmetry and harmony of the design.

The window symbolizes the devotion and faith of the people who worship Lunra.

I wait for a few minutes while the moon slowly creeps into the opening of the glass before I rise and turn to my subjects.

The room falls silent when I turn my back to the inferno tree behind me.

"Today, we've come together to offer Lunra, Goddess of the Moon and Love, a sacrifice. Since my father, King Obsidian, left a gaping emptiness on the Crymzon Throne, I've decided to spend the last fourteen years in mourning before summoning Lunra again. So tonight, we're gathered here to witness our sacrifice to our Goddess under a full moon. May Lunra grant us our wishes and bless us by bestowing us the magic that pulsates through our land."

The full moon shines brightly in the night sky as it perfectly aligns with the window, creating a circular frame around the lunar orb and illuminating the room with a soft light.

This is the moment I've been waiting for. The casted light streams through the fire of the Heiligbaum and fills the room with a red glow.

I snap my fingers and see Myra emerge from the crowd with a man trailing behind her.

Aemilius.

She followed me at a great distance from the palace to avoid distracting my subjects from my silent invitation to pursue me.

With the help of guards, she put a gag into his mouth to stop his screaming. Even though he couldn't use his voice anymore, he fought with all his might against her until one of the guards, who still had enough magic left, penetrated his conscience and forced him into submission.

My gaze lingers on them as they draw closer.

ius.

He's for sure not a Crymzonian, as he claims, which could only mean he's from Eternitie.

But why did he lie?

I exhale sharply, reeling my mind back in.

It doesn't matter why he lied.

In just a few more minutes, he will walk through the warm water surrounding the fire to cleanse his soul and climb the steps of the Heiligbaum to offer himself to Lunra. And In return, the Goddess will grant us what we need.

More magic.

I need it to get rid of the white hair hiding beneath the red-colored mud. For that, I need magic which will hopefully extend my life long enough to attack and defeat Keres for sending my brother to kill me.

Myra, dressed in an elegant tight dress that hugs her gracefully aging skin, leads the prisoner behind her. Her long gray hair waves behind her with each step.

Aemilius's brown eyes rest on me, but they're empty. All the anger I saw in his gaze in my chamber is gone.

The citizens hold their breaths as Myra comes to a halt before me, bows deeply, and speaks loudly, "My Queen, I present to you the sacrifice. He's a traitor who dared to plot against the kingdoms by fleeing into the Confines to live as an Ordinary."

I study him closer with a stony gaze. His brown hair is dyed red to signify the color of my kingdom. Short stubbles cover his face, and the silky clothes stick to his sweaty body, underlining every muscle.

Just as I reach out to release the gag, something flickers in his eyes, and I look over his shoulder to see the guard struggling to keep him under control.

I grab his head and close my eyes as I force my magic through my fingers into his skull.

Aemilius' mind is strong, but I'm stronger.

Finding his conscience inside his mind only takes a few silent moments. Once found, I force it back to sleep.

My hands tremble slightly as the magic pulls from my energy.

I feel my magic slowly depleting inside me. If this small use drains me so quickly, the guard must have saved up and used all his given magic to escort him from the palace to the temple.

I must act quickly before the last ounce leaves my body and breaks my control over him.

Slowly, I release my hands to pull the gag out and lower them to my hips, curling them into fists to hide the tremors.

Only a few more minutes, and I will get more magic from Lunra in return for his soul.

I turn to the Heiligbaum and concentrate on Aemilius' body. "Move," I whisper, watching as he takes one step after another, heading for the water.

A sharp pain rushes through my body, and I close my eyes to keep Aemilius in motion while concentrating on the speech expected of me.

"Great and powerful Lunra. We come before You today to humbly request Your favor and guidance. We have always looked to You as a symbol of beauty and grace and have been in awe of Your power over us and the night sky. We ask that You grant us more of Your power so that we may use it to bring peace and harmony to our lives and those around us. We promise to use this power responsibly and always honor and worship You. Please hear our plea and grant us Your blessings."

The anticipation in the hall is palpable.

The only noise filling the room comes from Aemilius walking through the hip-deep water slowly and steadily. The liquid is calm and clear, lapping against his body. The moon shines down on him, creating sparkling ripples and highlighting his silhouette as he moves forward.

Something I haven't felt in years bubbles up inside me, drowning out the pain caused by clutching onto the reins of his mind.

Excitement.

This is my first time offering a sacrifice to Lunra, and it feels even better than executing a horrid person.

Low voices enter my mind and almost make me lose control over Aemilius.

I strain my ears to listen to what they say until a woman screams, "It's the Prince!"

The murmurs turn into shouts.

"She's killing the Prince," a man yells to my right, pointing at me.

My mind races as I take his accusation in, and the second I realize what's going on, my connection to Aemilius snaps.

He tumbles forward and catches himself just in time to avoid falling face-first into the water. He whips his head around, and our eyes meet.

"You bastard!" I scream at the top of my lungs and lunge forward.

It takes him a second to regain complete control over his body parts, and once they work, he takes off running.

"Restrain him," I yell to the guards hiding among the citizens.

The screams of my subjects fill the hall, followed by armor pounding on stone as the guards give chase.

My knees almost buckle when I jump into the water, hitting the slick ground hard while my dress soaks with water and slows me down.

I search deep inside myself and find the last bit of magic I tucked away.

While I wade through the water, holding my hands out to keep myself steady, I have to make a decision.

Is the Prince really worth using up all my magic I need for something greater?

But the decision is made for me when I watch Aemilius fall to the ground, unconscious. Someone has used their power to knock him out without touching him.

I climb out of the water and look down on his unmoving body and smile.

He's mine now.

FIFTEEN

CYRUS

Cold water rips me out of sleep, and it takes me a few blinks to clear my vision. My breath hitches when I stare into the soulless eyes of Monsteress.

"What should I do with you, Cyrus Matrus, Prince of Eternitie?" she asks, kneeling before me. "Or do you prefer the name Aemilius?"

Hearing my real name from Monsteress' mouth sends ice through my veins.

No. It can't be.

How did she figure out who I am?

I'm back in the windowless room I found myself in after leaving her chambers. The warm stone beneath me seeps into my body, and I scramble to my feet.

Slowly, Monsteress lifts herself off the ground, and I'm startled at how tall she is. I didn't notice it during our last encounter in her chambers.

She steps forward, and I flinch before remembering who I am, building myself up to my entire height.

"Does your father know?" Monsteress asks, her lips curling into a smile. "Oh, no. He doesn't know where you are, does he?"

I don't give her the satisfaction of answering, but she doesn't give up.

"This whole '*my poor son Cyrus died, Goddess Odine bless his soul*' was just an act to cover up that his son is a traitor. A runaway." Her eyes flicker with excitement. "I can't wait to deliver you back to him. I wonder what your subjects think of you when they find out you're alive."

Her laugh vibrates through my body.

"You can't do that," I growl, her eyebrows shooting into the sky.

"Is that so?"

The silence between us is sharper than cut glass until she breaks it. "Name one good reason I shouldn't hand you over."

Every reason shooting through my head benefits me, but that won't satisfy Monsteress. So I need to dig deeper to save my ass.

Before leaving Eternitie in the dead of night, I did my homework researching all the other kingdoms for a case like this. I spent hours in the forbidden library gaining vital information I can use to keep my head on my shoulders if I get caught by my enemies.

It only takes me a moment to recall everything I know about Crymzon. Besides the fact that the Blood Queen is the youngest ruler ever to claim a throne, her kingdom functions through magic. Like every other kingdom, this one relies on the power of its Goddess. The Heiligbaum is the connection point between the domain and Lunra. Without it, the connection between the head of state and the higher entity dies, which would mean destruction in Crymzon's case.

My gut wrenches when I recall seeing the Heiligbaum with my own eyes. The heat radiating off it was overpowering, and I was so close to being sacrificed to call upon their Goddess.

I open my mouth to answer, my eyes falling onto the fine dust piled up in the room's corner. My gaze wanders to a crack from the previous earthquake blemishing the ceiling, and a better idea pops into my head.

"I know that you're dying."

She holds my stare briefly before she laughs, clapping her hands. "Everyone knows that."

She's bluffing.

She has to be.

Her subjects wouldn't have followed her into the temple if they knew they were trailing their death sentence. If the Sovereign dies without an heir to fill the throne, the kingdom falls with the crown. Everyone knows that.

But I can't risk being wrong.

"I know where you can find Painite," I add, and Monsteress' nostrils flare.

"Everyone knows where to find it. Terminus is full of it."

"But do you know where to look?" I counter and see in her angry face that I have the upper hand.

"Why did you flee?" she asks, and her question catches me off guard.

For a few moments, I consider what to say next.

I can't tell her the real reason I left. If I did, she would have even more leverage against me. So I tell her the second reason I left Eternitie behind.

"The thought of making the Connection Ceremony with the Monsteress herself and giving her even more magic than she deserves made me leave."

Her eyebrows shoot into the sky, and...she laughs.

"Don't flatter yourself. You wouldn't have survived a single night in my chambers, let alone turn out to be my Soulmate," she says, coldness lacing every word.

Just thinking about finding myself in her bed revolts me, and yet, my hands are eager to touch her smooth skin and bury them in her curls while staring into her green-golden eyes.

Her vibrant hair and tanned skin are more luminous than anything I've seen in Eternitie or any other part of the land.

I'm used to seeing females walk the halls back home, and I lived with Liza for a year in the smallest hut imaginable. But those females dressed according to their environment.

The gadgeteers need to cover as much skin as possible to avoid burns from the blazing hot steam and torches they use to build their inventions.

And Liza was required to cover her delicate pale skin from the burning sun to protect herself.

Monsteress' dress is as useless as me being a Prince, and the amount of skin showing is overwhelming when you're used to being surrounded by not-so-scantly dressed women.

I snarl and push the thought aside.

Whatever magic trick Monsteress uses on me to make me feel this way, she needs to try harder.

The Blood Queen circles me. "What irony to find you in a village so close to my kingdom while you try to claim you left your home because of me."

Truthfully though, there is no irony in it.

I couldn't stay close to Eternitie because every person behind those metal gates knows my face.

Tenacoro was my first choice, but when I arrived at the river separating Eternitie and Tenacoro, I noticed guards hidden deep inside the jungle, just waiting for me to cross.

Oceris and Starstrand weren't an option because I had neither wings nor fins. And Terminus' cold mountain landscape would have killed me before I had time to find shelter.

So my only option was to hide in plain sight, just a half day's ride away from the three people I despise the most.

"You need my help to find the gem," I say, trying to lure her back to what's essential.

Do I know where to find Painite?

Yes, kind of.

Is it worth lying about to save my life and get closer to Monsteress to kill her?

Absolutely.

"Why should I trust you?" Monsteress asks sweetly, playing with a strand of her hair. "After all, it was so easy for you to betray your own father."

My eyes are glued to her finger, but my mind stays clear of her attempt to distract me. "If you don't, the flame of the Heiligbaum will extinguish, and your subjects will finally figure out that Crymzon is done for."

The truth behind my words makes her drop her hand and recoil.

I see in her wild eyes that she didn't expect me to know so much about her land.

For the first time, I'm glad I listened to all the rumors circulating through Eternitie. It would have been my end without the old lady on the street whispering tales about the Crymzon Queen to scare little children never to leave the kingdom.

Monsteress doesn't deny my accusation, confirming what I already know. She needs that gem to hold her appearance of being untouchable.

If I were in a better position with Eternitie, I would spread the truth about her to watch her land corrupt and die from the inside out.

But I'm not.

All I can do now is to hold on to the sliver of hope that she believes my gamble.

Once I'm outside the kingdom, I will find a way to escape to return to Liza and flee with her again until we have a solid plan to save the other villagers if I don't get the chance to kill Monsteress first.

"We're departing in two days," she says, her eyes filled with hatred. "And if you're wrong, I will skin you alive right before your father."

Her words hold the right amount of menace to know it's not an intimidating tactic but a genuine threat. Despite that, the wrinkles between my brows deepen when I think about my father.

Monsteress will be the least of my problems if *he* finds out where I am.

SIXTEEN

KHAOS

G oosebumps race over my skin when I hear a fist hammering against my door.

"You don't need to escort me out. I know the way," I yell, taking off the gambeson, a padded protective jacket under my armor, to leave behind on my bed.

After what I did, there's only one thing left: resigning my position as Grand General.

Beating the man half to death for touching Soulin is something I can live with, but disobeying a command from the Queen is unacceptable, and I need to pay for my mistake. She ordered me to get off him, and I didn't listen.

A drift of air ruffles my hair, and instantly I'm aware I'm not alone.

"I said I don't need an escort," I growl through clenched teeth as I spin around, and my breath catches in my throat.

Soulin closes the door behind her and prowls in my direction, her eyes resting on the shining armor sprawled out on the bed. "I didn't release you of your oath," she says, her voice thick and soft at the same time.

I straighten my posture and bow. "You didn't need to, my Queen."

"Then why are you taking off your armor?"

Her eyes drift from my naked upper body to the loose silk pants bound around my hips.

I can't remember the last time she saw me without my protective clothing. It must have been right before I joined the royal guard to become a soldier, or when we used to swim in the fountain in the courtyard until her father demanded us to come out.

She's just an arm's length away from me, and a fresh, calming floral scent with a note of orange peels finds its way into my nose as she comes to a halt.

I drop to one knee and bow my head. "I apologize, my Queen. My actions were rash, and I should've thought them through."

Her expression softens slightly, "You must understand the importance of obedience in these times." She studies me wearily. "But, I accept your apology. Rise."

I shake my head slightly, trying to figure out if I heard her correctly. Her reaction is not the one played in my head repeatedly.

Through all those years growing up together, we transformed from sharing everything to courtly distance.

The moment her father asked me to address her as 'my Princess' at her eighth-year celebration comes back into my mind.

That's when we started to distance ourselves from each other. Even though social standings mean nothing in Crymzon, I noticed for the first time that she's royal and I'm just a stable boy.

It didn't stop me though, from trying to impress her. From making sure her horse was ready and shiny like a polished diamond to guarding her room even though I wasn't assigned to it.

Soulin didn't use to be this cruel monster. Her laughter lit up entire halls, and her love for her family was endless.

Until the day everything changed.

I look up to meet her eyes and rise off the ground.

There is silence between us for a moment, and as much as I try to mind my own business and be grateful to have her blessing, my fear of losing her takes over.

"You need to find your Soulmate," I press out before I can overthink my words.

Her lips curl into a cold smirk. "I tried that. Remember what happened to the last male?" She shrugs her shoulders. "You almost killed him."

Warmth rushes into my cheeks, recalling his naked body on the ground. "I'm sorry," I say, lowering my head to the ground. "I won't interfere again. But, with that being said, you need to find someone to complete the Connection Ceremony before it's too late."

Before you die, those are the words I don't say, but they hang in the room between us like deadly smoke.

"Let me guess. You think *you* are my Soulmate?" she asks, and her white teeth flash in my direction as she takes another step closer.

I can't move.

How did my concern for her well-being turn into an interrogation?

My eyes are fixated on her moving chest as she chuckles. "You think I don't notice the way you look at me?" Her hand shoots forward, and my air supply cuts off when she grabs my dick through the fabric. "How your cock twitches every time I'm around you? How your eyes linger on my bare skin?"

The feeling of her fingers curling around my shaft, pressing it slightly, sends warm waves of pleasure through my veins, but I don't react.

She's my Queen, and I'm her Grand General.

She's royal, and I'm nothing.

I stare at the ceiling to avoid eye contact.

If I look at her now, I will take her. I will grind my cock into her hand until she can't suppress the need for him inside her. I will make her mine, and no one will ever touch her again.

My throat burns as I swallow my desire to throw her over the edge of the bed and spread her legs just for me to see.

This can only be a dream. Another one of those that keeps me wrapped inside my wildest fantasies, making every move and every breath feel like reality.

I welcome those dreams. It's the only time I have control over my life; the only time I get the woman of my dreams.

She squeezes harder, rubbing her hand up and down my shaft, and I suppress a moan.

My instincts are about to take over, and I lower my head to give her a warning.

When I look at her, her eyes are distant and cold—colder than any of the versions I encountered in my dreams.

That's when the realization sets in.

This isn't one of my dreams.

This is *actually* happening.

Soulin is in my room and has her grip on my dick.

The urge to move my hips almost breaks my willpower.

She's my Queen, I repeat over and over in my head, and when I follow her gaze, my heart stops.

Her eyes rest on the faint scar of her outstretched arm, on the wound that almost claimed her. The reminder that I killed Felix, her brother.

Immediately, she retreats, taking away the touch I want the most. She takes a few steps back to put a safe distance between us.

The animalistic smile on her face dies when she clears her throat. "I came here to see you because I need to know if the prisoner, Aemilius, lived alone in the village. I was told you were the guard who brought him in."

In an instant, the lust for her crumbles into little pieces when she mentions another man's name.

"I'm not familiar with the name," I answer truthfully, trying to keep my voice steady and act as if nothing happened.

"He has brown hair and dark eyes."

"That sums up about all the men I brought in that day."

"The one I saw trying to escape before the throne room door shut all the way," she clarifies, impatiens rippling through her voice.

That's all the info I need to remember the man she's talking about. I hoped Soulin didn't see the struggle between my guard and the man. I was sure the doors closed before it happened, but I was wrong.

Now the prisoner has a name.

Aemilius.

I try to recall the moment I saw him for the first time. I found him right after I watched a girl kill one of my guards with a sword. She rushed to his aid.

Slowly, the vision of the hut I found him in comes back to life inside my head.

"I found him in a one-room hut. He wasn't alone. A girl came to help him. She didn't seem to live with him, but I noticed the table had two chairs, and the bed was big enough for two."

I try to remember every detail of the moment I used the dead soldier's magic to knock him out. If my instinct is right, he didn't live alone.

But why is it important?

Soulin looks around my room. "Could he have hidden a person inside the hut?"

"Not that I can tell. The hut was tinier than this room."

"But did you search it?"

Irritation starts to seep into my chest. "No. There was no need. We gathered all the surviving villagers."

Soulin takes another step back. "I need you to go back and turn his place upside down. I need to know for sure that you didn't leave a person behind."

She raises her hand, and her fingers glide between her boobs. I try to look away, but the sound of crackling paper catches my attention. Soulin pulls out a sealed envelope and hands it to me. My fingers close around the warm paper, and I stare at it.

"And leave this behind," she says, releasing the envelope.

Another command.

Her stony expression tells me she's done talking to me, and I'm aware that I can't disobey her again, so I say the only thing I can. "Yes, my Queen."

SEVENTEEN

QUEEN SOULIN

Behind the Crymzon Throne, hidden behind a silk-woven tapestry showing the lunar cycle and pictures of lifelike moths, is the door to my most precious room.

I tuck the fabric aside and push myself through a small opening of the door.

Instantly, the rustling of wings fills my ears, slowing my pounding heart rate to a slow beat.

"Good night, my babies," I whisper as hundreds of silk moths surround me, drawn to me like I'm their flame.

Soft, velvety textured wings, coated in a thin layer of crimson hair, flap against my skin, and I inspect their slender little bodies covered in tiny scales and the feathery antennae atop their heads.

The room is dimly lit, with only a few moonlight shafts filtering through narrow windows.

As I walk further into the room, the sweet, musky air of moths and mulberry leaves fills my nostrils. The walls and ceiling are covered in silken webs and cocoons, some torn open and some still waiting to reveal the growing moth inside. They glimmer and sparkle in the light as I reach out and touch one of the webs, letting the soft and silky material run through my fingers.

In the distance, I hear the tussling sound of more enormous wings and the army of silk moths flap away to make space for their Queen.

With a few giant wings strokes, Adira comes into view, and my heart leaps when I get a sight of my oldest Fighter Moth.

She's beautiful.

Wings in a deep, vibrant red, with delicate black veins running throughout and covered in tiny scales, are attached to her six-foot-long rounded fuzzy crimson body.

Adira flaps a few more times, blowing warm air into my face, before she folds her wings neatly over her body, revealing a bold white stripe that runs down the middle of her back.

Before I can lift my hand to greet her, she rubs her head against mine while eyeing me with her round, black eyes.

"I know. I've been gone way too long. But I hope Myra took good care of you."

The fine hair on her face brushes against my cheek, forcing me to close my eyes.

"Of course I have," Myra says, strolling into the silk room unannounced.

I whip around to meet her smiling face. "I told you we'll meet in the courtyard," I mumble, turning back to Adira.

"Can't I check on *my Queen*?"

She doesn't flinch when my icy gaze meets her. "You're acting like I'm going to tip over and die any moment," I say, scratching Adira. "I'm fine. Just give me a few minutes to breathe."

Myra comes to a halt beside me, a gray cloak hugging her delicate frame while worry clouds her eyes. "It's not far-fetched. You're running out of time."

I huff. "A reminder is unnecessary. I know what I'm doing."

"But do you?" She holds my stare for a moment before turning her attention to Adira. "We must replace the Painite soon, or the Heiligbaum's flame will extinguish. Lunra will turn her back on us if the flame goes out and stops sending her a signal. And Keres should be strong enough now to attack any kingdom."

I roll my eyes. "Lunra has forsaken us years ago. She doesn't care if that tree burns or not," I answer, straightening my blood-red dress. "And I'll convince the other Council members to join me. He's a threat to all of us."

As much as I want to kick his ass myself, there is no way around it. I need the other kingdoms' support. Without the full range of my magic, he'll crush my army before having me as a dessert.

"How confident are you that you'll convince them?"

I scoff. "They won't have any other chance than to fight. They must fight, or Escela will be destroyed."

Myra pulls back and straightens her shoulder. "I'm coming with you to the meeting." I lift an eyebrow, and she wrinkles her nose in return. "I'm your advisor. No one is better qualified than me. You'll need me to sway them. You know that I—"

I lift my hand, and Myra stops abruptly. "It was never in question for you to join me."

"But—"

"Why would you assume I leave you behind?"

Myra's cheeks glow. "I thought you'll take Khaos instead."

I think about her implication momentarily, seeing the error in my calculation.

Yes, Khaos is my advisor for battle and anything concerning my army, but this task needs a softer touch than willpower and strength. Those Council members are frail and never had to fight a day of their lives. Taking Khaos with me would scare them off.

"It's bold of you to come here to bargain. You, of all people, should know I don't change my mind at the request of others." I watch her expression tighten. "Grand General Khaos has other matters to take care of," I respond. "I'll meet you in the courtyard in just a moment."

Myra nods slowly before she silently leaves the room.

Alone again, I face Adira and lean closer to her. "What do you think? Are you ready for another adventure, or shall I take Storm or Barin?"

Adira's wings shoot forward, missing me by an inch.

Gently, I rub the spot behind her antennae, and she presses herself against me for a better scratch. "That's what I thought."

A sharp pain stings my heart when I think about how much time I still have left with her.

Moths are not designed to live longer than a few days after crawling out of the cocoon. Their only goal is to reproduce before dying. Their offspring, the silkworms, feed on mulberry bushes I grow in the North Wing to produce the shimmering cocoons we use to spin into silk.

Storm, Adira, Velda, and Barin are unlike the other moths. I nurtured them with the help of my magic and gave them working mouthparts and intestines to outlive the others. Because of their size, they earned the name *Fighter Moths* even though they have never seen battle.

But even though I gave them everything they need to survive the initial few days after hatching, I'm uncertain how long their lifespan is.

Adira was my first creation. I kept her in my chambers to attend to her daily, and it surprised me how big she got with the inconsiderable amount of magic I used.

After three weeks, I moved her back to the Silk Keep. But she seemed lonely among all the other moths, so I decided to give her company.

Our bond is stronger than the ones with Barin, Velda, and Storm. Maybe because the others were raised inside the Silk Keep, or because Adira is the strongest and oldest fighter I have, and she's very affectionate.

I drop my hand and walk to a massive stone-carved lantern in the middle of the room. With one flick of my hand, a fire ignites behind the fingernail-big holes hammered into the lantern—big enough to let light seep through but small enough not to harm any of my insects—and instantly, the small moths follow the crackling flame.

When I reach the door, I open it wide enough for Adira to walk through on her fuzzy legs, and that's when Barin, Velda, and Storm soar in our direction.

As the only male, Barin is smaller than the other three. He's also the calmest of them inside the Keep but very playful when he's outside.

Storm earned her name.

Not only is she fast, but she's also unpredictable and loves throwing people off mid-flight.

Velda is the most obedient and my first choice for transporting important cargo.

The moths halt before me, and I smirk at them. "You guys better behave today. I'll need the guards to get there safely."

Barin dances on his legs as if he can't wait to stretch his wings while Storm pushes herself past me, hitting me with her wing right in the face.

I scoff, and she stops for a moment before she continues to follow Adira into the Throne Room.

"I have no problem replacing you with a new moth," I growl, but she knows I would have done it long ago if I really wanted to.

Barin stares at me, his legs dribbling on the ground, and I move out of the way to let him through. He bolts through the door and crashes head-first into Storm. She flaps her wings vigorously, and he backs away from her.

Velda's gentle eyes rest on me, and I scratch her head before she follows me out of the Keep. I close the door behind me, and my face drops when I see the guards lined up at the end of the hall, waiting for us.

This time, I must choose my guards wisely because if Keres is as close as I suspect, my Fighter Moths may experience their first battle, and I'm in no state to win a fight.

EIGHTEEN

Khaos

My ass hurts, and my legs are numb from the day's ride.

With a handful of guards, I made my way through the desert in the scorching heat. At this point, my clothes beneath the armor are clinging to my body, and I feel the dust finding its way under my clothing to stick to my sweat.

But all I can think about is Soulin's hand on my cock. The feeling of her grip on the fabric was almost unbearable.

Thankful for the long ride to clear my thoughts, I repeat our conversation in my head over and over again.

What's so important about the prisoner that I must ride all this way to search his hut?

The thought of the prisoner turns me off faster than water killing a flame.

"Over there," whispers Remy, pointing his finger at the village in the distance.

"Halt!" I command, loud enough for everyone to hear. "We're going the rest by foot."

Groans erupt around me but die down the second my eyes fly over the soldiers.

"If we left someone in that village behind, we can't announce ourselves with hooves and metal," I explain, dismounting my horse.

The guards know better than to disobey my orders. Especially Remy and Jeremia have been in the royal army long enough to follow any given order without objection.

I hand-picked every soldier guarding Crymzon after Soulin started to build an army after ascending the throne.

Before Soulin 1 started, King Obsidian didn't need protectors because his reign was laced with love and peace. But Soulin brought a new age to Crymzon, and not every citizen welcomed her reign with an open heart after what she did to the King and his heir.

The day of her ascension, someone tried to kill her with an arrow. Luckily, I heard the whistling sound before it found its target and was able to put up a protective shield around the Queen, resulting in the arrow deflecting and hitting the ground.

That's when I still had magic.

The shooter was never confirmed, but over a dozen men were executed in the belief of being the person drawing the arrow.

That's also the day Soulin asked me to build a royal army to protect her and her kingdom from harm, and I was eager to defend my Queen.

Finding new men to join the royal guard is easy, but finding individuals with enough magic left to protect our kingdom without using weapons to cause suspicion among the other domains is almost impossible.

"What's so important about that guy, anyway?" a guard asks, voicing the same question I have been asking myself the entire ride.

I whirl around to face the newest member of my guard, a black-haired, brown-eyed youngling with the fierce energy of a puppy. "That's none of your concern. Your job is to search his housing for any clues."

"Clues for what?" the soldier asks.

"Bellamy, right?" I ask in return, trying to remember his name from the day he introduced himself just a few moons ago.

He straightens his shoulders in answer, his uniform clinking as the metal crashes together.

"If you ask me one more dumb question, I swear you'll leave this village without your tongue."

Bellamy's shoulders slump, and I catch a glimpse of Jeremia trying to hide a smile behind the new guard.

Whipping new soldiers into shape is the best part of my duty as a Grand General. It tells me everything I need to know about a person.

My threat can only be countered by two actions. Either Bellamy submits to me, showing me he's spineless and unsuitable to become one of the Queen's wall guards. Or he will retaliate and demonstrate a quality I'm searching for in my soldiers.

Everyone can obey rules and follow a leader like a puppy. But that's not what I need. I need men who are alert. Who ask questions to inform themselves about everything that happens around them. Who presents a strong will to work as a team and yet feel comfortable enough to take matters into their own hands when needed.

I attach the reins to a dead tree on the ground, fully aware that it won't secure my horse if it decides to take off, when Remy appears before me, binding his steed to the same piece of wood.

"Why are we here?" he whispers, taking his time to fasten the reins.

"Queen Soulin sends us to search his hut for any signs of a companion."

"For what?"

"Leverage."

Remy cocks his head and meets my eyes. "Don't you think she's going too far? At first, she let us search the Kingdom for corpses, knowing that no Crymzonian has the guts to withhold a trapped soul. And now she sends us on a quest to turn a prisoner's home upside down, completely disregarding the real problem."

He doesn't have to tell me what the problem is. Unlike me, Remy and Jeremia still have some magic left to defend themselves. At least if they haven't used it since the last time I tested them. Not only are the citizens becoming suspicious of the fading magic, but also the soldiers started to ask questions.

"It's not her fault," I say, building myself up to my entire height.

"Then whose is it? Everyone knows the Sovereign is connected to Crymzon. So there must be something she isn't telling you."

Remy is wrong. I know exactly what is going on and how close Crymzon's ruin is, but I can't tell him that, nor my soldiers. Panic is the last thing I need to add to the already dire situation.

There's still time to fix everything.

"Is the Queen going to attempt another ceremony again?" another guard asks as he dismounts his horse. "I wasn't there last time because you sent me to deal with the other prisoners, but I heard a rumor that she tried to sacrifice a prince. Is that true?"

I let out a laugh. "A prince? The prisoner is no prince. I would know," I answer, hearing the rumor for the first time. His eyebrows are drawn together in disbelief. "I'll prove it to you."

We march through the flat, dusty terrain for a few minutes in silence, the only noise coming from our rattling armor. The air is dry, and the ground radiates heat, making it unbearable to move on foot for long, so I pick up the pace to find cover inside the prisoner's hut.

I motion for the others to halt as we approach the first hut. I crouch down and examine the ground, my eyes scanning the area for any signs of new footprints.

Satisfied that the sand layer between the huts is untouched, I rise to my feet and draw closer to the rickety wooden door where I found the prisoner after slaying one of my soldiers. Then, without hesitation, I lift my foot and kick the door with all my might, causing it to splinter and fly off its hinges.

"Do you think a prince would choose to live like this?" I ask, not expecting a response, as my soldiers rush forward, their weapons drawn.

The inside of the hut is cramped and dimly lit, with a musty smell that makes my nose wrinkle in disgust. It's sparsely furnished, with a single cot in one corner, some pans and pots stacked in another, and a small table with two chairs in the center of the room.

As my eyes adjust to the darkness, I notice a few trash-filled crates stacked against one wall and several empty bowls of food littered on the ground.

Clearly, someone has been living here after we raided the village, but they are nowhere to be found.

I sign for us to fan out and search the area. We move quickly and efficiently, our eyes scanning the small room for any signs of movement, but there's no hiding spot in here where a person could hide.

"Someone was here," Jeremia whispers, pointing at the bowls on the ground.

"I can see that," I growl, kicking a bowl to the side. "But this evidence doesn't give away if it's someone who lived with the prisoner or if the person just happened to come through here and ate whatever they could find before moving on. So it could have been anyone."

Frustrated, I push over a chair, and it falls to the ground. What am I supposed to tell Soulin? That we found nothing? That we found food leftovers from a person who could be related to the prisoner, but we have no proof?

"I'm going to check the other huts," Remy says in a low voice, and the rest of my soldiers follow him to regroup outside.

I exhale sharply, trying to come up with my next step.

I can't go back empty-handed. Soulin is persistent and will send me back in a few days to check again.

This entire mission has been a disaster, from the excruciating ride to the torturous heat and the missing trace of any evidence to present to my Queen.

I pull out the envelope Soulin gave me and slam it onto the table before I take one last look around.

My eyes land on the wooden crates in the corner, and I clench and unclench my hands at my sides. I step forward and raise my arms above my head, my muscles tensing as I grip the crate tightly. Then, with a primal roar, I hurl it with all my might against the wall.

The impact sends a shockwave through the room, rattling the walls, and the trash spills out from the crate onto the floor.

Something catches my attention as it clatters and clangs against the hard ground, bouncing and rolling until it comes to a rest.

I watch as a tiny piece of it slides under the little bed in the room's corner, disappearing from my view.

For a moment, I stand there, breathing hard, my eyes locked on the object that is hidden beneath crumbled papers, dirty fabric, and spoiled food.

What in Lunra's name is that?

As I approach the item on the ground, I notice it's a strange contraption that looks straight out of this world. The object is made of rusted copper and brass and has intricate gears and cogs that turn and rotate in a rhythmic pattern.

The device is about the size of my hand and has a cylindrical shape with little metal pieces attached to it. Moving closer, I hear a faint whirring noise and a low hum emanating from within.

Upon closer inspection, I notice several dials and gauges on the front panel, each labeled with obscure symbols and markings that I can't decipher. The center of the device is dominated by a large, circular glass chamber filled with a mysterious liquid that glows with an eerie white light. I jump back as a burst of steam shoots out from one of the openings in the side.

What purpose does this strange machine serve, and why was it hidden inside a crate? Is it a weapon or something else entirely?

I heard a rumor that she tried to sacrifice a prince. Is that true? The soldier's words tumble back into my memory, and my breath hitches.

This isn't just any object. It's a gadget, and there's only one place in Escela where you can acquire it: Eternitie.

A kingdom forged of brass and steam, filled with mad scientists and gadgeteers.

Outside, I hear the clanging sound of armor coming closer. I reach for the gadget, my fingers hesitantly curling around the warm metal, and I stuff it between my chest and the breastplate.

"You ready?" Remy calls into the hut, and I jump off the ground, hoping he hasn't seen me store the foreign device away.

"One second," I press out between clenched teeth and scramble to the bed to search for the missing piece.

When I present Soulin with my find, I must ensure that all pieces are accounted for. What if the missing shred was a vital component to make it work?

I fall to my knees beside the bed and reach under it to feel for the metal fragment. I run my hands over the dust-covered ground, and to my surprise, my fingers catch on a metal ring.

Looping my finger into the hole to get a better grip, I try to lift it, but it's stuck.

"Need help?" Jeremia asks, startling me.

"Push the bed over," I snarl, trying to brush off the cold sweat covering my skin as I let go of the metal and search for the little missing piece before he can see it.

Jeremia doesn't hesitate, and with one push, the bed screeches over the floor, revealing the little brass fragment I've been searching for. I snatch it off the ground, and my heart stops when I hear Jeremia unsheathe his sword.

"What are you doing?" I growl, turning to face him while hiding the metal piece in my fist.

Did he see what I did?

His eyes are glued to the ground behind me, and I spin around to see what made him so rigid that he drew his weapon.

Under the fragile-looking bed is a wooden square with a metal pull handle as a latch. The same ring I pulled on without success.

Scrambling to my feet, I stuff the broken metal piece between my stomach and armor and pull my sword.

In my ignorance of how primitive the villagers live in these small huts, I haven't thought about searching for a hidden door.

"Ready?" I whisper to Jeremia, slowly closing in on the pull handle.

It's useless to lower my voice after I made our presence known when I smashed the crate, but if someone is hiding down there, I can still hope for the element of surprise that we found the trapdoor.

As I pull on the ring, the wooden door flings open, and with it, a woman flies in my direction, equipped with a knife. She lashes out, but the blade bounces off my armor.

"Stand down!" I yell at Jeremia and hear Remy and the others rush into the room.

The stranger jumps at me again, her knife aiming for my unprotected face, but before she can reach me, I bang the backside of my hand against her temple, and she drops to the ground, unresponsive.

I scan the woman before me. Her blonde hair is matted and filthy with dirt. She's wearing leather pants and a shirt that used to be white but is now stained with red desert soot. Her limbs are long and skinny as if she hasn't eaten in weeks.

"Who in the seven Gods' names is that?" Remy hisses as he comes to a halt beside me, his sword gleaming in the sunlight falling in through the open door.

I'm aware that the Ordinaries living in the Confines between the kingdoms are refugees. They belonged to a domain before running away or being exiled.

So who is the man I took prisoner? Why does he possess a gadget from Eternitie? And why does he have a woman hidden beneath his bed?

All I know is that he has to be more than just an average citizen if Soulin is interested in him.

NINETEEN

QUEEN SOULIN

If magic rushes through my veins as powerful as my subjects believe, there would be an entire army of Fighter Moths instead of just four.

Therefore, I can only take Myra and two guards with me. Hoping no one questions my abilities when I arrive understaffed, I chose two young soldiers still eager to maintain ground to get promoted.

Khaos was my first option, but he's the only one I trust to find what Cyrus is hiding, if it's anything at all. I need more leverage against the Prince of Eternitie to wipe that smug smile off King Citeus' face.

Adira waits patiently in the shade of a mulberry tree in the courtyard, her wings folded against her body.

I hear the hesitation in the guards' footsteps as we approach the moths. "Whatever you do, hold on tight," I say, a smile forming on my lips.

Under the visors, I can only see their eyes, but it's enough to detect the fear flickering inside them.

So far, no one besides Khaos, Myra, and I had the pleasure of mounting the Fighter Moths.

Storm had tried a few times to buck me off during our first flight and finally caved during our second. That didn't stop her from trying it on Myra while I was occupied breaking Barin in.

"Which one of you is the better rider?" I ask, stopping beside Storm and Barin, who buzz in excitement.

The guards look at each other until the sturdier one raises a shaking hand.

"Good." I point at Storm. "You're going to fly her."

His hand drops, and he stops before her.

With bare feet, I go to Adira and wait until she lowers her legs and lifts her wings. Then, grabbing her fine hair, I heave myself up and clench my feet against her fuzzy body.

Both soldiers watch me attentively, and another guard is needed to help them onto the moths with their heavy armor.

Myra is already mounted on Velda on the other side of the courtyard, and I watch as she drives her hands through the velvety hair.

Finally mounted, I give Adira a soft kick with my heels, signaling to her I'm ready.

Adira's flapping wings stir up the dust beneath us, and I close my eyes to protect them from the particles and to take the moment in.

My body relaxes with the rustling sound of her wings, and the air washes over my body with each blow.

For a moment, I'm no one. Not the Queen of Crymzon. Not Monsteress.

I'm just a little kid again, trying to take in the wonders of the land.

A loud metallic impact makes me rip my eyes open, and a laugh escapes my throat when I see Storm's rider with his back on the ground while Storm flutters below us, no sign of turning back for him.

"One guard will be sufficient," I bellow, leaving the fallen soldier behind.

No.

One guard won't cut it.

But I don't have the time to return, teach the soldier how to keep himself on Storm, and fly out.

I'm already late—just enough to provoke some reaction out of the council members—and I can't drag the wait out any longer if I want to be heard.

Plus, I have Myra by my side. She isn't trained for combat if needed, but if I'm right, she still has some magic hiding inside her, which will be helpful.

It doesn't take long until Starstrand appears in the sky.

From below, the foundation of the kingdom sits on a large, fluffy cloud. But it doesn't drift away like the others. Instead, it's anchored in the same spot above the ocean since Zorus created Escela.

Getting closer, the city surrounding the palace surfaces.

Starstrand is a beacon, shining bright in the sky, symbolizing their Queen's unwavering commitment to their well-being and wishes.

The bright sun illuminates the palace, casting a warm, ethereal glow across its marble walls, which glisten in the sunlight and sparkle like diamonds. The many towers and turrets, each adorned with shining flags that flutter in the breeze, seem to stretch into the sky forever.

I hear the guard's breath catch.

So far, Barin has behaved. I expected more resistance, especially after Storm's reaction, but I'm relieved to reach Queen Caecilia's kingdom with no more trouble.

Finally reaching my destination, Adira lands on the fluffy ground, her legs pressing firmly into the soft, white floor. Velda lands beside me, and Myra hops off her back in one fluent motion.

I jump to my feet, still surprised at how solid yet soft the cloud feels beneath my feet, cushioning my every step.

A man in golden armor approaches us, his wings neatly folded against his back, feathers swaying in the wind. The pale blonde hair falling into his face gives him away as a Starstrandian. It's the same color as his Queen's and anyone else's in this floating kingdom.

"This way, Your Majesty," the tall, wide-shouldered Starstrandian says, pointing at a cloud-made drawbridge leading into Starstrand.

"I expected Queen Caecilia to receive me," I snarl, strolling past him.

He hurries after me. "I'm sorry to disappoint you, Your Majesty. Queen Caecilia is occupied with the other Council members who arrived quite some time ago."

I hear the insult in his growling voice and ignore it.

As I walk through the clouds and over the drawbridge, I survey the marble houses that line the streets. The gleaming white structures soar towards the sky and are buzzing with life. A gentle breeze caresses my face, and the sweet fragrance of the garden flowers fills my nostrils. The sound of flapping wings and cheerful chatter fills the air as the winged people go about their day.

Just a few moments later, a grand silhouette comes into view.

Queen Caecilia's palace.

As I make my way up the steps and through the halls, I'm greeted by ornate arches, each one more intricate than the last. The ceiling rises high above me, painted with images of wing Starstrandians and mythical creatures, all frozen in time. I hear the whispers of their wings as they swirl in the updrafts of the palace, carrying my thoughts with them.

My guard walks behind me like a waterfall of silken robes and clanging armor, his steps echoing off the walls, and Myra falls into line beside me.

The glass ceiling lets the soft, white light of the sky pour in, illuminating every corner of the palace.

The halls are lined with beautiful tapestries woven from the finest silk—my silk—that depict scenes from this kingdom's history.

We approach a grand staircase carved from the same white marble. The steps are wide and shallow, spiraling up into the clouds. I ascend, my hand tracing the smooth banister, taking the building in from a new perspective.

At the top awaits a balcony overlooking the kingdoms below.

The view is breathtaking, as far as my eye can see. A crimson desert encloses my kingdom before the red seeps into the turquoise color of the ocean and the rivers surrounding Tenacoro.

In the depths of the still water, I can make out Oceris, the underwater kingdom.

Two winged guards catch my attention on the other side of the balcony as they open the doors to a room.

As I stand there, taking in the view, I remind myself why I'm here.

"Queen Soulin SinClaret. Ruler of Crymzon. Protector of Lunra," a guard announces, and I step into the room bathed in clouds and sunlight. "Accompanied by Myra Eslene, her royal adviser," the guard bellows behind me.

Queen Caecilia has done her homework since the last time I saw her. Until now, Myra has been my hidden gem.

But not anymore.

TWENTY

QUEEN SOULIN

"You made it," Queen Caecilia welcomes me with outstretched arms and a fake smile. "I considered sending a few of my guards to Crymzon to retrieve you like the other members."

Ignoring her gesture, I stir toward the last empty chair at the round crystal table between King Citcus and Queen Synadena.

"I hope you started without me to talk about all the unnecessary matters while I was absent," I smirk back, taking my seat.

Queen Caecilia's wings vibrate with anger, and I take the opportunity to scan the room.

All the Council members are here and awaiting my arrival just as planned.

My breath hitches when my eyes fall on the woman standing in the corner of the room.

She stands tall and proud, her dark skin, a testament to her royal heritage, shining in the sunlight filtering through the glass ceiling. Her hair, an ebony mane, cascades down her back in loose waves. Her piercing brown eyes survey me.

She moves with the grace of a big cat, her lithe form seemingly effortlessly gliding through the room as she approaches me. Her green dress, made from the finest silk, flows behind her like a river as she walks.

"I can't believe we meet again," Princess Opaline says, leaning down to kiss my cheek.

Starstruck by her beauty, I can't move away fast enough to escape her. Her lips burn on my skin like the Crymzon midday sun. I pull back and stare at her, finally regaining my composure.

I turn to Queen Synadena, her lips curled into a knowing smile. "It's time that Opaline learns more about the Council. Some day, she will lead our people, our kingdom. Until then, she has a lot to learn."

Seeing my childhood friend all grown up sends a shooting pain through my chest. Whenever my parents took me out of Crymzon to meet with the other rulers, Opaline was there. Together, we stole away from the tedious meetings and courtyard formalities to venture through the unknown cities of other kingdoms.

Back then, all five kingdoms were tightly intertwined with trading and peaceful alliances.

But after the day of my deadly magic surge, the other four kingdoms slowly retreated from interacting with me, and when an unknown ruler from the North started attacking the first village outside Eternitie's walls, the harmony in the land crumpled like loose rocks into the ocean.

I inhale sharply. "How time flies. It must have been a decade since I've seen you last," I answer, my voice laced with boredom. "You haven't changed."

But Opaline is no fool. She can see right through my attempt to shut her down. "Thirteen years, to be precise."

She twists a strand of my hair between her fingers before dropping it. I pull back, trying to hide the uneven red tone hidden beneath my curls.

"You're just as beautiful as your mother," Opaline says, and my insides catch fire.

I jump to my feet, my face just inches away from Opaline. "I thought your mother would have taught you better than to talk about the dead," I hiss, sizing her up.

She steps back and walks around the table, running her fingers over the long backrests of the chairs before coming to a halt on the opposite side to face me. "Isn't that why we're here? To talk about the King who brings the dead back to life to do his bidding?"

King Citeus cuts in. "We're still unsure if he *is* a necromancer."

"How much more evidence do you need?" King Usiel asks, tapping his finger on the table. "His kingdom stretches over the uninhabitable part of the land. No one can survive those extreme temperatures for long."

King Citeus rolls his mustache between his fingers. "Maybe their God protects them?"

Queen Synadena rolls her eyes and leans back in her chair. "The only God who hasn't shown his face is Otyx."

Queen Caecilia's eyebrows shoot into the air. "The God of the Underworld?"

He nods. "Keres has to be his creation. And if that's the case, we will need more than the protection our deities offer. I'm still in shock that it took Otyx this long to draw attention to himself."

King Citeus raises from his chair. "My deepest apologies, but I must ask. What evidence do you have of this threat? Of course, we know he has settled in Terminus, but do you have any proof of an army?"

Standing up from my chair, I match his height. "As I said during our last meeting, I have received credible reports from my scouts. Keres is gathering strength, and his intent is clear. He's working his way around our kingdoms to form an army of Ordinaries, and it's just a matter of time until he attacks one of us."

King Usiel's fist collides with the table. "Perhaps he's just helping us solve our problem by getting rid of the traitors."

I sit back down and scan Queen Synadena's face for support, but her face is blank.

Now or never.

"It doesn't matter what he is or who created him. The threat in the North grows stronger with each passing day. We cannot stand idly by while he marches towards us. So I implore you, join me in this fight against Keres and let us return Escela to its old glory."

Queen Caecilia clears her throat and looks right at me. "Why your sudden interest in saving your subjects? Aren't you a bigger threat to them than Keres?"

"If you don't take this seriously, you will regret it," I hiss through clenched teeth.

She spreads her wings, her eyes blazing with fury. "While I sympathize with your plight, I won't let you threaten me." She folds her wings back in. "I cannot spare any troops at this time."

"I agree," King Citeus says, returning to his seat. "Our resources are stretched thin, and we cannot risk a conflict that doesn't involve us."

I chuckle, and his nose wrinkles.

This is my opportunity to call him out on his lie. To point out his fake grief about his secondborn, who is alive, sitting in a cell inside Crymzon. To tell the other council members about his attempt to cover up that his son is a traitor to his own kingdom and that I almost sacrificed him not knowing who he was.

Giving the King of Eternitie one more smirk, I move my head to the other members. "Rulers," I say in a firm voice. "I understand your reservations, but consider this - if we do not act now, we may not have kingdoms left to return to. The North poses a direct threat to us all. Therefore, I urge you to join me."

Queen Synadena straightens in her seat, twisting a rich brown wooden ring around her finger. "Let's say we agree; what do you propose?"

I face her. "That we join forces, unite our armies, and defeat this common enemy."

King Usiel yawns. "And what do you offer in return for our aid?"

A huff escapes my throat. "What do *I* offer *you*? I'm the one saving us from doom. The question is, what are you offering me?"

The wrinkles on King Usiel's forehead deepen. "You're requesting assistance in a war that doesn't even pose a threat to us. This is a conflict only you seem to have with a faceless ruler in the North."

My cheeks heat as I take his accusation in.

I have proof. Felix came back from the dead. He wasn't alive, so to speak, but he was there.

Yet, openly discussing the incident with my brother in front of the Council members is impossible.

Myra steps beside me at the table. "We offer our sincerest gratitude and the promise of a lasting alliance. In this time of need, we must set aside our differences and work towards a common goal."

King Usiel massages his eyebrow with one hand while tapping the other on the table. "That won't be enough to spare any of my troops to aid your war in the ridged climate of the North."

Rage flushes through me. My eyes land on Queen Synadena, the only one still anonymous. She shakes her head slowly, lowering it.

Hot blood flushes through my veins, and I push the chair back, pointing at every single one of them. "And you call yourselves Kings and Queens, Protectors of your kingdoms," I snarl, making my way to the door without being dismissed.

Myra trails me quietly, and the sound of wings rustling in the air pierces my ears. I know Queen Caecilia is about to unleash living hell on me for disrespecting her court, but I don't care. I must get out of here before I use the last of my magic to strangle them all.

Instead of hearing the high voice of the Queen, Myra takes the stand. "We need you," she pleads, turning to the Council. "Otyx sends him to punish us. Zorus, the God of the Gods, promised in the prophecy that the day will come when Otyx claims his throne amongst the Gods to be deemed the strongest."

I jerk her arm to stop her from saying more, but Myra breaks loose and pushes away from me to get closer to the table. "We need your help! Please."

"We do not beg!" I bellow, moving around her, and I strike her face with my flat hand.

The slapping sound echoing off the marble walls sends a shiver down my spine and into my core.

Immediately her face reddens, and she holds her hand to her cheek in disbelief. Her eyes widen, and her mouth opens before she rushes out of the room.

I register the silence from the Council. Everyone watched me mute my advisor with my bare hand.

"How can we trust you if you don't even trust your people?" King Usiel asks, standing up from his chair and shaking his head. "Don't you think you're going too far? We watched your game for years and let you lead without interjecting, hoping you would pick the right path and follow in your parent's footsteps. But this..." He points to my throbbing hand. "Is that how you want your people to remember you? Do you want your legacy to be blood and death?"

I curl my fingers into fists. "At least I'm not a coward. Even your subjects will remember *me* as the only ruler with the guts to do something about Keres. But, of course, that would mean your kingdoms survive his attacks. Mark my words: Your kingdoms will fall, one by one, and I will be watching."

Through the pounding heartbeat in my ears, I can't make out a word from the uproar behind me.

My gaze wanders to the stone columns alongside the wall, and my eyes land on Princess Opaline. A single tear runs down her cheek, glittering in the beaming sunlight streaming in from the windows. Her shoulders are tense, and her hands balled into fists.

That's not how I imagined our reunion to unfold. To be honest, I never expected to see her again after how abruptly I dropped her after my mother's death.

Opaline wipes away the lone tear with the back of her hand, and that's the last image I see before the guards close the heavy doors behind me.

TWENTY-ONE

CYRUS

I'm not sure how much time has passed since Monsteress slid out of my room, leaving me and my thoughts behind. I tried to run every worst-case scenario through my head during my wait.

What if she tricks me and my father enters the room the next time this door opens? What if she changed her mind and decided to execute me instead of accepting my assistance in finding a gem I don't know how to locate? If Monsteress dies while I'm in this room, and the guards overlook me, what then?

I scoff when thinking about the last option. *No. I won't be lucky enough for that to happen.*

I would know if something happened to her. Even though I can't figure out what caused the palace's earthquakes I experienced, it has something to do with her. I'm sure of it.

Shuffling footsteps pull me back into reality.

"My Queen," a hushed voice says through the crack of the door, and I watch as it opens, revealing a candle-lit hallway.

I step forward, readying myself to bolt through the door, but my view gets blocked by a silhouette.

"Good, you're still breathing," Monsteress snarls as she enters my room, and the door behind her falls shut.

"I would say it's a pleasure to see you again, but welcoming death with open arms seems too cruel even for my taste," I hiss, straightening my shoulders.

The image of her trying to sacrifice me to a burning tree still haunts me, and I can still feel the heat penetrating through my clothes. I shake my head to clear it.

She smiles at me, revealing her bone-white teeth. "I always thought your father was the most annoying person on this planet, but you're able to claim his place with a single sentence," Monsteress growls back.

My eyes are fixed on my escape route to freedom. "What do you want?"

She takes a few steps in my direction. "Is that how you talk to the person who saved your life?"

I shake my head and look at her. "You almost burned me alive."

"But I changed my mind," she whispers. "You did this to yourself when you ran away, Prince. I just happened to find you before your father did." An evil smile hushes over her face, forcing me to step back. "Speaking of your father. He's sending his regards."

The sickening feeling that I have to throw up crawls through my stomach as the blood rushes from my face. "You didn't." I search her face for a sign that she's lying, but no muscle moves.

"It only took him two minutes to bring your death up during the meeting," she muses, circling her hands in the air as if those words are music to her ears. "How could I pass on the opportunity to tell him that you belong to me now, just like he wanted?"

My knees wobble thinking about my father. If he knows where I am, he will send my brother to retrieve me, and Cyprian will ensure I never reach Eternitie in one piece.

"Aren't you happy I don't force you to complete the Connection Ceremony with me like your father wanted? I mean, he must've been the one who decided to offer you to me if the thought of spending the rest of your life with me made you flee Eternitie."

My mouth is so dry I can't get a word out.

She studies me. "What do you think? Is he going to send your siblings to haul you back?" She shakes her head. "No. He's too much of a coward to send all of his heirs into my territory. Maybe a few soldiers?" She clicks her tongue, weighing her question. "No. He said his resources are stretched thin, which makes me believe he doesn't even have a royal army at his disposal."

"You're a fool," I whisper, and her eyes flicker in delight at my insult. "He'll send every single one of his soldiers if that means my return."

"Oh, don't worry. I can take on his handful of untrained men with a flick of my fingers," she muses back, snapping her fingers together, and I flinch.

Cold sweat forms on my skin. "You don't understand. He's obsessed with raising the biggest army in the land, and his weapons are nothing like you've ever seen."

The smile she gives me unnerves me. "I'm not worried about his little gadgets."

"You should be," I mumble back, trying to focus on her instead of the image of my blood-covered hands.

For a year, I've tried to suppress that memory, and I've been successful by keeping myself busy building hidden shelters in the village. But knowing my father will come for me throws me back into the spiral I so desperately tried to escape.

It's not me he wants. It's what's inside my head—the reason I had to flee my home.

"You can't do this," I mutter, fighting against more flashbacks flooding my head.

Monsteress presses her lips together as she considers my words. "You think you're worth your father's entire army?"

I throw my hands in the air. "Why does that matter?" I bark. "Even if he sends all his men, he won't attack you until he has me."

Her face turns into stone. "But if you want me to keep you safe, I need to know how many soldiers to expect so I can prepare my army."

I almost start laughing when I hear the word *safe* come out of her mouth.

This can't be true. I can't be having this conversation with Monsteress. There's nothing safe about her besides a certain death.

Slowly, the realization of my situation sets in. I'm about to beg the worst human on this planet to save me from an equal monster—my father.

But what better option do I have?

My first plan to kill Monsteress vanishes in a blink of an eye. She's useless to me if she's dead because she's the only one standing between me and my father. So my only chance of survival is to convince her I'm helpful to her long enough until I find a way to escape and leave Crymzon and Eternitie behind once and for all.

I can start new somewhere else, far away from all the insanity.

"He has about two thousand soldiers. But that was a year ago. By now, you could expect about double."

Her green, golden eyes pierce right into my soul as if she's searching for the truth. Then, finally, she exhales and drops her gaze while she steps closer.

With each step, my throat constricts, and I can't keep my eyes off her elegant, moving body. "If you promise to help me find the Painite," she says, touching my arm with warm fingers. "I promise to deny that you're my prisoner. After all, it shouldn't be a problem to convince him that I said it to get under his skin."

I focus on the door, trying to keep my senses sharp as she walks around me, branding my back with her fingers. The touch is soft and compelling, but it also feels like she's dragging cut glass over my skin.

I flinch away from her touch, breaking the spell she has on me. "Stop trying to seduce me," I growl, facing her. "And there's no way he's going to believe you. You already sparked his curiosity by mentioning that I'm alive when the entire land thinks I'm dead. He's not stupid. He will see right through your cover-up and send his soldiers to get me back by force."

The corner of her mouth moves up. "You give your father too much credit."

I huff. "And you don't give him enough. His brain is designed to find mistakes to make improvements. He's a mastermind even if he doesn't look like it."

"But you're not like him. Apparently, you know little about magic. A single spell is enough to make him forget that the conversation ever happened."

I bite my lip but can't hold back the words building up inside me. "If you're so powerful, why haven't you forced me to do your bidding? Why sacrifice so much precious time with a fallen prince when you only need to flick your hand to make me submit to you?"

The color rushes out of her face. "Where would be the fun of doing that?"

"You're a horrible liar," I grin back, reveling in the feeling of watching her clench her teeth.

I'm going to die through her or my father's hands, so why not embrace the little time I have left to give Monsteress some of her own medicine?

She strides to the door and presses her hand firmly against it without giving me another glance. "I feel generous, so here's my offer: Help me find the Painite, and I'll take care of your father."

"And what if I don't accept?"

"If you're unwilling to comply, I will return you to Eternitie." Her voice is laced with anger. "I'll give you until sunrise to decide."

"That's not an offer," I laugh, knowing full well that I don't have another choice.

"Then it should be easy to accept it," she answers as she opens the door. "Rest up. Once the sun rises, we'll be heading to Terminus."

She knows she won. I hear it in her voice. But two can play this game. Agreeing with her plan opens up my only way to make an escape.

So technically, my plan hasn't changed. It just got more urgent that I find a way to get away from Monsteress.

If I calculate it right, we're a four-day ride away from Terminus. That will give me four days to devise a plan, and with luck, I can pick out the fastest horse and disappear into the night before anyone notices.

She walks through the door, her blood-red dress trailing her like flowing honey, and my following words make her stop. "You know you can't win this fight. Death has you by the throat, and it's just a matter of time until it claims you."

She grabs the stony door and faces me. "I'm not scared of death," Monsteress says, fire flickering in her eyes. "The only thing bothering me is that Otyx favors another person over me, and it's my duty to remind him of who his real champion is."

And with that, the door shuts behind her, leaving me once more in total darkness.

TWENTY-TWO

QUEEN SOULIN

C onvincing Cyrus that his father is after him was easy. I had the feeling that something was amiss when I heard him mentioning Eternitie's ruler in a bitter tone. I know what a broken heart sounds like when I hear it. He uses the same tone I use when talking about my father.

Finding out how strong Eternities' army is, in case King Citeus decides to cross me, was even easier. If Cyrus is right, his father's army surpasses mine.

But Crymzonians possess magic, equaling one Crymzonian for at least four Eternians, maybe even more.

That means Eternitie is a threat if the King moves against me, but not enough that I have to worry about it. Once I restore the Heiligbaum to its full potential, I will make his army fall like a sack of rocks.

My mind wanders back to the man held in my palace. There would never be a real chance of trust between the Prince and me, but somehow he bought my lie and thinks I'm the one keeping him alive.

I needed to infuse fear to keep him on a tight leash and win his faith to help me find the Painite. With the help of the gem, I'm one step closer to strengthening Crymzon's bond with Lunra again, and hopefully, she will return the favor and boost our magic to face Keres.

As I walk down the halls, I hear the whispers of the guards behind me.

What gossip is spreading now through the palace? Is it my encounter with my brother, my health, or what happened in the temple?

The footsteps trailing me are more distant than I'm used to, so I spin around to address the two guards marching behind me. "It has come to my attention that rumors are circulating about me. Share them with me?" I demand as the guards stop abruptly to keep their distance.

"I'm not sure what you're referring to, Your Majesty," the older one says, bowing his head.

"I know when my subjects talk behind my back. What are they saying?"

Over the years, I've learned to listen silently to the whispered conversations between the guards, maids, servants, and anyone entering the palace. No one is immune to the frenzy of rumors and speculations. It's an integrated system of knowledge, all interwoven with information and details each person adds to decode any situation inside and outside the Crymzon Wall.

It's also the best way to influence the gossip by feeding them lies.

It never fails.

It takes less than a day for my lies to trickle down the rumor funnel until my version circulates throughout the kingdom.

Myra doesn't understand why I interfere with ordinary folks. She's an excellent advisor but doesn't see the importance of meddling with gossip. Therefore, her knowledge is limited to what she can tickle out of some trusted servants and our spies hidden deep inside each kingdom.

The guards shuffle their feet. "Your Majesty. We're not here to take part in any gossip."

"And yet you've heard it. So tell me: what are the people saying about me?" They keep their heads bowed and their eyes downcast when I try to meet their gazes. "We can either do it painlessly by speaking up now, or I can send Grand General Khaos to extract it from you."

The boy's Adam's apple moves nervously as he finds his voice. "They're saying you brought back Eternitie's Prince to sacrifice him to Lunra to spark a reaction out of King Citeus," he says, and the older guard gives him a stern look, but he continues. "And you tried to kill yourself on the rooftop because you know you're the reason magic is dying, and you wanted to end your suffering."

The laugh bursting out of me startles the boy.

"Dear Lunra," I laugh, trying to buy myself some time to figure out the perfect lies.

Someone must have seen me looking out from the tower before I was attacked. But had they seen the undead version of my brother?

Apparently not; otherwise, the rumor would be harder to turn around.

But the watcher knew that something happened to me.

We haven't experienced an earthquake since the day my father died. It's a sign that the Sovereign is severely injured or has died. It wouldn't surprise me if some of my subjects are over five hundred years old and experienced the quake following my grandmother's death, marking a new era of King Obsidian 1.

"The magic isn't dying," I smirk, my mind still working on the right words. "It's as strong as ever, but I'm preserving it to use it against the darkness brewing in the North. I must ensure we're strong enough to face what's coming to keep my kingdom safe." The lie slips as comfortably over my tongue as water. "And the speculation that I tried to kill myself is outrageous. Why would I do that? I'm the Queen of the most powerful kingdom in the land."

C.K. FRANZISKA

The older guard moves his shoulders like he must build the courage to speak again. "Then why did the palace shake?"

My grin widens. "The Prince, or whatever the people call him, he's nothing more than an intruder who tried to kill me. So the question is: how did he find a way into my palace with no one noticing? Don't I pay you enough copper to protect me from threats like him?"

No one dares to say a word or move.

The fastest way to kill a rumor is to focus on a bigger, unrelated problem. Unfortunately, this strategy won't give me much time because, eventually, people will ask more questions and start wondering how a simple man could injure me badly enough that my connection to Crymzon crumbled for a moment. Or why I haven't used my magic to defend myself.

Until that moment comes, I will have returned from Terminus with the Painite, restored the Heiligbaum, and Cyrus will be dead and left behind in the North to stop the rumors ultimately.

No body, no proof.

I point my palms up to the ceiling. "What are you waiting for? Spread the word to your fellow guards," I continue. "Keep your eyes and ears open, and report anything suspicious to me immediately. And find the guards who were on wall duty that day. I will select one of them for the next ceremony."

I turn on my heels to return to my chambers and listen to them frantically scurry down the hallway to find those innocent men.

They will be occupied for a few hours trying to round them up, and on the way, they will start spreading the newest gossip to every listening ear.

Smiling to myself, I think about my words, which will send shockwaves through the palace. Without them knowing yet, I have given them the hope that another ceremony will follow during the next moon.

140

As I turn the corner, I see Myra standing before my door, her hand raised to announce herself with her usual knock. But her hand freezes midair when she notices my arrival.

"Go in," I say, without waiting for her greeting.

Myra pushes the door open, and I follow her into my chamber, shutting the door silently.

"I have news from the prison. The newest add-on was just completed. That means we can finally gather more prisoners," Myra says as she scans my bright room.

"How many are we talking about?"

"About one hundred," she guesses, turning to face me.

"That's not enough," I say in a low voice.

Myra lowers her gaze. "I know. I just handed over the sketches for the two new projects you approved, and the construction starts as we speak."

"How long will it take until they're done?"

"It's hard to say. We're talking about three hundred additional cells."

I wrinkle my nose. "I know because I came up with those improvements. We need to get it done sooner."

"It's not possible. The prisoners are exhausted. If you run them ragged, we won't have any workers left."

"Then add more people."

Myra stares at me. "What do you want me to do? Pluck some random citizens off the street?"

"Oh, not random. Pick the young ones," I say, studying her face for a reaction. "We don't need more old people wasting a good cell. They've lived long enough and are useless workers."

"But—"

I cut her off. "This is not a discussion. It's a command," I say wearily, wiping my face.

The wrinkles around her eyes deepen. "Wait a minute," Myra says, lifting a finger to her chin. "Why are you in your chambers? If I didn't know better, I would think you're hiding. But you don't cower, so what happened?" She asks, her eyes searching my body for fresh injuries.

"I'm just exhausted," I whisper, the room suddenly spinning around me. I lean against the door to catch my breath.

Myra jumps forward and grabs me by the arm. "What do you need?" she asks in a soft voice.

I close my eyes. "Nothing."

When I open them again, I see the red mark on her cheek where I struck her. My fingers still sting from the slap, even though it has been hours since we landed.

"It looks worse than it feels," Myra says as she notices my lingering eyes on her. "But why did you have to strike me so hard?"

"What were you thinking?" I demand instead. "You had no right to address the Council that way. I was so close to getting what I needed."

Her eyes search mine, and her forehead wrinkles. "It didn't look that way. You were grabbing for straws." She hesitates for a moment, taking a step back. Then, finally, she speaks up again, her voice measured and calm. "Your Majesty, I'm sorry if I offended you. I didn't mean to speak out of turn."

I raise an eyebrow, confused about her sudden mood change. It's atypical for Myra to step down from a confrontation and even rarer for her to address me so formally.

Her compassion for righteousness is the quality that made me choose her as my advisor.

It wasn't right for me to lay a finger on her; she knows that as well as I do. So why isn't she fighting back?

Crossing my arms, I let out an exaggerated sigh. Usually, that's enough to get her blood boiling, but she doesn't take the bait.

"Very well," I say, irritated by her defeat. "Apology accepted. But remember: the consequences will be much worse next time you cross me in front of an audience."

Myra bows her head in submission, walks over to the bed, and gestures to follow her.

"Stop doing that. I'm not a child anymore," I growl, ripping the blanket out of her hand and shaking it to undo the neatly made bedding.

"Why do you have to be so damn stubborn?" Myra hisses as she snatches a pillow from the mattress and fluffs it up. "I'm trying so hard to help you. Why can't you accept it?"

My nostrils flare as adrenaline rushes through my veins.

There's the Myra I know. The feisty woman who used to go after me when I was younger.

"I never asked you for help. I'm capable of taking care of myself."

"By dying?" Myra barks, her face distorted with anger.

I inhale sharply and watch as her face crumbles. Myra sits down on the bed and buries her face in her hands. "How am I supposed to help you?" she whispers through her thin fingers. "It's not supposed to end like this. You're just a child."

I wouldn't say twenty-seven is a child's age, but I'm still a juvenile against Myra, who has served over two-hundred years at my mother's side.

"Whatever happens to me shouldn't concern you," I snarl back and walk around the bed to the window.

The sun burns on my skin when I gather the silky curtains in my hands and pull them shut, leaving the tiniest sliver of light behind to find my way back to my bed. Immediately, the room cools down.

Making my way back to the bed, I watch Myra in the darkness as she rises from it. "This affects all of us. You have little time left."

"That's why I'm leaving for Terminus in the morning."

"Have you lost your mind? You can't fly in this state," she says, pointing at me as I heave myself into bed. "Not to mention the danger lurking in the North. I will not let you leave."

"I don't need your permission. I'm leaving."

Myra curls her hands into fists and steps closer, her eyes shimmering in the ray of sunlight filtering through a slit between the fabrics like emeralds. "Then I'm going with you."

I shake my head. "No. Your presence is requested here."

Her dark eyebrows almost touch her silver hairline. "Excuse me?"

"You heard me right. I need you to prepare the temple."

Her mouth pops open. "For what? The last ceremony was a disaster. It would be best to take your duty as the High Priestess and Queen more seriously. You weren't prepared the last time you tried to summon Lunra, and you will fail again if you don't practice."

If I wasn't so darn tired, I would put Myra into her place, but the last few days have been exhausting, and I feel my body screaming for rest. Sleep is the only thing my body needs to have a chance of surviving tomorrow's voyage.

I pull the silky blanket up to my chin and find the fluffiest part of the pillow to rest my head on. "Make sure the common folk sees you during the preparations. Once I return, they will want to witness how I restore the Heiligbaum with a new Painite, and after, we will offer Lunra not one but two godless souls."

Myra crosses her arms. "And how will you find Painite, if I may ask?"

"That prisoner I tried to offer to Lunra, turns out he's more vital for my plans than I thought."

Even as my advisor, Myra doesn't need to know every little detail of my life. Sometimes it's better to keep a clear invisible line between my subjects and me, especially when it comes to another royal under my roof.

Cyrus isn't just any prince. He's the one who was promised to me since I took my first breath. And now it will be less than a day before he takes his last breath, and I'm free.

The less Myra knows, the better. If she knew, she would try to convince me to let him live, and I can't do that.

She can't find out who he really is.

"I put all my faith in you that the temple will be ready for the biggest ceremony Crymzon has seen in decades. And after I reclaim my perfect image, Lunra will gift us more magic."

"I'm not sure if you know what you're doing," Myra whispers, rubbing her forehead. "Praying to Lunra once won't put you in her favor. She will see right through you."

"Then pray that my intentions are clear enough and she realizes that I only need enough magic to kill that bastard in the North," I answer, repositioning my head on the pillow. "There's one more thing. Please prepare an extra prisoner for my return, and this time make sure he can defend himself if needed. Lunra wouldn't pick a weakling for me."

"She probably also disapproves of your method of finding your Soulmate without even trying to connect with that person."

I shrug. "I'm connecting with them the only way I know. There isn't anything deeper than what I'm offering."

Myra clicks her tongue. "You know what I mean. Of course, the connection through mating is important, and that's how you seal it, but the link between two people only appears when you're most vulnerable. That can't happen if you face a wall while he takes you from behind."

"So you saw?" I ask, closing my eyes to shut her out.

"I did." Her mouth turns into a thin line. "But I also know how it feels when the connection takes over."

My mouth goes dry when I open my eyes again and watch tears forming in hers.

Myra was gifted with one of the strongest connections I ever experienced. Her Soulmate was lovely and way too young when she died.

I know the pain Myra felt when Elia passed. I was there when it happened.

There's only one Soulmate out there for everyone, and when you lose them, it feels like you're dying with them.

Every unloved ounce that was reserved for Elia, she put into me.

"I need to sleep," I whisper, my voice raspy.

Myra looks me over, and I sense the request to stay a little longer in her eyes. Instead of answering her request, I pull the blanket up and turn to my other side to face the wall.

Whatever Myra needs, I can't give it to her. After years of shutting everyone out of my heart, I won't cave now.

Myra must have regained her composure because her voice sounds strong and eager when she speaks again. "I'll be there to see you off tomorrow morning, Your Majesty," she says, stepping away.

TWENTY-THREE

KHAOS

W aiting for the girl to wake is torture.

　　After knocking her unconscious, Jeremia asked me what to do with her.

My mission was to figure out if the prisoner lived alone. Unfortunately, Soulin didn't mention what to do if I found another person inside his hut.

Am I supposed to return with her, or is it my job to kill her and leave her body behind?

I waited outside while my soldiers turned every building inside the village upside down, finding hidden trapdoors in every hut.

To my surprise, the girl hanging limp in my arms is the only survivor from the day we raided the village.

"Who is she?" Jeremia asks as we make our way back to our horses.

I grunt in return, deflecting his question. The sun begins to dip below the horizon, coloring the already colorful desert blood red. "If we want to return before the sun sets again, we need to hurry."

The following hours feel like an eternity. The soldiers' questions linger in the air like thick smoke, yet no one is brave enough to speak them out loud.

As we ride through the dry, unforgiving desert, the only sounds are the steady clip-clop of the horse's hooves and the occasional rustle of the wind carrying the dunes away.

Even though the woman is only skin and bones, I feel the weight of her unconscious body lying across my lap, her short blonde hair splayed across my leg. I can't see her features clearly, but I can tell that she's about my age.

Who are you? I whisper to myself, studying her dirt-covered face for clues to her identity.

She's clearly not a soldier like some of the other women we retrieved from her village. Is she a victim of war, or did she get caught up in a different type of violence? Maybe she was a prisoner before we even found her and he kept her hidden in the small room beneath the bed for a reason.

But why?

Her pale skin can only mean one thing: she's from Eternitie, the city where no one ever leaves their homes because they are too busy inventing unnecessary gadgets like the one pressing against my chest beneath my armor.

Eternitie, though, it doesn't feel right. Blonde hair like hers is rare in any other kingdom than Starstrand. But to be a Starstrandian, she must have wings. I don't see any.

That means the gadget must belong to the man living in the hut. But how are they related to each other?

They must be lovers.

Despite my uncertainty about her origins, I'm determined to deliver the woman to Soulin. It's not my place to question the importance of finding her.

I urge my horse on, eager to get us out of the Confines before the moonrise. Our horses plod on, their hooves kicking up dust clouds behind us. As far as I can see, we're surrounded by a barren landscape.

"We need to rest," Remy says beside me, his eyes glazed with tiredness.

"Don't act like this is your first mission outside the Wall. You know better than anyone that we can't rest in the desert," I answer, tightening my grip around the reins.

Remy accompanied me on my first mission, scouting the desert. That ride taught me many lessons and showed me how foolish I was, thinking I could leave Crymzon unprepared.

Memories of the deadly creatures lurking in this unforgiving terrain flood my mind. Venomous snakes that can strike without warning, their deadly fangs capable of killing a man in seconds. Scorpions, their tails tipped with a venomous sting that can cause excruciating pain and paralysis. Spiders, their oversized bodies and sharp, pointy legs capable of inflicting deep wounds.

And those are just the tiny land creatures and don't even cover the airborne threats that haunt the desert skies.

I've lost too many soldiers to nature's cruel ways to balance the scale.

Despite the constant threat of danger, I need to remain focused and vigilant, ready to face any challenge that comes our way because I can't risk losing more.

As the night progresses, I sharpen my senses, yet I'm not ready for what comes next.

The woman stirs.

I slow my horse and try to steady her.

But before I can come to a stop, the woman springs up, surprising me with her sudden movement. Then, with a burst of energy, she leaps off the horse and takes off running, leaving me momentarily stunned.

Realizing what's happening, I quickly regain my composure and give chase to the fleeing woman, followed by the trampling hooves of my soldiers' horses.

"Grab her!" Jeremia yells behind me, and that's when it hits me.

"Stop!" I command, balling my hand into a fist, signaling the soldiers to fall back.

Instantly, the clapping hooves around me fall silent, and I pull on the reins to bring my horse to an abrupt halt.

I watch as she runs with determination, her feet pounding the desert sand as she tries to escape us.

"You're letting her get away?" one soldier asks, his finger pointing at the hysterical female.

"She won't escape," I answer loud enough for her to hear, pointing at the treacherous terrain. "She's as good as dead out here without shelter or our help."

We're halfway to Crymzon, meaning there's nothing else out here for hours besides sand and hungry creatures.

I watch as the woman stumbles over the ground, getting further away from us. With each step, she slows down until she comes to a standstill.

It's the exact moment she notices I'm right.

Her eyes wander over the moonlit landscape, and a desert lion—the Confines most lethal predator, whose powerful jaws and sharp claws make it a formidable opponent—roars in the distance.

She breathes heavily, her chest rising and falling as she turns to inspect her surroundings further. The desert stretches for miles without a single sign of life.

I scratch my head, waiting for her to face us finally.

Knocking her unconscious again isn't an option. She would never let me near her again. Not freely. If I had magic, this would be so much easier.

Another option is to ask a soldier to tranquilize her with magic, but I can't do that either. So far, I have been able to keep my depleted magic unknown, and I will do everything in my power to keep it that way.

"Let's go," I roar, turning my horse to head south.

"We can't just leave her here," Remy whispers, catching up with me.

I smirk at him. "Trust me. She'll make it to Crymzon," I whisper, and it only takes a few moments until the rest of the soldiers appear beside me.

"What's the plan?" Jeremia asks in a hushed voice, leaning over his horse.

"Just wait," I mumble, ensuring that my horse walks at a comfortable pace.

I don't look over my shoulder.

If I'm right, it will only take a few minutes until she realizes she won't survive a night out here.

I feel the soldiers' eyes burning on my face as they question my command. There's no way I will cave. This has to work, for my sake and hers.

To loosen up the uncomfortable silence, I start whistling. The melody carries my mind back to the stables, and I hear my father pipe the same tune as he brushes the horses.

Back then, I wasn't sure if I enjoyed his music more or the four-legged animals surrounding us.

"How did you know?" Jeremia whispers, and I look over as he rotates his head to meet my eyes.

I rub my lips against each other to mask my grin. "That she'll follow us?"

"Yes."

"Because she's smarter than you think."

"What does that even mean?" Remy asks as he watches the female stumbling behind us.

"Any man would have chosen to die out here instead of relying on another person. But this woman, she's smart enough to swallow her pride, knowing that we're the enemy, and yet she decided to trail us in hopes we keep her safe. That demands much courage."

Besides showing courage, it also gives me more insight into her character. Soulin would never trail the enemy. She's aware of her strength; even without magic, she's educated enough to defend herself.

This woman slowly creeping behind us is not a fighter.

She's a follower.

And there is only one kingdom known for intelligent but otherwise useless citizens—this woman belonged to Eternitie before she fled to the Confines.

This also means that the gadget tucked underneath my armor belongs to her, and I will find a way to make her confess what it does.

TWENTY-FOUR

CYRUS

Trusting a gigantic, winged creature to bring me safely through the land is even worse than facing Monsteress.

The plan to escape by horse vanished into thin air when Monsteress' guards led me to a generous bug with wings and told me to mount it.

How am I supposed to flee now? Flying hundreds of feet in the air isn't something I planned on.

Dropping from this height would mean my inevitable death, and from what I gathered, we won't stop until we reach Terminus.

As we fly over the river dividing Crymzon and Eternitie, high in the sky to avoid any attention, my mind races, trying to come up with a new solution.

A bright gleam catches my attention below us. I see it even so high above the land, far away from prying eyes.

A bustling maze of a kingdom in hilly scenery, filled with towering buildings with intricate brass and copper details and steam-powered inventions. The streets are crowded with people, all moving about on artificial paths.

The air is thick with the smell of coal and the sound of engines. Steam rises from every chimney, creating a veil between us.

I can see gears turning and hot air billowing everywhere I look as the city runs on the power of steam.

And right in the middle of all the commotion stands the Brass Palace.

My veins turn into ice as I watch ant-sized people stream in and out of the palace's gates.

If someone sees me, I'm done for.

The creature beneath me buckles, and I form a tighter fist around its fine hair to hold myself in place.

"Why is yours not trying to throw you off?" I scream after Eternitie lies behind us.

"Because she knows who's in charge," Monsteress yells over her shoulder, an evil smile curling her lips.

The further we get north, the colder the wind whips around my body. My flesh and bones are frozen to the core, making it almost impossible to hold on to the feisty beast beneath me.

The only reason I agreed to this plan was to escape. But, with no chance of ever getting out of my personal prison chamber and Crymzon alive while hundreds of guards patrol the palace and the Wall, Terminus gives me a better opportunity to vanish.

Ahead of me, a range of massive, pointy mountains looms, their peaks hidden in a thick blanket of clouds. I pull my silky shirt around my body, my breath is visible in the crisp mountain air.

The surrounding light dims as if the scenery before us consumes it, leaving only darkness behind.

Slowly, we descend.

"Where?" the guard yells at me, pointing at Terminus.

I'm about to shrug my shoulders when I remember what I told Monsteress.

She brought me with her because I claimed to know where to find a Painite.

It's only a partial lie.

Everyone knows Painite is hidden beneath those unyielding stone formations.

Finding it *is* the problem.

With Painite being the rarest gem in Escela, it's almost impossible to get your hands on it.

When I told her she needed me to retrieve it, I didn't expect her to accept my offer.

Clueless, I point at the nearest clearing.

A shiver runs down my spine as a gust of freezing wind hits me, whipping my hair around my face. I release the creature's fuzz to wipe my face, and that's the moment the giant insect twists beneath me, throwing me off.

My scream rips the air. Before I can lower my head to watch the ground grow closer as I fall to my death, my stomach hits the ground, pressing the air out of my lungs.

I scramble to my feet, in shock and ashamed.

Monsteress' beast lands beside me, and I watch as she throws her leg over its soft body and jumps to the ground with a smirk curling her lips.

"I wish we were higher," she snarls, turning her back to me.

Rubbing my sore stomach, I step closer to her. "You need me. Without me, you're dead."

She spins around, her eyes throwing daggers at me before her gaze moves to the guard still in landing. "Watch your tongue, or I will cut it out!"

The flying demon opens its wings behind me, and I stumble forward, almost crashing into her. I whirl around to swat the monstrous insect, but a hand curls around my wrist, holding me back.

"And if you touch Storm, I will take your hand too," Monsteress whispers in my ear, releasing me.

"For the love of Odione! This flying creature has a name?"

"It's a moth, and yes. She's more loyal than you'll ever be."

Her words sting, but I'm hung up on something else.

Monsteress hasn't shown a single weakness besides her dying magic. Until now.

Those moths mean something to her—more than I can wrap my head around.

Tucking the knowledge away, I straighten my clothes and face her.

Surprise hits me when I see her dressed in a black furry coat, pants, and high boots, which she wasn't wearing a minute ago.

"I didn't know you own anything besides revealing fabric and blood-red," I spit out, jealousy forming inside my stomach seeing her wrapped in warm clothes.

She turns to her moth, pulls another set of clothes and boots out of a bag attached to its body, and flings them at me. "Put it on."

Hastily, I slip the pants on and cover my shivering body with the coat. My fingers shake when I thrust into the fuzzy boots and pull the coat's sleeves over my purplish hands.

The soldier comes to a halt beside me. "Done?" he asks, resting his hand on the handle of his sword.

I nod, trying to match his taciturnity.

I'm starting to think he's not the smartest with his limited word usage, and I hope his fighting skills are equal.

I have to figure a way out to distract both of them to slip away. The guard is no match to my swift feet in his heavy armor, but Soulin...if she catches me, she will kill me faster than I can beg for my life.

"What are you waiting for?" Monsteress snarls at me.

Aimless, I move toward the mountains, my boots slipping on the wet stone beneath me, trying to find a way that looks like I know what I'm doing.

Another freezing gust of wind hits my face, and I lower my head to shield it.

How can someone live under those conditions?

Terminus is even crueler than any stories I've heard. There's no way a king reigns over this part of Escela, and even less believable that he has an entire army behind him.

My mind drifts back to what's essential.

If I was a rare gem, where would I hide?

I scan my surroundings again.

As far as I can see, we're enclosed by black rock. There are no signs of vegetation or wildlife anywhere.

My body finally regains a comfortable temperature, and I press forward. The guard grunts as I pick up speed. With each step, he falls further behind, but I feel Monsteress' eyes resting on my back.

How long until she notices I'm clueless about where to find the mineral?

They trail behind me, the metallic footsteps softening with each passing minute.

That's when panic spreads through my body.

Even if I manage to lose the soldier, there's nothing but sharp rocks and steep cliffs for miles. If Monsteress doesn't kill me, the bitter cold will while I hide with no prospect of anything edible for an unforeseen time.

A faint sound makes me stop in my tracks. I raise my fist to signal to stop, but Soulin is so close to me that she bumps into me.

A hiss escapes her throat, and with the speed of steam running an engine, I whirl around and press my hand on her mouth.

Sealing her lips with my hand, I scan the towers of stone reaching into the sky.

Another far-off sound rings in my ears.

We're not alone.

I'm so close to Monsteress' face that I can count her silver freckles. Then, realizing the short distance between us, I pull back.

"We need to hide," I whisper, looking over her shoulder at the guard fighting his way up the steep incline.

He hasn't noticed the danger yet. Muttering under his breath, his eyes are glued to the slippery ground.

What in all seven Gods' names is he doing?

I wave my hands over my head to catch his attention, to no avail. Finally, I open my mouth to call out for him, and the words catch in my throat when I hear a whistling sound, followed by metal meeting metal.

The guard's eyes widen when an arrow pierces through his armor right into his heart. He tips over, dead before his body can hit the ground with an ear-shattering metallic thud that echoes through the sloping walls.

Another arrow whistles through the air, coming right at us, and I squeeze my eyes shut, preparing for the impact.

TWENTY-FIVE

QUEEN SOULIN

I lift my hands, and the arrow aimed right at my heart stops mid-air before it falls to the ground.

Cyrus' body trembles, his eyes frantically running over the lifeless body on the ground behind me.

Great. Another coward.

I roll my eyes and push him behind me.

I will never find the Painite to keep the Heiligbaum alive if he dies.

His hands curl around my arms, and I wrench myself free. "Where is the stone?" I hiss over my shoulder while searching the slopes and peaks for the archer.

Cyrus shuffles behind me. "I lied." His voice shakes as he scrambles back.

"You...what?" I hiss over my shoulder, holding my hands outstretched to counter another arrow.

"I lied, okay?" he yells. "I panicked. Technically, I know it's hidden here in Terminus; I don't know where exactly."

Anger rushes through my veins, heating my cheeks. "And you didn't think it's wise to let me know before we enter the deadliest part of the land?"

"I never thought you would take me with you!" he screams, and I whirl around to face him.

His eyes are glued to the mountain peaks above us as he searches for the attacker.

"Good luck," I snarl, bumping into his shoulder to return to Adira.

I could stay and face the lone archer to continue looking for the Painite, but it's useless. Combing through the mountains would take me days, maybe weeks, without a hint of where to find the mineral.

I don't have that time.

Another hissing arrow flies in our direction, and I divert it. The wood explodes into a million splinters when it impacts the stone.

"You can't leave me here." His voice reaches a high note as he scrambles behind me, hunched forward to reduce his height.

I keep my pace steady as I walk further away from him. "Watch me."

Cyrus stumbles behind me. "Then what about the guard? Are you just going to let him rot here?"

My eyes land on the lifeless armored body on the ground just a few feet away. "It's the highest honor to fall in battle."

"What about his family? He deserves to have a proper burial."

I swirl around, diverting another deadly arrow with a flick of my wrist. "Maybe your kingdom is different and thrives on death, but in Crymzon, we don't celebrate the dead. Instead, the dead are dragged outside the Wall to be burned."

His face crunches up in disgust. "That's the cruelest thing I've heard you say so far."

I spin back around to continue to Adira. "If the blood runs cold and seeps into Crymzon's soil, it will corrupt its magic. But I don't expect you to understand our cultural customs."

"Stop," Cyrus yells behind me, and another arrow misses us by a hair.

I chuckle when I hear the panic in his voice. "You brought this upon yourself."

My teeth click with every footstep as the wind picks up around me.

How could I believe a traitor? Why did I think something would finally benefit me?

Out of desperation to save at least the Heiligbaum to avoid severing the connection to Lunra, I put my faith into a man who fled his kingdom to escape me.

From *me!*

I should have known it was a trick.

Stomping down the steep path back to Adira, Cyrus follows me like a desperate moth chasing a light.

"I'm sorry," Cyrus whispers, stepping onto my boot.

I trip and catch myself. "Back off before I—"

My throat closes when I round the slope and look into the pitch-black eyes of a woman.

Her face is pale and distorted. Yellow teeth snarl in my direction as she lunges forward, gripping me by the hair. Her fingers intertwine with my red curls, and she pulls, almost making me lose my footing.

I punch her right in the chest, and with the help of a magical impulse, she flies through the air...

And crashes into a wall of soldiers.

"Shit," Cyrus hisses behind me.

After twenty, I stop counting.

"What are we going to do?" he whimpers behind me.

Yes, what am *I* going to do?

I have enough magic to take down one or two for sure.

But over two dozen?

I'm not sure it will be enough.

There's only one way to find out. I need to make it to the moths and out of here.

I part my legs and search deep inside for the magic I have hidden inside me.

If I use it all, everything will be different.

If it's gone, everything will change.

But I can't think about that right now, being stared down by soulless eyes.

The only way to get to Adira is through them.

Anger amplifies the magic rushing through my veins in violent pulses. My hands warm, and the tingling sensation of power makes me close my eyes.

This is what I was born for.

Cyrus grabs my shoulder and pulls me back. "What in Odione's name are you doing?"

Swishing my shoulder out of his grip, I march forward, and I'm met with the screams of the attackers bolting in my direction.

"What no one else will do!" I yell, my walk turning into a sprint.

I've heard stories about my ancestors' war. It was gruesome and long. Battle after battle, they tried to defend Crymzon against the other kingdoms.

But that was way before my time, even my father's, and since then, our kingdoms' borders have been established and trading agreements signed.

My lungs burn from the cold, but I keep going. Before the first man can reach me, his face torn up and black sud foaming out of his mouth, I blast a red orb straight through him. He falls to his knees and lands on his face, unmoving.

One.

I aim for two other Undead and watch my magic rip them into pieces. Two. Three.

More follow, and I raise my hands before I force my magic down and into the ground. The rock beneath us shakes, sending little pebbles flying into my face until the magic submerges feet away from me. Long strands of crimson waves stream out of the ground and curl around the soldiers' legs, cutting them clean off.

It takes me a moment to get back up. Then, out of breath, I look over my shoulder, and to my surprise, I see Cyrus still alive.

One of the Undead is charging at him with a sword, and with another flick of my hand, the ugly man tips over, sending the sword skittering over the ground.

Cyrus' eyes widen when they meet mine.

I turn my back on him to assess the situation. I lost track of how many Undead I slayed with my last attack, but seeing another dozen rush towards me, I don't have time to waste on rationing my magic.

With a clap, I press my hands together and rip them apart.

The world comes to a halt.

In slow motion, I watch the hate-distorted faces of my attackers, each of them uglier than the other.

Hearing that Keres is a necromancer is one thing, but seeing his creations makes an icy shiver run down my spine.

Memories of Felix return.

His red curly hair; the beautiful freckles on his pale skin; the black eyes staring at me; and the hate radiating from his body.

It wasn't my brother.

A low scream rips the air, catapulting me back to Terminus.

The Undead have gotten closer, even while being slowed down by my magic. I release my hold on them and point my hands in their direction.

Light explodes from my palms, and I must close my watering eyes to avoid going blind.

I hear lifeless bodies fall to the ground, and my knees buckle.

The last attack required all of me. All of my power.

Emptiness builds up inside me, leaving a gaping hole where my magic used to be.

I've used all of it.

All of it!

This ambush depleted the magic I was hiding, and with it gone, everything I tried to suppress for the last fourteen years comes back to me.

The pain of loss overwhelms me, ripping my heart into pieces over and over again.

The feeling of loneliness and vulnerability pierces my chest like a hot knife.

My head fills with all the memories I concealed behind a wall of magic.

The pain makes my vision go blurry and forces me to my knees. Even though I'm wearing thick furry pants, the coldness of the stone beneath me seeps through the fabric and into my body.

I try to force my eyes open, but my head is throbbing, followed by a wave of nausea.

I need to get up!

Just the slightest movement of my leg sends another rush of bile into my throat, and before I can attempt another motion, darkness clouds my mind before it overwhelms me.

TWENTY-SIX

CYRUS

I only have a second to make a decision.

Monsteress' unmoving body is sprawled out in the middle of a pile of attackers.

While she was taking out handfuls of nasty-looking people, I'm struggling with just one of them.

Ice runs through my veins as the dead man stalks in my direction. Half his lip is missing, but that doesn't stop him from snarling at me.

He knows I'm no match.

I know it, too.

But I have to try.

Lunging forward, I grab the sword on the ground before me and point it at him.

Maybe I expected him to flinch or show the slightest fear, but he looks unfazed when I wave the sword between us.

Monsteress killed so many of them. The least I can do is take this one out.

The smell of rotten flesh and death creeps into my nose, making my stomach turn.

The man takes another step forward, and before he can reach out his hands to grab me, I push the blade into his abdomen. Bile rises in my throat when the metal collides with his bones.

I pick up my boot to give him a push to retrieve the sword for another stab, but he grabs the blade, his fingers digging into the metal, and pulls it deeper into himself. I stumble forward, and another crunching noise rips the air.

Instead of pain, I see amusement flicker in his eyes as he lets go of the blade to grab my throat.

"No!" I scream out, pushing myself away from him as I let go of the handle.

How is he not dead yet?

That's when it dawns on me. How am I supposed to kill a man who is already dead?

Stumbling backward, I search my surroundings. Only a handful of attackers remain, one still grinning at me.

Adrenaline rushes through my body, and I bolt forward, missing the man's grip by arm's length.

My gaze lands on Monsteress, who's still lying on the floor, her face flat on the ground.

To save myself, I need to leave her.

My legs carry me past her as I dodge another one of the disgusting creatures.

I take another step, and my muscles tense when I hear the gut-wrenching scream of a woman.

Shit.

I whirl around and look at the woman aiming for Monsteress with a dagger. She's about thirty feet away from her and shows no signs of stopping.

"Odione, help me," I scream, leaping forward.

Within seconds, I reach Monsteress and wrap my arms around her shoulders and legs to hoist her up.

"Why are you so damn heavy?" I snarl through clenched teeth, stumbling forward under her weight.

The sound of flapping wings appears behind me. Her beast is just a few feet away, and it steps closer, lowering its wings to help me throw its owner over its body.

Another scream erupts behind me, and I hear the whistle of an arrow right before I jump.

Landing hard on the scale-covered back behind Monsteress, I thrust my heels into the creature as if it were a horse.

Wings flapping, it rises into the air with ease.

"Get us out of reach!" I scream through the whipping cold air while pressing Monsteress against its back.

I'm not sure if that thing beneath me even speaks our language, but it intensifies its strokes, and before I know it, we're out of the danger zone.

In the air, I notice the other two insects waiting for us.

With another kick of my heels, my beast turns around, still gaining height, and I watch as the screaming attackers on the ground become specks.

"We made it," I whisper to myself. "We fucking made it."

But the excitement dies immediately when I notice whom I am talking to.

Her face pressed against the hairy body of her creature, she hangs over its body like fallen prey.

I didn't intend to save her. I should have let her die and taken off with one of her moths to make it to Liza, and then finally to Devana.

But I couldn't.

Those soldiers...no...those soulless shells of dead people are indestructible. The memory of the sword driving through his belly while the man laughed into my face turns my stomach again.

I look down. The land slowly regains its color as we fly further and further south. At this height, a fall would be fatal.

My eyes scan Monsteress' body, and the urge to grab and toss her down is soul-crushing.

My fingers curl around her arms...

And I pull her closer to me.

It would be the right thing to drop her. She needs to pay for everything she has done. If evil has a face, it's hers, and this is my opportunity to rid this land of the most vicious ruler known to this day.

Yet, I can't.

If more dead, yet alive, creatures are roaming Terminus, we will need magic, because even my invention I had to leave behind in Eternitie isn't strong enough to injure them.

How can it be if the person is already decomposing and indestructible?

Holding on to her tightly, I close my eyes to think.

Once I'm back in Crymzon, I will plead for my life again in return for saving hers.

It has to work.

After all, without me, she would be lying at the foot of the mountains without a heartbeat.

But that's not the reason I let her live.

We need her.

I need her.

If I want to protect my sister and Eternitie from the North, Monsteress is my only course of action.

If Keres starts attacking kingdoms once his army is ready, he'll go for Eternitie first because it's the closest kingdom to Terminus.

My stomach clenches.

I can't let my people die.

The only thing able to kill an undead person is magic. And if Monsteress dies and her kingdom with it, we're screwed.

As we pass over Eternitie, I stay further away from my home kingdom. My father might not be able to tell it's me flying over his territory, but I know that the intrusion won't go unnoticed. His spies are everywhere.

My body shakes when the legs of the creature come into contact with the ground. Immediately, guards storm in from all directions, and I hold my hands high in the air, away from the precious cargo.

This is it.

They're going to rip me off this beast and toss me back into the prison chamber to rot.

"What happened?" a guard yells, his sword aiming at me.

I swallow hard. "We were attacked. She fought off Keres' soldiers and then collapsed. I don't know what's wrong with her."

I'm pushed off the moth, and two soldiers carefully grab Monsteress's body to lay her on the ground.

"We need a healer," another guard yells, pushing a few armored soldiers out of the way.

My eyes rest on the peaceful sight of Monsteress. Her eyes are shut, covering her green-golden irises. Her hair is tangled, and her clothes are covered in black sud.

Everyone's attention is on her.

I look around, waiting to be seized.

The sun is shining down on me, casting a warm glow on the intricate stonework of crimson walls. I hear a fountain from somewhere nearby.

The creature brought us to the courtyard.

A grand archway leads up the stairs to the palace, and on the opposite side, there's another one. Through it, I see the sandstone-carved houses of the people of Crymzon.

My pulse quickens when I look back to the tumult around Monsteress. No one is paying attention to me.

On tiptoes, I creep toward the city and away from the palace. A few steps in, I look over my shoulder and notice I'm still unsupervised and almost out of sight behind a tree.

I sprint for it and expect someone to charge after me...

Nothing happens.

Skittering around the corner of the courtyard wall, I press myself against it, closing my eyes to listen for any signs of metallic clacking.

Nothing.

I bite down a smile and open my eyes to see a little girl standing on the other side of the uneven road, her mouth parted and her eyes big.

Every story told in Eternitie portrays Crymzon as a night kingdom, just like Starstrand. But, while the Starstrandians use the night to read destinies in flickering stars, Crymzonians come to life under the moon.

So why is a child standing in broad daylight in the streets?

I can't make it through the kingdom if everyone is awake.

I press my finger to my mouth and let out a quiet 'psst' before I run down the empty street, far away from the kingdom's center.

TWENTY-SEVEN

CYRUS

I know Crymzon's layout by heart.

A city embedded into a sandstone bowl surrounded by a massive, circular wall. In the center towers the palace, and to the south, the temple resides to catch the highest point of the moon.

There's no plausible explanation for why the prison was built outside the kingdom's wall. Maybe because they ran out of space when Monsteress started incarcerating her subjects. Or because she didn't care if the building is destroyed first if the kingdom ever goes to war.

Sneaking undetected into the dungeon under the palace, where I was held when I arrived, is impossible. It's highly guarded.

Plus, I'm sure Devana isn't being held there.

When I awoke in the dungeon, I only noticed male prisoners.

If I'm right, Monsteress sends the females off to rot in prison outside the Wall.

That's where I need to go.

As I go through the empty streets, I realize the tales about Crymzon are true. The girl by the courtyard is the only soul I've seen since I started bolting to the south part of the Wall where the prison stands.

Piece by piece, I take off the overheating coat, boots, and pants Monsteress tossed to me and throw them into different alleyways to scatter the evidence of my path.

The Wall grows in size as I near the southern border, and I take a deep breath, my eyes fixed on the towering red sandstone barrier in front of me as I assess the obstacle. My heart pounds when I visualize what would happen to my body if I lose grip before I can reach the top. The Wall must be at least fifty feet high. One misstep and I'm done for.

But I have no other choice. I must get to the prison; it's my only way out.

With a firm grip on the rough surface, I climb, my muscles straining with each upward movement. Sweat pours down my face, but I keep going.

The red sandstone is coarse, and my hands and feet soon ache from the blazing surface's roughness.

Devana's determined eyes flash before mine, and it's enough encouragement to make me keep going, driven by the desire to at least free one other person.

As I climb higher, I can see the kingdom stretching out behind me, its buildings and streets like a miniature model far below.

Monsteress' soldiers will soon be after me. I can't give up.

Finally, after what seems like an eternity, I reach the top of the Wall. With one last push, I roll myself over it and land hard on my side, every muscle in my body aching.

For a moment, I just lay there, catching my breath.

The clicking sound of boots sends a fresh push of adrenaline through my body, and I scramble to my knees to analyze where the sound is coming from.

The heads of two soldiers appear, their gazes wandering over the kingdom. I can hear them whisper to each other, and one of them lets out a quiet laugh before they turn around again to march back in the direction they came from.

I would laugh too, if my job is to guard a kingdom that hasn't been under attack for centuries. Those soldiers are as useless as bent gears for an invention.

Slowly, I crawl to the other side of the Wall and peek over the stone railing into the desert landscape.

To my surprise, I see the smallest curved bridge leading to another building outside the Wall, just twenty feet away from me. Actually, I wouldn't call it a bridge. It's a one-foot-wide stony connection between the Wall and the prison.

How am I supposed to cross it unnoticed? Crawling isn't an option because of its width, and if I slip or stumble while running across it, the fifty-foot drop will claim me.

I scan the building again. Armed soldiers guard the heavy iron gate. Entering through the entrance is also off the table.

The windows are only narrow slits, too small to squeeze through.

The prison walls are darker than the rest of the kingdom, and the deep-red color reminds me of the lush dress Monsteress wore the first time I set eyes on her.

From within, I hear the prisoners shuffling in their cells, their moans and cries for help lost in the wind.

Deep down, I can feel that Devana is inside those walls, but I can't help her if I get caught.

Trying to find a weak spot that might have escaped my initial observation, I inspect the prison a few moments longer. Without a sword or backup, I'm just unmarked flesh for the gleaming blades wrapped around the soldiers' hips.

I strain my ears and hold my breath, trying to make out any familiar voices fleeing through the windows into the open, and my heart breaks when I fail.

I'm so close to freeing my people; the people who had taken me—a stranger—in without asking questions about my heritage, and who have given me clothes and a bed to sleep on.

Still, it's impossible to release them without getting myself killed. Those soldiers don't know who I am, and setting off Monsteress' suspicion about why the prison is so important to me is another danger I can't risk.

My throat closes, and my stomach turns when I look over my shoulder and watch the two soldiers still marching away from me.

I'll come back for you; I whisper as I crawl in the opposite direction to find the hidden staircase leading down to the stables marked on a map I've seen in Eternitie.

I'll come back, Devana.

TWENTY-EIGHT

KHAOS

S he can't be here.

I inquired about Soulin's whereabouts the moment I returned and was told she would be in Terminus until the night begins.

The thought of her leaving me behind to take the prisoner with her while I had to ride all the way back to his village to search his hut turns my stomach into a knot.

At least, my mission was fruitful, and I have something to show for it.

Exhausted from the long ride, sand crammed into every skinfold of my body, I took the liberty of using her water room. I've done it countless times to escape the glares from other soldiers in the little waterhole that is assigned to us. Soulin offered to let me use her personal water room during the day when she's fast asleep, but it seems she has forgotten her offer.

The red silky dress swirls around her as she storms into the sand-stone-covered room, and I press myself against the rough stonewall of the handmade cave in the water to stay out of her sight.

If Soulin is already back from Terminus, something is wrong.

Holding my breath, I watch her pace through the room. Her anger fills the air like a raging sandstorm.

Flitting footsteps echo through the hall. I clench my teeth when Soulin screams at the servants who are trying to aid her until they scramble away like beaten animals.

I can't be here. If Soulin finds me, I don't know what she will do to me.

I watch as Soulin rips on her dress, splitting it in half, and her breasts pop out of the torn fabric.

The sight of the delicate rounded skin sends blood rushing into my dick, and I press my hand to my mouth to hold my breath. My lip hurts as I bite down on it and force myself to look away.

But I can't.

Soulin pulls the dress down over her wide hips and lets it fall to the floor before marching to the pool entrance.

I should make my presence known, but I can't move.

She descends into the warm water. My eyes are fixated on her as the liquid slowly rises up her calves, then her thighs, her vagina, her hips, and finally, her breast.

She dives under the water, and the faint sound of a scream vibrates through it, sending bubbles floating to the surface.

What happened in Terminus?

As Soulin emerges again, my breath catches.

The water enclosing her is blood-red.

I jolt forward.

How did I fail to notice she was injured?

Her eyes widen when she notices me rushing through the water in her direction. Confusion clouds her face, and it takes me a second to come to a halt.

"What are you doing here?" she hisses, her green eyes formed into small slits.

That's when I see it. It's not her blood staining the water. A snow-white strand of hair is now visible between her wet colorful curls.

I swallow hard, trying to save myself. "Once, you offered me to use the pool during the day when you're asleep."

Her face turns to stone. "Do I look asleep to you, Grand General?"

I shake my head, everting my eyes from her naked shoulders hovering over the surface.

"Turn around," she commands.

I follow her demand without thinking.

Water splashes, the sound moving further away from me. That's when panic sets in.

She's leaving. Why is she leaving? This is her room.

I can't think straight.

The memory of her, undressed and vulnerable, makes me look over my shoulder. Every fiber in my body tells me to touch her bare skin. To claim her. To take the pain away from her.

I can still feel her hand around my cock as if an invisible hand has stayed behind after she released me.

As if she can feel my gaze on her, she spins around and looks me straight in the eyes. "You can't even follow the easiest of commands now?"

I know I should listen to her. Yet, I hold her icy gaze and step forward.

"Stop looking at me like that," I whisper, and the smirk on her lip intensifies.

"How am I looking at you?" she asks, her eyebrow raised.

"You used to give me that look when you're trying to cover up your pain."

Her eyes widen for a moment before her smile dies off. "You shouldn't be here."

"Neither should you."

"You know I could hang you for this?"

I study her face, searching for what is causing the pain behind those bright eyes. "I have nothing to lose," I say in a clear voice.

In three large steps, I reach her and climb the steps to build myself up in front of her.

Her eyes wander over my face, down my chest, and belly until they rest on my dick.

Her body shivers as she takes me in, and I can't help but get harder knowing she sees me—all of me.

Her gaze lingers on me for a moment longer until she jolts her head up, stepping back until her back collides with the stone wall.

"You can't be here," she repeats, her chest heaving with every breath.

Closing my eyes, I exhale sharply.

I know her. I know the real Soulin.

Behind that façade of the unbreakable Queen is a woman who fights her battles in silence until they eat her alive.

I open my eyes. "I'm right where I'm supposed to be," I whisper, watching as goosebumps form on her skin.

"You don't understand. You need to go," she growls back, but something in her voice sounds different from usual.

There's no way I'm going to force my help on her. Especially since we're both still naked.

I'm about to turn away to grab the linen I had on to sneak down here, but my limbs won't listen.

"Why the prisoner?" I ask, my heart breaking as I think of the moment I crashed through her chamber's door.

It's not my place to ask her for a reason, but I need to know so I can finally release her. I need to know why she doesn't feel the same way I do after everything we've been through together.

My heart pounds in my chest as I wait for an answer. After a few seconds, I give up and lower my eyes to the ground.

The feeling of my heart being ripped out of my chest almost brings me to my knees, but I straighten my shoulders instead.

That's when her voice reaches me. "I won't let a connection with another person weaken me. You know what I would have done to the man if he turned out to be my Soulmate?" She pauses for a moment before she continues. "I would've killed him because I don't need a Soulmate. I just need to fulfill the Connection Ceremony with the right person to regain my magic."

That's when it dawns on me.

The image of Soulin's face pressed against the wall with closed eyes appears before my eyes.

She didn't enjoy it.

There was no passion between her and that guy.

Her goal is to sleep with as many men as it takes to find her Soulmate, just to kill him after.

How many men did she test so far? Is that the reason she discharged me as her personal guard because she knows how I feel about her?

The thought of other men inside of her disgusts me. But it also ignites the instinct to protect her.

"I would rather be a dead man for loving you than spending the rest of my life without you," I say, looking into her eyes one more time before finally letting her go.

It will be hard to be her Grand General, knowing she doesn't return my feelings, but I will do it for her. I need her close, even though it's eating me up on the inside.

Just as I want to walk off, something blazes in her eyes, a shimmer of anger and fear. "I'm dying."

Hearing those words coming out of her mouth catches me off guard. I stiffen. "You're not. We will find a man to save you."

Soulin shakes her head. "No, Khaos."

The sound of my name coming out of her mouth turns me into stone.

I can't recall the last time she called me by my name. I'm catapulted back to the time when we ran through the halls, laughing. When the land was at peace, and her family was still alive. When she promised me, it would always be us, Soulin and Khaos.

Forever.

Her expression sobers. "I'm dying, and my magic is gone. I couldn't find the Painite to keep the Heiligbaum alive." She closes her eyes. "In a few days, Crymzon will consume me."

"No." My breath catches. "No. That can't be true."

Her eyes soften for just a moment—one blink—and that's when I realize the old Soulin I have known before magic overtook her is still inside her.

The expression in her eyes tells me she's speaking the truth.

Rage fuels my veins. Before I can get it under control, my fist collides with the wall right beside her head. She doesn't move, as if she knew what I was about to do.

My vision tunnels as I take her words in.

How is this fair?

She can't die.

She can't!

Gently, she takes my hand and rubs over my throbbing knuckles. Her touch sends me over the edge.

I lose myself as the spark of lust inside of me reignites.

Without thinking, I lean down and cover her mouth with mine.

The moment our lips touch, she tilts her head to the side, but I grab her by the neck and press her into me, my gentle kiss turning into something desperate.

Slowly, her body relaxes and presses against mine, a moan escaping her throat. The desire to thrust into her consumes me, but instead, I put all my anger, my fear, and my love for her into this kiss.

I pull back, and her hooded gaze meets mine.

"Tell me you want this," I whisper against her mouth between ragged breaths.

Instead of answering, she weaves her fingers through my hair and fists it tightly, pulling me back to her mouth.

Her lips are soft as she parts them to welcome my tongue. With each passing stroke of our tongues, our kiss grows deeper.

Her other hand slides down my torso. I moan when she grabs my cock, slowly sliding her hand up and down.

My skin is on fire, and I can barely breathe.

Desperately, I fill my hand with her breast, her nipple hard against my rough palm. I squeeze it between my thumb and forefinger, and she buckles against me.

A deep throb grows between my legs. I hook my hands around the back of her thighs and hoist her up, pressing her against the wall. She wraps her legs around me and tilts her head back to let out a primal groan.

My erection pressing against her leg, I dip my head down to take in the other nipple. Her moan deepens as I slide my tongue over her delicate skin before I tease her lightly with my teeth.

Her thighs tighten around me as she grinds against me with each bite. The heavy pulse between my legs intensifies when she scratches her nails over my shoulders. The pain drives me wild and makes me drip with need.

Her fingers find their way back into my hair, and she pulls my head up before I can suck on her nipple.

Fire blazing in her eyes, she leans into me and whispers. "I want this."

Those words are almost enough to make me cum.

I slide my cock along her slit, the tip lining up with the entrance...

And thrust into her.

Her vagina is so tight I have to push into her, again and again, to slide in deeper. Her wetness drips down my cock as I draw my hips back and forth to completely fill her.

Her groans make me ache. I readjust my hands to grip her ass, squeezing it tightly.

I pump into her in a slow and steady rhythm, my swollen cock circling with each thrust.

"Harder," she moans between clenched teeth.

I widen my stance and pick up speed, her breasts bouncing to the rhythm.

This woman makes me lose my mind and control.

My stomach muscle tense as warmth spreads through my body.

We're moving fast.

The urge to touch her body, to feel every inch of her, almost makes me stop in my tracks, but I want to see her face when she comes undone.

Her lips part as her moans deepen, and her nails bury into my arms as I pump into her.

Her face is distorted with pain and pleasure, and it's hard to take my eyes off her.

Slamming into her, the skin-slapping sound echoes through the room. My breath is labored, and my muscles burn when her grip tightens around me.

That's when it hits me.

She's finally mine.

Soulin is mine.

Years of anticipation for this exact moment rush through my body. I feel my cock swelling as I'm flooded with heat, my muscles pulsing.

Her mouth opens wider. I lean forward to caress her neck with my lips before biting into her delicate, sweat-covered skin.

Her vagina clutches around my dick with each bite. She throws her head back even further to let out a loud moan.

I want to drag this moment out, to stay inside her forever, but her naked skin on my fingers and the clapping sound from my hips colliding with her butt robs me of all senses.

She rocks her hips against mine. Each thrust makes it more unbearable to hold my pleasure in.

"I'm so close," I moan as my dick throbs, and at that moment, her vagina tightens around me, and she erupts.

TWENTY-NINE

QUEEN SOULIN

Warmth spreads through my body, and my vagina clenches around his cock. I tighten my legs around his hips and pull his face closer to mine as a tingling sensation ripples through me in waves.

This feeling, it's like nothing I ever felt before.

I try to keep my mouth closed with all my might because the sounds escaping my throat feel so foreign to me.

That's when I hear his breath quicken as his mouth presses against my ear. The primal groans rushing over his lips make my body shake with lust, and I feel his cock throbbing inside of my convulsing core.

After a few more thrusts of his hips, his tensed body relaxes under my touch. Our breaths are the only sound surrounding us as we cool down.

I expect him to drop me, but he holds onto me tightly, our sweat-beaded skin burning against each other.

Is this how it feels when a connection between two souls snaps into place?

It has to.

184

It felt like the entire universe revolved around us when he came inside me.

My head leaning against his broad shoulder, his cock still inside me, and his hands grabbing my ass, I wait for the magic to surge through me.

That intense sensation had to be the sign that I found my Soulmate.

If I search deep inside me, I suspected Khaos could be my missing piece.

No.

I've known it was Khaos since I looked into his deep brown eyes for the first time, and if my magic hadn't killed my entire family, it wouldn't have taken me fourteen years to figure it out.

But the moment I watched my brother burn to ashes, I pulled all the magic that destroyed the throne room back inside me and used it to shield my heart.

Love killed my mother.

My brother's love for me turned him into a cruel memory of burning flesh and agonizing screams.

Love is the villain in every story. It turns you into a servant. All your senses are numbed or only directed to one person. Your mind wanders to your Soulmate whenever you're awake. It's a distraction I didn't want or need.

For fourteen years, I've successfully suppressed any emotion that made me vulnerable.

It all worked out until Terminus.

I could feel the magic slipping through my fingers when I took down the last of the Undead, releasing the feelings I concealed inside me all at once back into my heart. The only barrier between my heart's desire and my longing for revenge vanished instantly.

Khaos' chuckle pulls me back into the water chamber. His warm touch on my skin makes me curl my toes. I inhale his smell deeply before I rest my shoulder against the wall to look into his brown eyes.

"I can't get enough of you," he whispers, his eyes flickering with lust and something I can't put my finger on.

My core heats again. All I want to do is jump into the water and feel his hands all over my body again.

I drop one of my legs to find a grip on the floor, but he holds me tightly as he searches my face.

Reaching inside me, I search for the refreshed magic that should fill my body now since I finally found my Soulmate.

But there is... nothing.

My heart races as I realize I'm still powerless.

No one ever told me how long it takes for the connection to establish. It may take a few minutes before the magic begins to rush through my veins again, or hours.

I inhale sharply, and with each breath, I feel the warmth dampen.

There is no connection between Khaos and me. All I experienced was lust and a weird sensation only he could lure out of me.

"Let me go," I say, pressing my hand against his chest to push him away.

His eyes darken. "What's wrong?" he asks, releasing the grip around my ass as he slowly lowers me.

"This was a mistake," I whisper, rushing to the ripped piece of fabric I tossed to the ground that used to be my dress.

"A mistake? What are you talking about?"

I hear his bare feet following me. "This wasn't supposed to happen. You're the Grand General of my army, nothing more and nothing less," I say, snatching the dress off the ground to cover myself.

"Soulin. Please," he pleads.

His warm hands touch my shoulder, and I spin around to face him.

"It's Queen Soulin SinClaret for you. Whatever this was…" I shrug my shoulders and point at the wall where my back and butt imprints still mark what we have done. "It's never going to happen again. Even better: it never happened in the first place."

My insides stir. I haven't felt guilt in such a long time that I forgot how painful the throbbing pain in the stomach and heat rising into your face feels like. I press my arm against my stomach to ease the pain.

"You can't do this to me," Khaos whispers, his eyes glazed. "I can't lose you again."

"I was never yours to begin with," I hiss back, deciding whether to cover my breast or vagina with the thin fabric.

"How can you say that?" his voice breaks, and the muscular man who held me against the wall just minutes ago crumbles before me.

"You're just another man I needed to try out to find my Soulmate."

The second those words come out of my mouth, I feel my heart break into a million pieces.

Khaos doesn't deserve that.

The moment he kissed me, I wanted nothing more than to feel him inside me and be closer to him than anyone else has ever been before.

But I'm dying, and if even Khaos isn't my match, I only have a few more days to avenge my brother before everything he has ever known dies with me.

"Pack your things and get out. I never want to see you again," I say, wrapping the torn dress around my body.

"You can't do this," he pleads again.

My stomach turns when I watch him tumble to the nearest wall to lean against it.

I spin in the door's direction to avoid eye contact. It takes everything out of me to walk with the confidence I used to have. "Before you leave, please select one of your closest soldiers as your replacement and send him to my chambers," I say, staggering through the door.

"Soulin!" Khaos yells after me, but my hand is already clenched around the door.

I swing it closed behind me before he can pursue me, or I do something I will later regret.

THIRTY

CYRUS

The map lied about how close the Wall's staircase is to the prison bridge. By the time I reach the wooden door let into the Wall, my knees are raw and excruciating pain shoots up my legs every time I lift them to move forward.

Behind me, I hear the beating footsteps of the soldiers. Without hesitation, I open the door and throw myself into the darkness. The door loudly falls into place, covering the loud grunts I let out when I drop the first few steps down the staircase.

I rest there for a moment, waiting for the soldiers to chase me down.

Did they see me?

If so, I'm not in any shape to defend myself. My knees and hands are scraped open and covered in dirt. My muscles are rendered useless from climbing the Wall.

They can't find me. Otherwise, all of this was for nothing.

It was so easy to think I could walk through Crymzon unnoticed, tackle the Wall without complications, enter the prison, and release my friends.

Only one of those steps turned out to be true if I don't count the little girl staring me down the second I escaped the courtyard.

While releasing the prisoners without notice becomes a daydream, fleeing seems even more challenging. I will never make it on foot through the desert.

Knowing the stables is right below the prison, I don't have to ride through Crymzon again. But how am I supposed to stay out of sight on the flattest landscape known to man?

The stables are located opposite where I need to go—home.

One step at a time, I whisper to myself as I stumble down the steep steps leading down inside the Wall. The dusty air stings in my lungs. I pick up the pace to escape this overheated hallway. Sweat runs down my back and my vision blurs. If I don't make it out of here within the next minute, my grand escape will be the least of my worries if I collapse first.

Then I see it.

The stairs lead to...

A dead end.

Where I imagined another wooden door is nothing but stone. I jump over the last few steps, and my knees buckle when my feet collide with the ground, throwing me forward. I'm not fast enough to shield my face from hitting the Wall, so I pull my shoulder forward to embrace the impact.

As my shoulder collides with the stone, it gives in, and I fall through nothingness until my body hits the ground.

Head spinning, I scramble to my knees, and I immediately regret my reaction when my kneecaps pulsate in pain.

Where am I?

I blink through the pain, and my eyes widen when I realize what happened. Somehow, I made it through the Wall without a door. How is that possible?

Breathing hard, I let myself down on my butt and look back at the piece of wall I must have fallen out of. The stone barrier is still intact, not showing any sign of weakness.

Silently swearing, I get up and walk back to the Wall. Hesitantly, I reach out to touch the uneven surface before me. To my surprise, my hand goes straight through the stone and disappears. I pull my hand out and stare at it before I repeat the process.

This isn't just any door. It's a passage forged by magic.

I look over my shoulder and see the stables' curved doorway. Luckily, it's not guarded. My eyes wander up the blood-red building until they reach the top. Fortunately, the excuse of a bridge blocks my view of the guards positioned in front of the gate leading into it.

I take a moment to unscramble my thoughts as I hid in the Wall's shade. Looking around me, I try to memorize every detail of my location for the future. I need to return to release my friends; this doorway might be helpful.

I reach down. The rock I find on the ground is rough and edgy, just what I need. At first, I thought about using a symbol to mark the entrance but then decided that a simple line is plenty enough.

Carefully, I carve into the stone beside the invisible door. It looks like someone accidentally came in contact with the sandstone while trying to enter the staircase.

I turn around and creep through the bridge's shadow toward the stable. I move quickly and quietly, my eyes darting back and forth as I scan the area around and above me, ensuring no one is watching me. Then, with practiced ease, I slipped inside the creaky door unseen.

I was known in Eternitie for my silent appearances. It was almost second nature to me to stalk my father and brother as they discussed any upcoming ceremonies that would otherwise only reach my ears once they were revealed to the public.

As a second-born, I knew it wasn't my place to demand to be a part of my father's Council. Cyprian is even further down the line of succession as a third-born. It's Catalina's birthright to be our father's advisor until it's time for her to climb the throne but my father never cared about that fact.

It wasn't a shocker that King Citeus favored Cyprian over my sister and me. After all, he was the one to present his invention before we did. But knowing the intentions my brother had to reach the throne eventually was the eye-opener I needed to fake my own death.

I attempted to persuade Catalina to accompany me, but our brother didn't intimidate my sister. On the contrary, my absence might have steered her on to go heads up against Cyprian.

The interior of the stable is dimly lit, with only one window serving as a light source. The air is surprisingly cool and damp, and the musty scent of hay and horse sweat fills my nostrils.

I scan each stall for the fittest horse as I sneak through the stable. My target is a beautiful chestnut stallion with a lean build, shiny coat, and sturdy legs.

A plan forms in my mind - I can rest inside the stable for the rest of the day and then steal the horse to continue my journey under the cover of the night.

If I'm lucky, Monsteress still hasn't regained consciousness, which means no one has noticed my absence yet.

I walk up to an empty stall in the back corner, hidden from view. With a sigh of relief, I creep into the stall and lay down on the soft hay, my eyes growing heavy as the sounds of the horses around me lull me to sleep.

Hours must have passed as I slept, my body weary from traveling to Terminus and my attempt to save the villagers. Outside the window, I can see nightfall approaching as the sun sets and the sky turns a deep shade of orange.

I peer out of my hiding place. The stable is quiet and even darker than before.

I can't waste any more time if I want to prepare the horse for my departure.

About forty bridles hang neatly lined up on the wall on hangers. I grab every single one of them but one, toss them inside the empty stall I slept in and cover them with hay.

Triumphantly, I grab the last one and approach the stallion I spotted earlier, whispering soothing words to calm him down.

The animal snorts and stomps its hooves, sensing that something is amiss. I quickly slip a rope around his neck, followed by a bridle, and lead him out of the stall.

As I mount the horse, my heart pounding in my chest, I feel the powerful muscles tense beneath me. I dig my heels into its side, urging him forward through the stable door and away from the prison and towards Crymzon to keep to the shadows of the Wall to avoid being seen. The animal surges forward, bolting out of the stable, leaving a cloud of dust in its wake.

The horse's hooves pound against the hard-packed earth as I race through the night, the wind whipping past me as I leave the stable behind. Adrenaline and relief rush through my veins. I'm finally free, even if it's just for a short time before I have to return to break into the prison.

I lean low over the animal's neck, urging it on faster and faster.

As I ride, I can't help but think of the consequences that would follow if I'm seen. The stallion's hooves are loud enough to wake the entire kingdom, so the problem isn't to be heard. The real danger lurks in what happens if I get caught.

I try to remember if the soldiers on the Wall had bows attached to their backs. It was a brilliant idea to hide the bridles to stop soldiers from following me by ground, but if arrows are involved, there's no way I'm going to outrun those.

I push those thoughts aside, focusing only on the urgent need to return to my village. There, I can hide with Liza for the next few days until Monsteress' army arrives to find me. It will give me enough time to devise a plan to free the other villagers.

But for that to happen, I must return to the village before sunrise. The desert is treacherous, with dunes and rocky terrain that could trip up even the most experienced riders.

I push on, urging the horse to go faster as I hear shouts from above. The animal responds, galloping across the sand with renewed energy.

I'm so close to leaving Crymzon behind.

Staying close to the Wall, I force myself not to look up. If arrows start to rain down on me, I don't want to see them coming.

Every muscle is tense as I clench my hurting legs around the stallion's sides. My hands burn as the reins rub over the already tortured skin of my palms.

That's when I see the enormous entrance door of the kingdom—the only known way into Crymzon until I found the magical doorway.

I pull on the reins to distance myself from the Wall and aim for the open desert stretching before me. Each hoove slap carries me further away from my deadly faith.

By now, I expected riders to chase me, or be struck down by magic or weapons.

Is it really that easy to flee from Crymzon? I had a more challenging time escaping my own kingdom without throwing magic into the mix.

Or maybe Monsteress acknowledged that she's in debt to me for saving her life and has decided to let me go. Perhaps she does have a heart and told the soldier to stand down and let me pass.

I could have killed or left her behind for those disgusting creatures to feast on. But she is crucial to Escela's survival. Only her magic can do enough damage to King Keres' resurrected army.

But just because I need her alive to go head-on with Terminus doesn't mean I have to be her prisoner in the meantime.

My heart races as fast as the stallion as I watch Crymzon shrink over my shoulder. Little silhouettes dance across the Wall, and I can see arrows flying in my direction, but they miss me.

What took them so long to attack? Clearly, Monsteress doesn't see my attempt to save her as a peace offering, and it's the guards' fault for their slow reaction. I couldn't have made it any easier for them to strike me down when I followed the Wall as a guide to find north.

But now, I'm hundreds of feet away from them.

Chuckling that I made it out alive in one piece, I sit up straight and give the horse a little slack...

And immediately regret my foolish decision.

The ground beneath us shakes. This is the part I have been waiting for. Finally, the Crymzonian soldiers use the weapon no other kingdom offers: their magic.

The landscape around me wobbles. The horse shies back from a gap forming right before its feet, almost throwing me off its back. I ram my feet into its sides, and it quickly jumps over the little crater separating us from my village.

Leaning down, I yell at the horse to pick up speed.

I hear the ground behind us grinding before it bursts wide open. But luckily, the desert before us stays untouched by the soldiers' attempt to kill us, and it's the first time in days that I can exhale as a free man again.

THIRTY-ONE

CYRUS

M y heart pounds frantically as I make my way through the desert. The faint sounds of lethal animals prowling keep me alert, even though all I want to do is close my eyes and trust the stallion to get me home safely.

We race under the stars, the wind in our hair, until finally, we reach the outskirts of the village.

Breathless and exhilarated, I finally pull up in front of the small hut, dismounting and leaving the horse outside. I clap the stallion on the behind to send him away, but he doesn't budge.

"Go," I say, waving my hands in front of his face to scare him away, but his brown eyes rest on me with no sign of fear. "I need you to go. If they find you here, I'm dead."

But the horse doesn't move.

I roll my eyes and point at the stable in the middle of the village, noticing all the horses are missing. "You should find some water and hay in there. Refresh and leave," I tell the horse and shake my head when I realize I'm talking to an animal.

As I watch it trot off, my body shakes in anticipation.

I made it home.

The excitement subsides when I push the door open and see what's inside.

The once neatly stacked crates in the corner of the room lay in splinters across the floor. One chair has fallen, and the bed is pushed over, revealing the most essential part of my home: the hidden trapdoor leading to our hideout.

My stomach turns.

No.

No!

Fear grips me as I cross the room in a few quick strides and kneel beside the trapdoor. I hesitate for just a moment before pulling it open.

Beneath the wood is a small space, just big enough for two people to hide. A handmade wooden shelf stacked with dried fruits, vegetables, and cans filled with water covers the wall, and an empty bucket stands in the corner. The space is filled with hay and a few linens for comfort in case we are stuck here for weeks.

I climb down the wooden ladder, already aware that I'm alone.

Liza isn't here.

Head spinning, I climb out of the hole and storm to the door when something on the table catches my attention. I draw up short and stumble towards it, my hands reaching for it before my brain can assemble what I'm about to touch.

It's a letter.

My fingers stop midair when I see the red seal with ornate swirls encircling a golden moth.

Monsteress.

Panic ripples through my body when my hands touch the smooth paper. Then, without hesitation, I rip the envelope open.

Of course, she uses red ink. That's the first thought that floats through my mind when I see the cursive handwriting sprawled across the paper inside.

My dearest Aemilius,

I am writing to you with a heavy heart as I have received news of your escape. I hope we can resolve this matter without such drastic measures.

However, I must inform you that you have left something very dear to you behind in your haste to flee. I have now come to possess something that I wanted to offer you in return for your kindness. Naturally, I do not wish to divulge what it is in case this letter ends up in the wrong hands. However, I am confident that you know exactly what I mean.

I implore you to return to me before the next sunrise if you wish to reclaim what is rightfully yours. I do not wish for any harm to come to you, but I must warn you that time is of the essence. If you do not return in time, I cannot guarantee the safe return of what you hold dear.

Talking about your freedom, I understand, it is a precious thing. But you must know that it cannot be granted without consequence. Your actions have brought harm to my kingdom, and it is my duty as the Queen to ensure that justice is served.

So, I urge you to consider your next move. The consequences of your actions will only grow more severe the longer you remain on the run. However, if you return before the next sunrise, I am willing to consider a more merciful punishment.

I understand that our past may be fraught with tension and conflict, but I beg you to put that aside for now. This is a matter of utmost importance, and I hope you will see it similarly.

I eagerly await your arrival and pray to Lunra that you will make the right decision.

By the Queen Soulin SinClaret, Ruler of Crymzon, Protector of Lunra

How did she know I would escape? Did she use her moths to fly here?

She must have because no horse is fast enough to reach the village before I did.

I slam my hand on the table. The sharp pain radiating through my body reminds me of one thing—the pain Liza will feel when I don't make it in time back to Crymzon.

"Fuck!" I yell, pulling on my hair.

I kick the standing chair over and watch it shatter on the ground, burying trash under it.

Trash?

I sprint to the wall and stumble over the other chair as I notice the missing top box.

"This can't be." My knees hit the hard floor, and I moan as I scan the ground for the only valuable thing inside our hut.

It can't be gone. *It can't!*

Rummaging through the trash, I search for something I know is gone. I would notice the copper and brass object I hid inside the crate just before the soldiers stormed the village.

I didn't have enough time to use it back then because I planned to hide under the trapdoor with Liza until the soldiers passed. At that time, I thought all the villagers would have the same idea. I didn't expect to hear the screams and witness the bloodshed outside my door.

The Soulkeeper was the first invention I came up with at twelve. Being trapped inside Eternitie's palace was dreary. All I was allowed to do was watch other children play outside in the streets.

So I had no other choice than to create a friend.

I spent years studying ancient texts and experimenting with magical devices to create this gadget.

Constructing a device that is little enough to fit into a backpack and yet powerful enough to store a person was impossible. However, building a trap for a soul was less challenging.

A year later, I trapped the first soul successfully inside the Soulkeeper. But it wasn't just any soul.

I had chosen a cruel-looking creature that entered our courtyard when I was allowed to stretch my legs for a bit.

At this point, I have effectively trapped eight souls behind the circular glass chamber. Three of them are actually quite entertaining, while the other five ignore my requests to get to know each other at all costs.

As I sit down for a moment to catch a break, thoughts of the mighty creatures trapped within consume my mind. I picture them in my mind - a gigantic bird-looking creature with scales and feathers as black as night; a shimmering woman with horns of purest silver and lies as deadly as venom; a sly, cunning cat creature with eyes that glittered like jewels and burning fangs.

Those are just a few of the nightmares imprisoned within the Soulkeeper, their magical energies harnessed and controlled by the intricate mechanisms inside.

My breath catches when the door pushes open, pulling me out of my thoughts. The head of the stallion appears in the doorframe, and I let out a sigh.

"You darn horse," I spit out, holding my chest to calm my heart.

The horse tries to squeeze through the frame and stomps its hooves on the ground when it gets stuck.

"Are you serious right now? Why won't you leave?" I say, jumping to my feet to help the trapped animal back up. Pressing my shoulder into the stallion's chest, I give it a big push. The horse tramples backward and breaks free.

My eyes linger on his as he looks at me with anticipation until it moves his head to look back toward Crymzon.

"I know. I don't want to go back there, either. But I must," I whisper, following its gaze.

The stallion eagerly clicks his hooves across the sandy ground, stirring up little dust clouds as if trying to communicate with me.

I wrinkle my nose. "You want to go back?"

His nostrils flare as it shakes its head in the direction again.

Why is the horse so eager to get back?

I can't fathom living inside Monsteress' terrain as enjoyable to any living being. Maybe the horse has developed positive feelings toward his captor over time and doesn't know a world without cruelty exists.

Positive feelings, I think to myself, petting his neck.

"That's it," I say, slapping a hand to my forehead.

Maybe some of my trapped souls inside the Soulkeeper have grown attached to me. I for sure care for them. If so, I can use them against Monsteress if she hasn't already unleashed them on her kingdom.

Hope reignites inside me, and I think of all the ways I can use my creatures against her.

"It's time we show *Her Majesty how* it feels to fight fire with fire." I spit out the title in mockery as I grab the reins and jump on the back of the stallion to make my way back to the evil Queen.

THIRTY-TWO

Queen Soulin

A knock on the door startles me.

"What now?" I yell, covering the last piece of white hair with red clay and inspecting the new silk dress I put on after storming out of the water chamber.

It was almost impossible to get back to my chambers without being noticed by servants or guards. If anyone saw me covering my body with a ripped dress, I would need to hang them to stop the spread of the rumor about what happened inside the chamber. The word about Khaos and I can't spread through my kingdom.

Myra walks in, slamming the door shut behind her. "What were you thinking?" she screams at me, the veins on her neck sticking out.

"You need to be more specific," I growl, thinking about whether she means I lost my magic or the *altercation* with Khaos just an hour ago.

"You know exactly what I'm talking about. I told you it was an idiotic plan to leave for Terminus. You could've been killed."

"You're just worried because you fear becoming homeless."

"I *am* homeless. My place on this planet died when you turned my love into ashes."

Bringing up her Soulmate as leverage against me makes me cringe on the inside every damn time.

"Did you come all this way to taunt me with something I'll never have?" I ask, facing her. "Not everyone's connection is as strong and uncomplicated as yours."

It takes one breath for her to cross the room. Her fingers jolt into my hair, and she balls a fist, plucking strands from my skull. The pain is excruciating, and I wince under her grip.

"Listen to me now carefully, Soulin. On her deathbed, I swore to your mother that I would care for you like you're my child. My vow to advise and protect you stands above everything else. And I never blamed you for Elia's death. She was just in the wrong place at the wrong time when the magic inside you lashed out." She tightens her grip and pulls me closer to her face. "But I will never forgive you if you mock her again. Do you understand me?"

I exhale sharply and try to use my magic to ease the pain, but it's not there.

I've never seen Myra this violent, even after all that happened to her.

Her breath is hot on my face, and I feel tears forming. "I'm sorry," I whisper, trying to reach her hand before she can pull more hair out.

Those words are enough for Myra to let me go and take a step back. Her emerald eyes squeeze almost shut as she takes me in.

"What was that?" she asks, her voice trembling.

"I said, *I'm sorry*," I repeat, my voice regaining its sharp edge.

She looks at me in disbelief. "Why didn't you use your magic to get free?"

Instantly, I realize the mistake I made. Myra wasn't aware that I depleted my magic in Terminus. As of now, she thought I still had some.

Feeling pain is only a small part that gave me away. Without my magic, I feel pain like every other person in Escela, and to add to it, I also can't heal myself.

But apologizing to her was the biggest misstep.

I've carried that apology inside my heart for fourteen years. I locked it behind an indestructible layer of magic—until my powers vanished.

"It's gone?" she whispers, her voice breaking.

I don't need to give her an answer because my face says it all.

She inches forward and is about to run her fingers under my chin. An inch away, she stops, her finger pointing at me. "So the rumors are true? Crymzon is falling?"

I'm trying to make sense of her. How did she go from plucking my hair out and scolding me like a mother to sadness within a blink of an eye?

"How do you know?" I croak out, my throat thick with emotions that I'm so used to suppressing.

She points to the window, and my gaze follows her finger. "Have you not looked outside? Last night, the ground around the Wall started to crumble when the prisoner left."

My heart stops. "What prisoner?"

"The one who brought you home safely. I thought you let him go."

The room closes in on me.

"Why would I do that?" I ask, trying to understand what she's referring to.

"You were unconscious when you arrived. When I tried to thank him, he wasn't in his chamber. So I thought you let him go for saving your life."

My hands go numb as all my blood rushes into my heart to pump faster. "You can't be serious."

"He had a horse," she mumbles, questioning her decision. "Somehow, he had a horse. And I told the guards to shoot the desert lion prowling the outskirts of Crymzon. It was about to rip him apart, and he didn't even notice."

None of this makes sense. How can she think I would let him leave? I've shown no signs of sympathy for anyone, so why does she think I'm that weak to grant him his life for not leaving me to rot in Terminus?

I brush my hand through my hair, catching a few loose strands from Myra's sudden outburst. "He *had* to return me home. Without me, the moths wouldn't have listened to him," I exclaim, jumping off the chair. "What were you thinking?"

"I wasn't," Myra answers, her eyes running over the desert as if she can still see him. "My focus was solely on you. I needed to ensure that you were taken care of. Then, I assumed you were just exhausted from your trip, but I didn't know you were actually drained. You're now human. *Just* a human."

Hearing those words out loud cut deeper than expected, and I steady myself before my knees can cave in.

Without my magic, I'm normal. I hurt, I feel, and I can't heal. Those are all the attributes I hate in the common folk—and now I'm one of them.

"Can you feel it?" Myra asks, pointing at my chest. "Do you know when it's going to happen?"

I take way too long to realize what she means.

"I can't feel when Crymzon is going to consume me. It's not like an internal timer started counting down until my death," I say, searching inside me. "But I know it's soon."

Myra steps in front of me and stops me from pacing through the room. "What do you want me to do?" she asks, her warm eyes searching my face.

I'm clueless about what my next step should be. I'm powerless, without a Soulmate, and I'm dying. So where can I go from here?

"This needs to stay between us," I say, grabbing her shoulders. "I can't have fear spread through the kingdom."

Myra shrugs my hands off, and her eyes widen. "But that won't stop you from killing everyone inside Crymzon's Wall. We need to evacuate now."

I look into her deep green eyes and shake my head before twisting away from her. "And where do you want them to go? To Tenacoro? Or even better: Eternitie?"

Myra bites her lip. "But the children—"

"Will be fine," I cut in as a plan forms in my head. "I released the Grand General from his oath, and he is on his way out of the palace as we speak. While I'm gone, I need you to wait here to instruct the new Grand General to round up my army and start marching north. I will meet them there."

Myra opens and closes her mouth repetitively, searching for the right words. Finally, she finds her voice. "We're going to die out there."

"You don't say," I smirk. "If we wait here, we'll die, and if we stand up against Keres, we'll die. So it doesn't matter what we do next. Death is knocking on our door."

"It matters to me," she shrieks.

"But you're not the Queen."

Myra crosses her arms, her face hardening. "I won't do it."

I expected those words. After all, Myra has been at my side since I can remember. But, unfortunately, I know her too well.

"Myra Eslene of Crymzon. I release you from your oath as my advisor. You have until sundown to pack your belongings and leave my kingdom."

Myra reaches out to grab my hands, but I pull them away.

"If you're spotted after the sun touches the horizon, your punishment will be death."

Her nostrils flare, and I watch all kinds of emotion overflow her body. Tears start forming in her eyes, her fists shake uncontrollably, and her jaw clenches. "After everything I've done for you, you can't just throw me away like I'm nothing. You *can't* do that."

"I just did," I say, my voice firm. "Guards," I yell. The door jolts open immediately. "Guide Myra back to her chamber and ensure not to make any detours on her way out of Crymzon."

The guards hesitate for a moment before stepping forward.

"You can't do this," Myra pleads as she shakes me by the shoulders. "It can't end like this."

"Get her out of my sight," I growl to the guards and shove her away.

My push is more potent than I expected, and she stumbles backward and falls to the ground. She looks up at me, tears running down her face. "I've always been there for you, and this is how you repay me? I've done horrible things in your name!"

"If you would really know me, you should have seen this coming," I snarl, waving my hand to gesture to the guards to seize her.

The guards approach Myra, grab her by her arms, and pull her to her feet. She launches forward, but one guard wraps his arm around her waist and pulls her back before she gets too close to me. "If your mother and Felix could see what a disappointment you have become, they would beg you to kill them again."

A laugh erupts out of my throat. "It would be impressive if my brother comes back from the dead just to die a third time," I say, wrinkling my nose. "Take her away."

"Let me go!" she yells at the men, but they enforce their hold on her.

I flick my hand to the door, and the guards drag her across the room.

"You will die! All of you will *die*! Do you hear me? *The Queen will kill you all!*" Myra screams at the top of her lungs as they pull her into the corridor and close the door behind them.

It takes a few minutes for her screams to subside as the guards drag her through the palace and out of reach of my chambers.

For a moment, I stand there and calculate how long it will take for her words to reach my subjects.

I shake my head.

Who would believe a woman who just fell from their Queen's grace? The Crymzonians have followed me even after I killed my family, after I stopped holding ceremonies, and after the magic wore out. After worshiping me for fourteen years, they won't turn their backs on me now.

My lips curve upwards as I think about the envelope I handed Khaos before he left to search Cyrus' hut.

Everything I wrote was in the hope Cyrus would try to escape and that Khaos would return with something valuable. And he did.

Cyrus was the only leverage I had against Eternitie. The only person who can force King Citeus into submission to join me against Keres.

I was told Khaos returned with a female he found inside the hut. I haven't had the chance to visit her because after I awoke, my head and body overrun by emotions I haven't felt in over a decade, I fled to the water chamber to wash my defeat and feelings away.

Thinking about Khaos' hands touching my body shatters me. I wanted it to be true. I wanted him to be the one I spent the rest of my life with.

Growling, I push the memory aside and concentrate on my following action.

I need to find out who that female is, and then I need to speak to Lunra. Only the Goddess can grant me enough power to avenge my brother and find the Painite to restore the Heiligbaum. Rehabilitating the Heiligbaum will give me more time to find a Soulmate.

Exhaling sharply, I clutch my hands into fists and release them as I look outside the window and over the Wall. The deep craters outside the gate are the first signs of my kingdom disintegrating.

"I'm Queen Soulin SinClaret. The Ruler of Crymzon. The Protector of Lunra. I'm the only SinClaret remaining. If I fail, so will an entire kingdom."

THIRTY-THREE

KHAOS

My fist collides with the wall. I hear a knuckle break before the pain shoots up my arm and into my chest.

"Fuck!" I yell, and the word echoes off the unscathed stone barrier back at me. Instead of grabbing my hand to ease the pain, I drop my fist and breathe through it.

Even a broken bone aches less than my broken heart.

There's no way I'm leaving. Soulin doesn't know what she's doing anymore, I think to myself as the sharp pain slowly turns into numbness.

After guarding her my entire life, even before I joined her army, she used me and spat me out like sour wine. But that isn't the worst. Her face—her expression filled with disgust and disappointment—burnt into my memory. It's all I see when I close my eyes.

When I heard her enter the room, I should have grabbed my clothes and left. I went too far. I know that.

Instead of backing her into a corner, I should have told her about the stranger hidden beneath the trapdoor or the gleaming gadget.

The gadget.

I turn around and scan my chamber for the saddleback, where I stored the weird contraption after returning my horse to the stable.

Where did I put it?

Retracing my steps, I try to figure out where I placed it when I was still in a haze of riding for an entire day. I rummage through the broken furniture pieces scattered on the floor I destroyed after rage overtook me. The ache in my hand forces tears into my eyes, and I grit my teeth to distract myself.

While I search for the only thing that can help me regain Soulin's favor, a scream in the corridor makes me pause.

"Get off me!" a woman yells.

I'm at the door with two big steps, tearing it open.

"What's going on here?" I demand as my eyes fall on Myra, who's being carried by two of my guards. "Drop her," I say, pointing at Myra.

The guards draw up short and blink at me. Confusion is written all over their faces, and I'm taken aback when they shake their heads.

"I'm sorry, Grand General Zedohr. The order to escort Myra to her chamber comes from the Queen."

"From the Queen?" I mumble, searching Myra's eyes for an answer.

"She's insane!" Myra screams as she tries to wiggle herself free. "She's going to get us all killed when she heads north! You must stop her! Save us!"

My mouth goes dry. "She's going back?"

"She's summoning her army as we speak. You have to do something. She can't leave Crymzon."

If this is the path Soulin is choosing, I need to intervene. She can't go back there. She almost didn't return from her last excursion.

"What order did the Queen give you?" I ask, my question directed at the soldier I recruited just a few moons ago.

"She stripped me of my oath and exiled me. I have until sundown to leave Crymzon," Myra answers as both soldiers scramble for an explanation.

"I'm sorry, but we can't stay here. If the Queen finds out we're wasting time, she will punish us," the other guard says, dragging Myra over the ground.

There's no time for further questions. I only have two options and lean to the nonassertive one first as I think about my broken knuckle.

"Let me escort her. Over the years, I had enough time to watch her. I know all of her moves and tricks," I say thickly.

As they pass me, I grab Myra's arm and yank her out of their grips. "But this better stay between us. If Her Majesty finds out, we're all in deep shit."

I'm not sure who's more shocked: the guards because I'm trying to help them, or Myra because she isn't used to me putting a finger on her.

She drops to the ground like a dead weight, and I reach down to pull her back up. "You better not fight me, or I will ruin your beautiful face," I spit out as I press down on her arm.

Her body stiffens under my grip as she lets out a whining sound. "Stop hurting me," she says, squirming under my touch.

"What are you waiting for? Alert the soldiers that we're leaving for Terminus before the sun sets," I bark at them, pulling Myra closer to me.

As the soldiers scramble around the corridor's corner, I release Myra.

"Are you okay?" I ask, pulling her into my chamber.

She rubs her arm. "I could ask you the same. She exiled you, too?"

I look up and down the corridor for any listening ears before closing the door. "Not officially. She never spoke the words to release me from my oath. So technically, I'm still her Grand General and servant," I whisper, leaning against the wall. "And that allows me to lead our army to Terminus."

"You can't be serious. Why would you still support her?"

"For the same reason you fought those guards to let you go. I can't stand around and watch her fail."

She straightens her emerald dress and points to the door. "That woman out there, that's not Soulin. She hasn't been since her mother died. So hanging on to the sliver of hope that we can bring her back is in vain. She's exactly who everyone says she is, Monsteress, and we were just too blind to see it."

My stomach turns at the thought of leaving Soulin and Crymzon behind.

"This is my home. I can't just walk away and watch it turn into rubble and dust."

She looks into my eyes, and a tear rolls down her face. "But you also don't have to fall with them," she says, wiping a tear away. "This is our chance to start over. To begin a life without serving, without being treated like vermin. We deserve so much more than that."

Is this it? Is this how Myra wants to part from Soulin and observe her downfall from afar?

Maybe she can, but I can't.

My mind floods with the memory of her pushing me away when she got hurt while playing in the stables. It was to ensure I wouldn't see her cry. But I sat beside her on the hot floor instead of leaving her. It took just a few minutes and many cuss words until she leaned against my shoulder and let her emotions run wild.

Her father taught her to never show any emotion other than happiness. So how could she not be happy being the Princess of an entire kingdom, living in a palace with servants and guards? Everything she ever wanted was handed to her before she knew she wanted it.

But the Soulin I know hates to be handed everything she desires. She wants to work for it. She wants to make it with her bare hands and her skills.

"She didn't choose this life. And she surely never prepared to take the throne," I whisper as my blood boils. "I know her, and so do you."

Myra moves her head slowly. "I'm not so sure anymore, Khaos. There is nothing we can do. It's too late."

Those are the words I have been waiting for.

While my brain knows the truth, my heart can't accept it.

Soulin is dying.

Crymzon is dying.

The destruction of everything inside the Wall is imminent.

Houses. Citizens. Magic.

And there is no way to stop it.

I march through the mess on the floor and pick up my chest plate.

"What are you doing?" Myra asks, observing me as I pull out my sword belt under the ripped curtains.

"I'm not asking you to stay. I can't. You've given so much to the throne, and you deserve to enjoy happiness as a free woman for the first time in your life." I inhale deeply. "But Soulin needs me. I don't care about her title. I don't care that she's not the Soulin I grew up with. She's still my best friend..." *My soulmate, even if destiny spoke otherwise,* but I keep that to myself. "She needs me as much as I need her, even when she pushes me away."

Myra's hands tremble when she wipes new tears off with her sleeve. "Damn it, Khaos. I was ready to walk away from this life—"

"Then do it. This is your chance," I cut in when I notice the change in her voice. "Leave this Lunra-forsaken place and take as many Crymzonians with you as possible."

"But—"

"Go, Myra." I point at the window to the sandstone-carved houses. "Those people out there need you. They will follow you." My throat constricts. "And I will miss you."

Those last words came over my lips before I realize it. That doesn't make them untrue.

Myra was one of the first palace servants I met after my father took me with him to the stables to help with the horses. Her smile and graying hair made it easy for me to see her as a loving family figure.

I remember the first time she took me to the side to demonstrate how to bow correctly before the King, just minutes before I had to perform it as he came to inspect the horses. Myra was also the one that kept getting Soulin and me out of trouble. She would cover for us or take the blame whenever we were caught stealing from the kitchen or used the palace walls as enormous canvases to practice art.

The smile on Myra's lips is the same one she gave me when she laid eyes on me for the first time. I feel the same warmth streaming through my body that I experienced back then.

"It's not too late to come with me," she says, her voice heavy.

I bow my head. "I'm sorry."

Her feet appear in my vision, and her hand reaches under my chin to lift it. "We will see each other again, Khaos Zedohr. Your journey is far from over." She pulls me into a hug, and for a moment, I forget to be the tough soldier everyone expects me to be.

I slump down and press her against me.

"I will miss you, too," she whispers into my chest as I feel my heart breaking. "You're one of the finest boys I had the pleasure of watching grow up. I'm truly sorry I didn't do more to save you from this place."

"Without *you* and *this* place, I would be an entirely different person. I don't regret any of it."

She exhales, and I feel her muscles relax under my touch. "She doesn't deserve you."

I let go of her and step back, only to regret it when I step on a splintered wood piece that used to be part of my bed.

Myra gives me one more smile, but her eyes are sorrowful. "May Lunra protect you and guide you safely through what's coming."

"May Lunra protect you and guide you safely through what's coming," I repeat as I watch her disappear through the door.

It only takes me a few moments to retrieve the rest of my armor, and just as I hear another set of metal boots clinking down the corridor, I'm outside.

"Jeremia," I say as monotone as possible to sound like the Grand General he knows.

"Is it true? Are we marching north?" he asks without hesitation.

I close the door behind me to block off the view of the mess I made after my encounter with Soulin and come to a halt beside him.

"It is. And I have to find the soldier with the strongest magic."

"That's you," Jeremia says, his brows drawn together. "What in Lunra's name is wrong with you?"

"With me?"

"Why are you acting so... weird?" he asks, pointing at my shifting feet.

"Can you help me or not?" I growl, annoyance bubbling up inside of me.

Every minute I waste on finding a replacement for my job gives Soulin more time to notice my scheme.

"Since I train with most soldiers, I think Remy might be the strongest after you."

Even though shame ripples through my body on the inside, I don't let it show. Jeremia, or any other soldier, has never experienced *my* magic. It was always borrowed or stolen magic I snatched from the people around me by touch, just like I had done when I used the dying guard's magic just before it could leave his body in the village.

"Are you sure he's the next in line?"

I know he speaks the truth because I had handpicked Remy after seeing him use his power to climb the Wall in a blink of an eye.

Yet, I want to be wrong.

Remy has grown on me since I recruited him. But if my plan fails, he will die with Soulin on the battlefield.

It's a risk I have to take.

"I'm worried about you," Jeremia says, but his facial expression goes blank when he sees the rage in my eyes. "Yes, I'm sure he's the one. Are you going to tell me what this is about?"

"I will tell you everything once we're on the way. Grab the warmest undergarments you can find and a handful of soldiers. Meet me at the stable and make sure no one notices you guys leaving the palace."

Jeremia's mouth pops open, but I continue. "Be fast and silent. All of this will make sense once we're out of Crymzon."

I whirl around and march toward the barracks, giving him no time to question me. The silence behind me tells me he's still trying to figure out what my babbling is about, but when I turn around the corner, I hear his feet stomping away.

Now, I only have to find Remy and deliver the news that he got promoted to Grand General for a critical mission. I'm not sure what lies I will feed him about why Soulin removed me as the Grand General of the Crymzon Army. No one gets demoted without severe charges. But if I play my cards right, he won't suspect anything.

THIRTY-FOUR

CYRUS

The fire inside my veins reignites when I lay eyes on Crymzon.

I'm so sick of this shithole of a kingdom.

Monsteress' lies, the sense of death surrounding her, and her cruelty make Eternitie look like paradise.

The guards shout distorted words at each other when I draw closer to the gate.

I never expected to return to this place freely. Well, *freely* isn't the fitting word to describe my situation. But, unfortunately, Monsteress is the one having the upper hand in this. By capturing Liza, she forces me to return, most likely with deadly consequences.

If they give me the option to flee from this place again, I'll take it.

No doubt.

The sun has just made its way over the horizon when my horse gallops through the open gate, and two dozen men inside the Wall greet me. The soldiers on guard duty quickly spring into action as they draw their weapons and take up defensive positions, wary of the potential danger I might pose.

"Missed us, huh?" a soldier calls out, his voice sharp with irritation.

I raise my hands in a gesture of surrender, my eyes darting from side to side as I assess the situation. "I'm here to turn myself in," I say, my voice hoarse and strained from the long ride.

The soldiers exchange skeptical glances, clearly not convinced by my story. They tighten their grips on their weapons and step forward, closing in on me.

How much do the guards know? Are they aware that Monsteress is holding Liza as a prisoner to lure me back?

"Queen Soulin will be delighted to see her favorite pet back," a man snarls out of the second row.

My nostrils flare when I recognize the soldier with the crooked nose. "How is that nose treating you? Do you need my help to restore it?" I smirk as I remember the cracking noise his bone made when my elbow collided with his face. He jolts forward, but another man holds him back.

Despite their best efforts to intimidate me, I remain calm and composed. I dismount from the horse and raise my hands in surrender once more, offering no resistance as two soldiers approach to apprehend me.

I'm led through the kingdom's streets into the courtyard where I delivered Monsteress and up the stairs to the palace. I keep my head hung low as two heavily armed guards escort me.

The moment we step through the palace gates, I start counting my steps while memorizing the way.

The palace is a labyrinth of corridors and rooms, each more opulent than the last. I'm able to fill in the missing parts of the palace map inside my mind as I keep my head low to avoid suspicion.

As we walk, I can't help but feel a sense of nostalgia as I pass by familiar rooms and furnishings which look so similar to my old home—Eternitie. The memories of my old life of luxury and privilege, which ultimately led to my imprisonment, float through my head, making it hurt.

But those reminiscences are quickly replaced with dread as we approach a chamber.

As the guards open the door, I step inside and feel a chill run down my spine. It's the same windowless room with only a small slit under the door for light and ventilation I occupied just days ago. The room is devoid of furniture save for a small straw mat on the floor.

I've hoped that Monsteress is dumb enough to hold Liza in this god-forsaken room, but that would have been too good to be true.

"Just like I remember," I say, faking the excitement in my voice as I try to figure out where Monsteress could hold her.

"Now, this is a public execution I can't wait to see," one guard says as he pushes me to the ground. "This chamber is already more than you deserve."

Chuckling, I roll my eyes. These guards are as primitive as the ones at home. Even though they know nothing about me and the circumstances that brought me here, they think I deserve this fate.

"What's so funny?" he asks, drilling his metal glove into my collarbone.

"I can't wait for it either," I lie through clenched teeth.

Stop stirring the pot, Cyrus.

Relief flushes through me when the guard eases the pressure. They hurry back to the door and push it shut behind them. I don't need to turn around to know there is no way out of this chamber. It's just me, that damn straw bed, and darkness.

I sit on the mat, my mind racing with regret. I thought I could escape my fate, but I only managed to return to where it all began.

As time flies by, I come to terms with my doom. I know I have to face punishment for taking Monsteress as a fool. But the thought of what she will do to Liza is almost too much to bear. None of this is her fault.

Just as my mind drifts off to find peace by resting, I hear footsteps approaching.

The air around me crackles with energy, and my eyes dart to the wall as it begins to shimmer and distort like a mirage in the desert. The stone seems to melt away, revealing a smooth, transparent surface like nothing I have ever seen.

The wall transforms into a sheet of glass, so clear that I can see through it to the other side. The glass is so perfectly formed that it looks almost like the hands of the finest glassmakers in Escela crafted it.

Slowly, I get off the mat. My eyes land on the cruel smile Monsteress throws back at me.

"For a moment, I thought you won't show. But I guess your whore means more to you than I expected," Monsteress snarls through the thin glass barrier between us as she snaps her finger at a guard. On command, he tosses a woman to the ground before her.

My heart stops when I watch Liza fall to her knees. Her body is much more delicate than I remember. Her clothes are ripped and stained with desert sand, her hair is dirty, and her feet are raw.

"What did you do to her?" I yell, jumping forward. I pound my hands against the glass, but the barrier doesn't budge.

"Me? What did *you* do to her?" Monsteress asks as she fists Liza's hair and pulls her head up to force her to look at me.

Liza's eyes are bloodshot, and her energetic blue irises are dull as they land on my face.

This isn't the Liza from my memory.

221

Why isn't she responding to seeing me? She must recognize me. So why doesn't she say anything? Can't she see me?

Monsteress pulls her fingers out of her hair, and Liza's head drops to the floor. "You're the one that kept her in a cell beneath your hut. So what is she? Your slave? Your concubine?"

My fists hurt as I keep banging them against the glass. "Leave her alone!"

"You know it's rude not to answer to your Queen," she hisses, her smile growing wider.

"You're *not* my Queen!" I spit back, my jaw in pain from clenching it too hard.

"That's too bad. I thought we made some progress in Terminus. But I guess we have to establish our *friendship* again." She unhooks a clasp on the bracelet around her wrists up to her forearm. "That blacksmith of yours...he does exquisite work. It needed some elbow grease to convince him to forge me a weapon, but his hard work paid off."

No...Wayne can't be working with her. He would rather cut his arms off than support the Crymzon Queen. While I know little about his and Devana's history, it's enough to know that they hate Monsteress as much as I do.

"What do you think? Are three lashes enough to change your mind?" Monsteress unravels the bracelet. Bile rises up my throat when I realize her jewelry piece is actually a weapon.

"No! Leave her alone," I say as I come back to my senses. "Please. No."

Monsteress clicks her tongue as she drives her finger over the gleaming metal chain edges decorated with little spikes as sharp as claws. "Lovers then," she snarls as she lifts her hand. "I didn't take you for a romantic."

I inhale deeply, and a scream gets stuck in my throat when the metal whip flies through the air and descends on Liza's back. Her eyes shoot up to the ceiling when the metal collides with her back.

Another lash follows before I can even comprehend what's happening.

"Stop!" I yell as I watch Liza close her eyes, her face distorted in pain.

Not a single sound leaves her lips. Her shirt is ripped in both places where the whip struck her, blood oozing out of the clean markings now exposed to my eyes.

Monsteress wrist is about to unleash the last lash when she freezes midair. Her eyes rest on Liza's shoulder blades, and her brows draw together.

"Take her shirt off," she demands, her eyes fleeting over Liza's body as a guard approaches her.

"Don't fucking touch her!" I scream, clawing at the glass. "Leave her alone!"

But it's too late. The soldier grabs her damaged shirt and rips it clean in the middle, exposing Liza's most vulnerable secret.

"A fallen warrior," Monsteress says with amusement as she scans her back. "I should have known. Look at her blond hair. Your concubine is a fallen warrior."

My throat closes, and my heart quickens when I see the delight in Monsteress' shimmering eyes.

Everyone knows the reason Queen Ria died. Her Starstrandian lover was the father of her third child, but the baby got stuck in the birth canal with its wings, leading to the death of both mother and child.

It's also known that Monsteress has since blamed the Starstrand Queen for their preventable deaths as if it's the ruler's responsibility to keep their suspects in check.

"Please, don't hurt her," I whisper through tears as I take in the two scared-over round patches of skin where her wings were clipped.

I've seen them a lot since Liza trusted me with her secret. When I met her, she still struggled to clean the slow-healing wounds on her back, which made no progress for a year before our paths crossed. With the help of a woman who fled Tenacoro, I mixed a thick paste to speed up the healing process.

"Who did this to you?" Monsteress asks as she runs her sharp nails over the broken skin. Liza flinches under her touch but says nothing.

"Please. Tell her to leave her alone," I plead to the soldier beside Monsteress. His eyes fill with hurt when he watches Monsteress press her nails into one of the scarred patches until she draws blood. The soldier diverts his eyes to look at his boots, and I bang against the glass to catch Monsteress' attention.

"Queen Caecilia has a backbone, after all. I didn't expect her to punish her citizens," she says, dragging her nail over Liza's spine to the other scar tissue.

"What do you want from me?" I yell, surprised that Monsteress lifts her head to look at me.

"You never knew where to find the Painite, did you?"

That damn rock. Of course, everything is about that damn piece of mineral.

She knows the truth. Lying would only turn into more violence. "I already told you. No, I don't know the exact spot," I say, lowering my head. "I only know where the highest success rate of finding one is."

"Let me guess. It was nowhere close to where we looked?"

My silence is enough to confirm her question. But I've already been through this. I confessed to her in Terminus right before she lost consciousness.

"I'm running out of patience with you," Monsteress hisses as she tightens her grip around the whip. "I don't think you quite understand what's at stake here." She grabs Liza's chin and forces her to look at me again.

I know what's at stake more than anyone. It's not just about saving Liza's life. It's about Crymzon and what Monsteress is about to lose when she doesn't get her hands on Painite. Liza is just her excuse to break me and to keep giving the impression that she has everything under control.

"Do you have a map of Terminus?" I ask, choking down all the other mean things I want to throw at her. But I can't. She has Liza firmly in her grip, and the rage inside Monsteress' eyes scares me.

Something changed since the last time I saw her. The irresistible pull I felt towards the Crymzon Queen is gone. The glowing silver freckles on her face are lightless and gray, nothing like the sparking silver I saw as she towered above us on the Crymzon Throne.

"If you get me a map, I can show you exactly where the Painite has to grow," I say, watching Liza breathe heavily through Monsteress' touch.

"I won't fall for that again," she snarls, letting go of Liza. She raises her hand, and the whip follows her movement.

"Wait, wait, wait," I scream, lifting my hands. "I know you can't trust me after what I've done. But I'm begging you to give me another chance."

Slowly, Monsteress lowers her arm, and I exhale sharply. She opens her mouth, but before a sound can form, the earth trembles beneath us, sending vibrations through the walls and floors. The air is filled with the sound of cracking stone and glass shattering.

Liza falls onto her side and lets out a groan while Monsteress and her guard find hold leaning against the corridor wall.

As the earthquake reaches its peak, a crunching noise rings in my ears. A fine black line shoots past my eyes just inches away. The line grows broader and deeper as if the earth is trying to break through the walls.

The Queen's guard rushes to her side, urging her to take cover, but she stands rooted to the spot, unable to tear her gaze away from the ominous crack in the glass. For a moment, it seems the entire barrier will shatter, sending a cascade of glass fragments down upon us.

But as quickly as it began, the earthquake subsides, leaving behind an eerie feeling. The palace walls are saturated with small cracks, the floors littered with debris, and the glass barrier before me is permanently scarred by the dark line, just like the open flesh wounds Monsteress inflicted on Liza's back.

My gaze falls back on Monsteress, and I catch the fear on her face just seconds before she regains control, and it vaporizes.

She turns to the guard and pulls him closer. "Get him the map and toss her in there. And make sure they receive new clothes."

The guard's face falters. "For what, Your Majesty?"

She curls the whip around her arm and latches the handle to hold the deadly jewelry in place. "We still have a ceremony to attend," she whispers before she walks off.

My stomach twists when I hear the last sentence, but it immediately eases when the guard picks Liza up. He steps to the glass barrier. Then, with one push of his hand, the glass transforms back into stone, and the door jolts open to let him in.

My instincts tell me to take him out and run, but when I see Liza's broken body inside his arms and how gently he lets her down on the mat, that plan nulls.

"I'm sorry," he whispers as he storms out of the room, shutting the door behind him, leaving Liza and me behind in almost complete darkness.

It takes a few heartbeats for my eyes to adjust. When my vision finally returns, I curl up behind Liza and carefully pull her into a hug.

Her body trembles against mine, and I use my weight to put pressure on her. I've done this countless nights to assure her she was safe. Whenever the nightmares about her wings returned, I was there to help her.

"I got you," I whisper into her ear, and the tension in her body slowly diminishes.

"She will kill me when she finds out who I am," Liza groans. The sound of her voice, raspy and hushed, breaks my heart.

"No matter what we do, she'll kill us," I say hushedly to cover my shaky voice. "I'm so sorry I pulled you into this."

"At least we'll die together," Liza says before her body goes limp in my arms.

THIRTY-FIVE

QUEEN SOULIN

I follow the dark, jagged crack in the stone floor that leads toward the East Tower. The gap is wide enough to slip a finger through, and as I make my way through the palace, I notice the strange quietness that hangs in the air. An eerie silence has replaced the usual sounds of bustling activity and conversation.

Most Crymzonians are asleep while the sun heats the sandstone buildings unmercifully, but I'm shocked that no one has woken up.

How?

By now, the corridors should be filled with guards and servants trying to understand what caused the tumult.

Suddenly, the ground beneath my feet shakes violently, throwing me off balance. I stumble forward, grabbing onto the nearest wall for support. Tiny cracks appear on the wall's surface and I pull my hand back to avoid a vein-thin gap forming beneath my palm.

Hesitantly, I consider my options before deciding to continue my way to the tower. I step over the deep chasm, my heart beating fast as I cross the precarious divide.

Determined to reach the tower to assess the damage, I almost run into the door that flings open, revealing a scared-looking servant.

"Your Majesty," she says, her eyes wide with fear. She reaches for her nightgown and attempts to curtsy, but the brutal waves shaking the place make her stagger in my direction. "I'm so sorry," she says quickly when my hands grab her by the shoulders to stop her from ramming into me.

She scrambles back, but I hold onto her tightly. I feel the magic flowing through her veins like a storm surge. Hypnotized by the urge to feel that kind of power inside me again, I close my eyes and pull on the invisible force running through her body. I feel the magic seeping through her pores into my fingertips and palms.

Only a few Crymzonians can pull magic from another individual. It is strictly reserved for healers *only* since the magic started to die inside the Crymzon Wall, and if caught stealing power from another being, it is punishable by death.

But that rule doesn't apply to me. I have taken the magic from the soldier who dragged the female to Cyrus' chamber, and the moment I walked away, I depleted the soldier's magic.

Pulling on her power one more time, I open my eyes. The maid's eyebrows are drawn together in disbelief. She opens and closes her mouth like a fish on desert land, and I push her away from me.

"Be glad I didn't do worse to you for touching me," I growl as the quake rippling through the palace disappears.

That's when I realize my connection to the quakes. Whenever the last drop of magic leaves my body, Crymzon reacts.

To think I had days to live without serving as the power source for my kingdom was foolish of me.

The maid scurries back into her chamber and pulls the door shut behind her without saying another word.

I continue my way through the corridor. Finally, after what feels like an eternity, I arrive at the tower. The structure appears to be unscathed by the earthquake, and I sigh in relief. I climb the stairs, my footsteps echoing in the quiet hall until I reach the top.

Felix was the one who made this spot my sanctuary. Unfortunately, he's also the one who ruined it.

Standing here, the only thing I can remember is his blood-red freckles and black void eyes. It's the last memory I have of my brother—forever.

Looking out from the tower, I survey the damage caused by my magic deficiency. A large black crack zigzags through the kingdom from the gate to the prison. Some houses look close to falling apart, while others are unharmed.

Despite being daytime, I see my subjects streaming into the streets, shouting and inspecting the destruction.

So they noticed after all. Damn it.

Soon, the maid's magic will wear off, and the demolition of Crymzon will continue.

I need magic. Somehow, I need to get more magic.

My eyes fall on the temple. From here, I can't see any damage to the building.

Of course not.

Lunra will protect her temple until the bitter end, no matter the cost.

And that's when my next steps form inside my head.

Making it through my kingdom's streets unnoticed is more challenging than expected. I throw the cloak I snatched from a soldier passing me in the courtyard over my shoulders to cover my signature red dress. The hood is big enough to conceal my face beneath it, and I slip my shiny shoes off to avoid any attention.

When I make my way through the streets, people bump into me, and I bite my tongue to suppress the urge to yell at them. My path is crowded with agitated Crymzonians. At some point, I have to elbow through a crowd overlooking the most significant part of the crack dividing the street in two.

I run up the stairs to the temple and sneak inside. My feet burn from the overheated ground, yet I restrain myself from using magic to cool them down.

Even though the temple has dozens of windows, the red stained glass dims the sunlight. It serves to set an ambiance but also as a sunblock.

Hastily, I shrug the cloak off and march to the Heiligbaum through the water and up the steps.

The flame consuming the tree from the inside out is nothing more than the size of a campfire spotted in the desert by individuals passing Crymzon to find a place in the Confines.

I remember the heat the Heiligbaum used to radiate from it, making its presence noticeable the second you step over the threshold. Being so close to it, I should feel the warmth seeping through my wet dress, but I feel nothing.

Without hesitation, I drag my fingernail over my palm until I draw blood, step closer to the Heiligbaum and press my bleeding hand against the burning tree trunk.

My flesh sizzles beneath the ever-burning wood. I inhale sharply to extinguish the pain rolling through my body.

Once the pain is manageable, I lift my chin to the sky and close my eyes.

"Lunra, Goddess of the Moon and Love. If you can hear me, please delight me with your presence. I need your guidance."

Nausea ripples through me, and the pain almost causes my knees to buckle. My breath quickens as I lift my other hand to enforce my connection with the Heiligbaum when a gentle hand pulls me backward.

"Oh my," a voice says behind me. It's sweet and yet authoritative, light and yet dooming.

I turn around slowly, and my breath catches in my throat when I look at her.

"I didn't think you had it in you to ask for help," Lunra says, her red-golden eyes flickering like candlelight.

She towers over me. Her skin is tinted in red, and a golden crown rests above her long dark hair cascading down past her buttocks. A golden amulet with a full moon hangs around her slim neck, and her burgundy dress clings to her body like melted wax.

The Goddess smiles at me as she grabs my hands to cup them in hers. She lowers her head and blows gently on my blistering palm.

Right away, the pain eases while I watch as my hand heals right before my eyes.

During my walk through the kingdom, I had enough time to find the right words to address the Goddess, but now that the moment is here, my mind goes blank.

"I've waited so long for this moment," Lunra says, pressing my hands against her chest with one hand while cupping my chin with her other. "Watching you turn your back on me was hard, but I understand. Love isn't always pretty. Losing a loved one is the hardest burden someone can carry, and learning to live with the weight of a loss takes time."

"You let them die," I whisper, holding her gaze.

She studies me for a heartbeat. "I don't decide when it's someone's time to go. But I was there to strengthen you to get through it. I watched over you."

"But why didn't you help?"

The Goddess lifts one side of her mouth. "Am I not here right now?"

My shoulders slump.

Of course, she's here now. But where was she when I needed her fourteen years ago? Why did she grant me a power I wasn't ready to wield at such a young age?

"I had the privilege of observing your family for generations. You are the first one to ignore me. Do you know how many countless nights I tried to reach you when you sat on the tower looking over our kingdom? Or how many times I helped ease your heart in hopes it would mend? You are the strongest SinClaret yet. Leading a kingdom without godly help is unheard of, yet you did it for so many years."

"And I'm tired of it," I say, lowering my head.

"I know, my child. But you must go on."

"I never wanted this." I look around the big empty hall filled with benches. "Any of this. The throne was supposed to go to my brother and not me. I wasn't born to rule."

"No. *You* were destined to rule," Lunra says, her words echoing through my head. "Felix played his part in this world. He showed you how to love and lead. But it was never his destiny to reign over Crymzon."

My heart hammers in my chest. "You knew? You knew he was going to die?"

"No one knows the future with certainty besides Zorus, God of Order and King of the Gods." She presses my hands tighter against hers. "But I felt it. The moment you were born under the lunar eclipse, I knew you were going to lead our kingdom."

"I wish you were wrong."

Lunra releases me and takes a step back. "You requested my help. Here I am. What is it you want?"

"I need more magic," I say, cutting Lunra off when she opens her mouth to answer. "I only need a few more days to find a Painite to fuel the Heiligbaum. Plus, I need it to defeat Keres. After that, you can do whatever you want with me after transferring the Crymzon Throne to someone worthy."

"You know I can't do that," Lunra says, her eyes searching mine.

"I don't need much. I just—"

"I can't exchange you. Only the SinClaret bloodline can wield the power of nurturing Crymzon with magic. No other bloodline will be strong enough to withstand the magic flowing through their veins and into the land. Unless..." Lunra bites her lower lip.

"Unless what?"

"If the connection between two Soulmates is strong enough to withstand death, the lowborn could potentially carry the weight of the Crymzon Throne."

The thought of finding my Soulmate before sunrise is laughable. Lunra knows that just as well as I do.

I try to collect my thoughts. "What do you mean, *withstand death*?"

Lunra chuckles. "That's the same question I asked Zorus when he told me about that loophole. After death, a soul departs into God Otyx's territory, and I can tell you, I've never heard of a soul slipping through his grip and back into the world. That being said, I'm not sure *if* it's possible to trick death."

I throw my hands in the air. "So why mention it? I don't have time for games."

"My child... every move you make is a decision set in stone since you took your first breath. You're just following the path laid out for you."

What bullshit.

No one is wicked enough to construct a path so cruel and lonely. I've chosen this life, no one else. Every step I take forward is because I *want* to take it.

My nostrils flare the longer I think about her words. "I'm running out of time. I need to leave *now*," I spit out, spinning to the entrance, but Lunra clears her throat.

"Seven nights," she says, bringing me to a halt. "I can extend your magic for seven nights."

My heart flutters uncontrollably.

Seven nights will be enough to send my army into the North and retrieve a piece of Painite. It also has to be enough to overthrow Keres.

"Thank you," I mumble.

Lunra straightens her shoulders. "I'm not sure what you're thanking me for. It only stretches out the inevitable. In seven days, your magic will disappear, and so will Crymzon. Without an heir or a Soulmate, our kingdom will consume you until there's nothing left of you."

The feeling of excitement subsides as fast as it appeared. "Then why are you helping me if you already know the outcome?"

"There's a long history between the God of the Underworld and I. As much as you want to make Keres pay for using your brother's corpse against you, I want to see Otyx tremble."

I never considered what the Gods do when they're not summoned by the kingdoms they rule over. Somehow, it seems childish to think that even Gods have their own lives, away from ceremonies and prayers.

"And what will become of you?" I ask, my eyes lingering on her flickering irises.

"Me?" Lunra's smile widens. "You think your kingdom is the first to fall? No, my child. I will lose my kingdom just to begin the process of restoring it all over again."

I watch Lunra step towards the Heiligbaum and into the flame dancing inside the tree hollow. I stretch my hand out to stop her, but before I can touch her, Lunra vanishes right before my eyes.

What did she mean Crymzon isn't the first kingdom to corrupt? How many times has it happened, and why don't I know anything about it?

A sharp pain rushes through my head, sending me falling to my knees. Screaming, I grab my hair and pull on it, the pulsating pain sending waves of nausea through my body. Just as I think I'll tip over to take my last breath sprawled out on the floor, the throbbing stops.

When I open my eyes, I feel the power stirring inside me. The power I haven't felt this strong since I was a little girl.

Lunra kept her word by granting me more magic; now it's time to keep mine.

Pressing my palms flat against the ground, I concentrate on my first task. I pull on the magic and wrap every emotion inside me—besides the rage filling every fiber of my body—into a neat little box before tucking it away.

Instantly, my body relaxes as the wild thoughts alleviate under the magical barrier, and for the first time since Terminus, I can think straight.

If I send my army before sundown, they will arrive in Terminus in four days. That's enough time for me to seek the person I have sworn never to visit again. The person who showed me my future before I ever set foot on the dais of the Crymzon Throne. The same person I imprisoned fourteen years ago and who hasn't seen a single ray of sunlight ever since.

It's time to pay the Lady of Fate a visit.

THIRTY-SIX

KHAOS

Telling Remy that his temporary status as Grand General is because of his fantastic performance during our village raid went almost smoothly. I predicted he would sense my lie, but his excitement was too intense, clouding his senses to read between the lines.

I told him the Queen awaited him in her chambers for his first command as the head of the army, and my stomach turned when I think about him entering her room. Few people are allowed to be in close proximity to Soulin, especially inside her own four walls, but it's Remy. He would never attempt to do anything reckless before the Queen.

He better not because otherwise, I will cut his balls and present them hung on the entrance gate for everyone to see.

No...no...He's a good soldier; I remind myself. Almost too good. He's precisely the kind of guard Soulin needs to support her right now.

As I'm about to use a secret door leading from the West Wing Tower into the desert surrounding the prison, my feet are glued to the ground as if pulled by an imaginary force. Panic sweeps through my body as I lean forward to free my limbs, but the force doubles, freezing my entire body.

What is happening?

My heart rate quickens when my thoughts go to Soulin. Does she think I'm abandoning her? Is she using someone else's magic to prevent me from leaving her kingdom?

The blood in my veins heats, and I let out a silent groan as my body shakes, taking in an unknown power coursing through my veins. It feels like I'm being boiled alive from the inside out.

I stretch my hand out to push against the hidden door built into the Wall when something crackles between my fingers, sending me sprawling back.

That's impossible!

I haven't touched another soul since letting Myra go.

My stomach drops.

Myra.

Have I stolen her magic unnoticed? Have I taken her remaining power, leaving her defenseless if Soulin finds her?

Usually, it only takes a blink of an eye for the magic to transfer from one person to another. If that was the case, I should have felt it the moment I released Myra.

The force holding me in place disappears as fast as it took hold of me. I stumble forward, right through the door into the desert.

After landing on my butt, I study my hands.

How is it possible?

Little sparks of magic coil around my fingers, and I feel the power rushing through my body like waves, ready to submerge whatever stands in its wake.

But I don't have time to waste figuring out what in Lunra's name is happening to me. I must be out of Soulin's reach before she notices what I'm about to do.

Nevertheless, the thought of robbing Myra of her only way to protect herself from Soulin and anyone outside of Crymzon makes my mouth go dry.

If this is really *her* magic I'm harboring, I should seek her out and transfer it back to her. But what if she gave it to me without me acknowledging it? What if she's still trying to save the little boy she once knew? The boy who still exists in her memory is only a faint reminiscence to me.

I look over my shoulder at the Wall. No matter what, I can't go back in there. It wasn't easy leaving the palace this time, and I'm unsure if I will find the strength again to do it a second time.

In a trance, I wander to the stables to ready the horses. I jump a little when someone appears behind me.

"What are we doing out here?" Jeremia asks, mounting the horse I prepared for him without waiting for my command.

This is the reason I picked him. While he does question my orders and motives, he never backs away from fulfilling his duty before inquiring about it. Whatever I tell him to do, he will do it.

When I watch four more soldiers enter the stable, my heart sinks. I've told him to recruit a handful of the most trustworthy men in our ranks, but somehow I hope for more manpower than just Blake, Kasen, Charli, and Rene.

Brushing my thoughts of the magic lingering inside me aside, I ready the last horse until I turn to mine.

"The Queen is sending her army north once the sun rises. It's our mission to secure the travel route," I lie, guiding my steed out of the stable. I secure the saddle bag with some essential items we will need and climb into the saddle.

Jeremia shrugs his shoulders. "There is nothing to secure," he says, falling back to come up beside me. "The other kingdoms won't attack us. Crymzon is the only one with a proper army. Besides, the creatures roam the land at night, so we have nothing to worry about."

I taught Jeremia well, maybe too well. Whatever awaits us on our journey won't be the beasts lurking in the dark but whatever is brewing in the North.

"Queen's orders," I answer, leaving no room for a discussion.

As we stand on the sandy dunes, I survey the barren desert stretching out behind us. We have overcome countless obstacles to reach this point - the blistering heat, the swirling sandstorms that threatened to swallow us whole, and the ever-looming sense of isolation in the vast desert. My water canteen is almost empty, and my body aches from the physical exertion of riding in harsh conditions.

But we have persevered, fueled by an unwavering determination to survive and complete Soulin's mission. At least, that's what the handful of soldiers believe.

Finally, after what feels like a lifetime, I spot a glimmer of hope in the distance - a ribbon of blue cutting through the monotonous landscape, and behind it, a lush green backdrop of trees and bushes. It's a river, a lifeline amid the unforgiving desert. A surge of relief and renewed determination washes over me as I quicken my horse's pace, driven by the promise of water and respite.

As we approach the river, I hear rushing water growing louder, a welcome melody to my ears. The sight of the glistening water is like a mirage coming to life, shimmering in the sunlight like a precious gem.

I guide my horse towards the riverbank, jump off, and sink to my knees. My parched lips crack into a smile as I dip my hands into the cool water and bring it to my lips, savoring the taste of life-giving hydration.

We have been traversing the desert for two days, and the sight of the verdant trees and glistening water is a welcome I will never forget.

"We have to hurry," Jeremia whispers beside me, splashing water into his face. "Queen Synadena won't be pleased to see us at her border."

My senses sharpened with his words.

We reached the pivotal milestone. Here, we will figure out if my plan is as reckless as I think it is. One wrong move can end our lives in seconds.

I gaze out at the river, its water flowing swiftly and decisively into the jungle landscape on the other shore.

"Fill up your canteens," I command as I muster the energy to stand up.

The scorching sun beats down relentlessly on us as we stand at the river's edge. I peer into the lush green jungle on the other side as my soldiers refill their canteens. Sweat trickles down my forehead as I eagerly scan the area for any signs of movement.

I grip the hilt of my sword when I catch a glimpse of movement in the foliage, and signal my men to be on alert.

And then, I see it. Perched high in the branches of a massive tree, its coat blending seamlessly with the emerald leaves, is a jungle cat. I hold my breath, knowing that this enormous feline is a formidable predator known for its stealth and power in Tenacoro.

The jungle cat remains perfectly still, its green feathers camouflaging the black undercoat among the leaves. Its sleek body is taut with coiled muscles, and its piercing gaze is fixed on us. Its eyes lock with mine and its tail twitches nervously. The tension in the air is palpable as I wait, my senses heightened and my sword's grip firmly in my hand.

"Don't move," I whisper.

The river is the only thing separating us from the feline, providing a natural barrier. The rushing water is wide and deep, with currents that would make crossing treacherous. But I'm well aware that jungle cats are excellent swimmers. I only hope that it already had an enormous meal today, so we don't end up on its menu.

Time seems to stand still as we engage in a silent standoff with the massive cat. I remain cautious, knowing that it could strike at any moment. The jungle cat seems to assess the situation, its keen eyes never leaving us.

A few minutes in, it finally breaks eye contact and leaps effortlessly from the tree, disappearing into the jungle's undergrowth. We let out a collective sigh of relief, but remain on high alert, knowing that it could still lurk nearby.

"I'm out," Rene says, mounting his horse to ride off. His slim yet skillful body looks small against the horse's mass.

Within three steps, I'm at his side. "Get down," I growl, pulling on his reins.

"You know what they say. The Tenacorian Queen is linked to the creatures living in her kingdom. She knows we are here."

"Don't believe in all the tales your mama tells you," Jeremia laughs, attaching his canteen to the saddle. "It's a freaking cat with feathers, not a spy."

"Mark my words," Rene says, pulling the reins out of my grip.

"We're still on our Queens territory. They can't reach us here," Charli says, spitting into the water.

A whistling noise pierces my ears. Instinctively, I pull my sword, but I'm not fast enough to counter the arrow which hits the sand just a hand's width away from the soldier's foot.

More arrows shoot through the sky in our direction, each missing its target by inches.

Slowly, I lower the sword. "Get off the horse," I say again, sheathing it carefully. "Those arrows were meant to miss us. I can't promise the next ones won't."

I can hear Rene dismounting behind me as I lift my empty hands and raise my voice. "We're here to request an audience with Queen Synadena," I say, scanning the jungle across the water.

The people of Tenacoro are as good at camouflaging as their beasts, making it impossible to spot them unmoving. I've heard stories about their endurance of shadowing their prey for hours without giving themselves away. They have probably watched us since we were tiny dots on the horizon.

"What the fuck are you doing?" Jeremia hisses through clenched teeth.

"Play along if you want to live," I growl back, taking a step forward. "Please," I yell over the rushing water. "We come in peace with a message from Queen Soulin SinClaret."

A loud chuckle thunders through the jungle, a mix of human laughter and animal screams, making my sweat turn cold.

"What was that?" Kasen asks behind me.

I shake my head slightly, hoping they will see the movement. "Stand still," I hush back.

That's when I notice ripples and splashes in the water. Curious, I focus my gaze on the source of the commotion, and my eyes widen when I see a head surface in the current.

A creature comes into view and emerges from the shimmering water. It's massive, easily over 6 feet long, with sleek, dark fur covered in green scales that glisten in the sunlight.

The animal has a long, sinuous body built for speed and agility in the water. Its mouth is lined with sharp teeth, revealing a playful grin as it emits a series of high-pitched chirps and whistles, communicating with someone on the other side of the river.

The sound sends shivers down my spine.

What is it saying?

The creature's head is enormous, adorned with a broad, flat snout, and its keen eyes are large, shining with curiosity and vitality. Its small and round ears perk up as it surveys its surroundings.

As the animal proceeds out of the river, it shakes its body, spraying water droplets in all directions before gracefully bounding onto the riverbank with surprising ease. It moves effortlessly on land with its short legs, which end in webbed feet resembling flippers, and I watch as it comes to a halt before me.

It opens its mouth, and I feel my soul leave my body when a human voice exits it. "We're both well aware that Queen Soulin would *never* send a message through a soldier. She loves to listen to herself during Council meetings way too much," the creature says.

My throat goes dry.

Shit.

I had two days to prepare for this moment and already blew it. How could I be so stupid as to believe that Tenacoro's Queen would buy my lie?

"I need to speak to Queen Synadena," I say when I regain my voice.

"For what purpose?" the creature asks, and my mind goes ragged, trying to understand how an animal can speak with a human voice.

Everyone else is hearing it speak, right? I can't tell if my soldiers are staring at the *animal* because they never crossed this particular one before, or because they can hear the words reverberating out of its throat as I can.

Focusing back on the wildlife, I swallow.

My plan was to only speak to the Queen about my idea, but without stating my business, the chance of facing the Queen might be destroyed before I ever get anywhere near her. I have to work with what I'm given.

"Join us in the war against King Keres," I say to the animal.

I hear my soldiers inhale sharply behind me.

For that reason, I haven't told them about our actual mission. Since Soulin made me gather an army to move away from thousands of years of peace inside the Crymzon Wall, most young lads were raised believing in strength and dominance rather than love and justice. They believe their ability to fight for their Queen is above everything else.

Maybe because I remember how Crymzon and Soulin used to be before she took on the throne. I was her only friend inside the palace. Or perhaps because my father parted ways with the crown after Soulin executed a handful of Crymzonians shortly after her brother's death, and my father begged me to leave with him. Instead, I took his job and worked my way up the ladder to where I am now.

"Does Queen Soulin know you're here?" the animal asks.

My silence says more than any words can.

The creature surveys me before turning to the water. "Follow the stream until you reach a bridge. I will be waiting for you there," it says, jumping into the water and disappearing out of sight.

"What in the actual God of the Underworld is wrong with you?" Jeremia barks at me, but the only thing I can think of is to get to the bridge as fast as possible.

THIRTY-SEVEN

QUEEN SOULIN

The air rushing through my lungs feels different as if the magic brought a fresh taste with it.

The sandstone-carved houses gleam dark red in the sunlight as I step down the temple's stairs onto the road. This time, I don't hide beneath a cloak. Instead, I want my subjects to look at me as I descend from the holiest places inside the Wall.

Finally, after passing a handful of buildings, a woman dressed in layers upon layers of fabric calls out my name. The bustling street falls silent.

"Queen Soulin," another man yells, falling to his knees. "Are you here to save us from Otyx?" He points at the massive crack in the ground.

I should've known that people suspect the God of the Underworld for causing such destruction to the kingdom. And that assumption comes just in time to use it to my advantage.

I raise my hands to the advancing night sky and raise my voice. "Lunra has spoken to me. With her help, we will defeat the so-called King Keres and banish his evil God back into the Realm of Gods." I lower my hands and scan the fearful faces of the people crowding now around me. "Every Crymzonian who can wield a sword, follow me."

A murmur runs through the crowd. Their hesitation causes anger to ripple through my veins. Again, I'm reminded of the new magic running through my body.

I lower myself to the ground and press my hands to the warm, stony ground beneath me. My spine tingles as I tap into the raw power of my newly acquired magic. It flows through my veins, my palms, and into the ground. A soft golden glow envelops my fingertips, and the crack in the road shimmers and pulses, as if responding to me.

I focus my energy, channeling the tiniest spark of power into the crevice. The crack slowly closes, piece by piece, as if knitting itself back together under my skillful touch.

Every Crymzonian watches me in amazement as the road mends before their eyes. The crack vanishes, leaving no trace of its existence. Gasps of wonder and applause erupt from the crowd, expressing their gratitude and admiration, and I'm here for it.

Even though the crack is healed, I keep going. I keep the magic flowing for a few more seconds, sending it straight into Crymzon's soil before straightening myself. I turn towards my subjects, my smile widening as I watch their awestruck faces.

With the crack in the road now healed, my subjects are filled with renewed respect for me. I can feel it. Magic is bringing once again hope and wonder to their lives. After years of hiding behind the palace's walls, they have finally witnessed my true potential, which in return repaired their faith in me.

I watch their faces light up even more when the magic I just stored in the soil seeps through its inhabitants.

"My magic is back," a man yells, watching his trembling hands.

More and more people speak out over their returning powers, and as I watch my subjects study me in disbelief, my shoulders straighten more. One after one, they kneel, lowering their heads in my direction.

In the distance, I can hear metal boots clicking over the ground as I walk through my submissive subjects.

"Your Majesty," the soldier leading a small group of guards says, bowing his head when he comes to a halt before me. "Khaos Zedohr sends me."

My eyes scan the soldier before me. Compared to Khaos, he's slim and looks fresh out of training. His long brown hair cascades down his shoulders, and his eyes are filled with eagerness and admiration.

I have seen him before, countless times if my memory serves me well. He's one of Khaos' favored soldiers and is always at his side.

"What do they call you?" I ask after inspecting his clean armor.

He tightens his grip around the pommel of his sword. "Remy Cengor, Your Highness."

"Grand General Cengor," I whisper, taking his name in. "I'm guessing you're here to receive your first order?"

He nods silently, his breath quickening.

I lean closer, close enough to notice the fine stubbles covering his chin. "Arrest everyone who's not willing to fight for me," I say in a hushed voice, dragging out every word.

His eyes widen. "My Queen?"

"You heard me," I say, inhaling his musky smell of sweat and fear. "I want to hear them scream from the prison. This kingdom has no place for cowards. Once I leave with my newest add-ons to my army, I want you to arrest the remaining subjects."

Remy's nostrils flare.

"Do we have a problem?" I ask, taking a step back to see his face.

His jaw twitches. "No, Your Majesty," he answers with distaste.

I whirl around to face my subjects once more. "You will receive your armor and sword inside the palace. Then, tomorrow at sunrise, we'll head out to show Otyx what Crymzonians are made of."

Thunderous jubilation resounds from streets, windows, and rooftops. The crowd has grown.

When I pass Remy, his face as cold as the north, I hear people falling into step with me.

Just as I round the corner, a trail of new army fodder follows me. Remy barks orders at his fellow soldiers, and I can't suppress the grin forming on my lips.

After leaving my newly recruited soldiers with a dozen trained guards to prepare them for tomorrow's march, it's finally time to visit the person who determined my fate even before everything went to shit.

As my footsteps echo through the dimly lit corridor, I approach the hidden door behind the throne's tapestry that guards the entrance to the Silk Keep. Nothing is a more formidable barrier to my secrets than my Fighter Moths. Only a handful of people know about the locations of my moths, and even fewer are aware of what's hidden within the dark chamber inside the Silk Keep.

The fire I lit days ago has run cold, and the room is filled with flapping wings.

Adira flies in my direction and comes to a halt before me. She nudges her head into my shoulder until I push her playfully away.

"Just a few more hours, and I will take you for a spin," I say, walking past her into the room to a wall covered in little silk moths.

With a gentle command and a touch of magic, I tell the moths to move. Within seconds, they fly out of my view. My eyes zoom in on the little hole in the wall, almost too little to notice.

I retrieve a key from the jeweled whip strapped around my leg and insert it into the keyhole. It's the newest adjustment I had requested from the blacksmith.

To my knowledge, there's only one copy of this key inside Crymzon, which forces me always to carry it to ensure that my prisoner never leaves again.

I turn it slowly, feeling the weight of my decision. Then, finally, the locking mechanism inside the wall clicks open, and I push against the heavy stone slap with a determined force, revealing the darkness beyond.

Stepping inside, my eyes adjust to the lack of light, and I make out the faint outlines of the chamber. The air is musty, and the silence palpable, as if the room holds its breath, waiting for my next move.

At the center of the chamber stands a frail figure hunched over and clad in tattered rags. It's a woman, her back bent with age and her face obscured by shadows.

As I draw closer, I see her milky white eyes staring blankly into the void. The woman raises her head slightly, sensing my presence. Her lips move soundlessly as if trying to speak, but no words emerge.

The woman turns her face towards me, her blind eyes searching as if trying to discern who is before her.

As her eyes finally turn in my direction, the woman's gaze meets mine as if she can see me, and a faint smile crosses her lips. She reaches out a hand towards me, and this time, she finds her voice. It's frail, but the sound almost brings me to my knees. "It has been fourteen years, eleven months, and thirteen days since you damned me to rot in your godforsaken kingdom."

"But somehow, you look like you've aged a thousand years since then," I snarl back, moving my head slightly to check if she follows my movement.

She doesn't.

How is that possible? The woman I captured almost fifteen years ago looked young. Her hair was unnaturally blond, nothing like the gray floor-length hair streaming off her head. Her skin had been luminous and not shriveled with wrinkles, and her eyes had sparkled in a sky blue hue and not clouded with a silver cast.

This isn't the same woman who earned as many names as I have over the last centuries. The Lady of Fate. Destiny Forgeress. Oracle.

"You would age too if someone would take moonlight from you."

I'm at a loss. Moonlight?

Then it hits me.

The chamber I hold her in is deprived of all-natural light. I chose this room because her screaming would go unnoticed, being this deeply buried behind sandstone walls, and because her power grows stronger under starlight.

"Are you here to mock me?" the Lady of Fate asks, turning away from here. "Or have you finally made peace with your fate?"

Even though I'm stronger than ever, the magic I use to suppress my emotions slips momentarily. I feel my stomach twist before I can get it back under control. "Whatever you showed me, that wasn't my fate," I answer, pulling out a little bundle of wax I took from my chamber before questioning Cyrus, and I throw it to her feet. "I need you to forge another candle to read my future."

"Sadly, I have to decline your request."

"It's not a request. It's an order."

"If I recall correctly, I've already told you your fate. Your family died at your hands, and your kingdom is falling into ruins because you're unable to fulfill your duties as the sovereign. This means I only have to wait a few more days until these walls around me crumble, and I'm free. I'm guessing we're only one quake away from your dismay, right?"

My head fills with the memories of my father taking me to Starstrand to ask the Lady of Fate to read my destiny. But instead of fortuity, she showed me death and destruction. Her power displayed my mother's death during childbirth and my brother's and father's cruel ends. The last image was of Crymzon being swallowed back into the earth.

Back then, I returned to my father's arms crying, telling myself that the Lady of Fate was playing tricks on me.

That lasted until her first image came true. By then, I didn't know I would be the person sentencing my brother and father to death. If I had known my magic would claim their lives that day, I would have stayed away from them.

In my rage at losing my family, I tracked her down during one of her visitations to Crymzon to collect more wax from the market. With the help of my magic, I forced her to stay silent and follow me into the palace. I only wanted to show her the damage my magic brought upon the Throne Room. I wanted to show her the fate she had given me.

While scanning the burned ground, her unfazed expression sent me over the edge. I was helpless. I was a child. So why didn't she help me? Why didn't she approach me after leaving Starstrand to stop what was to come?

"If you're unable to make another candle, I need you to tell me if you see Keres in your visions," I say, suppressing the images floating through my head.

"You've never been good with someone else stealing your limelight," the old woman says, scratching her chin in disinterest.

I clench my hands to crush the urge to close them around her neck. "So you have seen him?"

"Of course I have. I also know you're holding a Starstrandian prisoner as we speak and have failed yet again to accept your Soulmate. I've never read a fate as wretched as yours."

I ignore her attempt to tickle an emotion out of me. "Is he going to survive?"

"I can tell you he's not the one dying on that battlefield you bring right to him."

"Who is?" I ask, already knowing the answer.

"Let me return to Starstrand, and I'll tell you," she says, her face covered with a big smile.

My nails cut into my palms. "I'm done with you," I say, turning around.

"If you head for King Keres, you will risk everything you hold dear," the Lady of Fate says as I walk away. "You're going into a battle you're destined to lose because you won't accept the truth."

I pull on the stone slap to close the opening in the wall, but her words are faster than my movement.

"Your fate is to bring death and destruction to Escela, and no one can stop it besides you."

THIRTY-EIGHT

KHAOS

"I have to rest," Charlie, the most muscular of my soldiers, says beside me.

He's leaning awkwardly to the side in his saddle, and his dark eyes roll back.

The night is closing in on us. Since we rode away from Crymzon to meet with the Tenacorian creature, I haven't allowed my soldiers to dismount their horses. Time is of the essence, so I can't waste precious minutes trying to stop for a break when I trained my soldiers to sleep on horseback.

"Once we reach the bridge," I growl back, searching the river for any sign of passage.

"That's what you said when we left the riverbank," Rene cuts in, and my patience dissolves into anger.

"What if that beast led us astray? What if it's a trick?" Jeremia asks, riding up beside me.

We haven't talked since we began our search for the bridge. Jeremia knows better than to question my orders, yet I can see the betrayal written on his face. It would have made my job more manageable if I had told him about my plan to request reinforcement from another kingdom after being stripped of my title. He could have helped me to convince the Queen to join us.

But he could have also rejected me after discovering I'm not the Grand General anymore. So technically, he doesn't have to listen to my commands with things being how they are.

"Because I've spent time with Queen Synadena in the same room. And while Tenacoro is known for its fearless warriors, their Queen is smitten by ours," I whisper to Jeremia.

"What happened back home? What aren't you telling me?"

"I'll allow you guys to rest while I speak to the Queen," I say loud enough for all of them to hear before I turn back to Jeremia. "And I will explain everything to you after."

I can't keep him in the dark any longer. If we fail, we have nothing to return to. Soulin won't take me back, and Crymzon...it might not be a kingdom anymore.

I look at my five soldiers. Their armors are muddied, and their faces smeared with dirt and sweat, evidence of the grueling journey we have been on.

The rushing river grows wider and more treacherous, the water splashing against our horses' legs. In a few minutes, the sun will disappear, making it impossible to follow the river safely. While the creature with the human voice looked cute, I don't want to know what else lives inside the water.

After hours of riding, I finally catch a glimpse of a rickety wooden structure in the distance. The bridge is barely holding on against the force of the raging river. I quicken my pace, the anticipation of reaching it palpable in the air.

As we approach the bridge, I signal for the soldiers to halt. I dismount and approach the structure cautiously, assessing its stability. I step on the first plank to test it with my boot, and I'm relieved that it holds my weight, despite it swaying slightly in the current.

"Find a suitable spot to make camp," I say, returning to my horse. Relief washes over their faces as I look at Jeremia. Instead of making his way away from the river with the others, he guides his horse to me. "If we're not back by sunrise, keep following the river until you reach the iron bridge and wait for the Crymzon Army to arrive. It's the only connection between the north and the south."

The soldiers are too tired to ask questions or worry about our safety. They only want to get off their horses and sleep the night away.

I motion for Jeremia to proceed while remounting my horse.

One by one, we ride across the bridge, our horses' hooves clattering loudly against the wooden planks. The water rushes beneath us, threatening to swallow the bridge with each passing moment. My eyes are fixed on the other side, scanning the trees and bushes for an ambush.

"Do you really believe they won't attack us?" Jeremia asks, his voice hushed.

"I'm not sure what to expect," I answer honestly, kicking my horse forward.

Crossing the bridge from the scorching desert into the lush rainforest, my horse moves swiftly, despite the precarious conditions.

The transition is abrupt; the air grows thick with humidity, and the temperature drops significantly. We're met with a cacophony of un-familiar sounds. Loud chirping noises fill my ears, and weird-looking animals jump from tree to tree while screaming.

The forest seems to close in around us; the trees towering above, their branches creating a canopy that partially obscures the last sunlight.

I keep a watchful eye, my senses heightened, ready to react to any sudden movements, but it's not enough. I pull on my reins to stop my horse when a spear points toward my face. Slowly, I lower my head, following the hand-carved wooden staff leading to the person holding the other end of it.

I exhale sharply when I notice who it is.

"You should have seen your face," Princess Opaline laughs, lowering the spear. "You looked like you were going to pee your pants."

A loud chuckle escapes my throat. Jeremia almost falls off his horse when he turns to look back at me.

"Look at you," I say, swinging my leg over my horse's neck to jump off. "You're a woman."

"And you're still the same old grumpy sack of bones," she squeals, jumping into my arms.

"Excuse me? What's happening?" Jeremia asks, coming up behind me.

I release Opaline, and my heart skips a beat. "Meet my old friend, Opaline Roja. Crown Princess of Tenacoro."

"Wait. You're telling me you know him?" he asks, pointing at me.

"Every inch of him," she laughs, scanning my body from top to bottom with a smirk.

"Be quiet. He'll believe something happened between us," I say, shaking my head.

"Only you're dumb enough to turn this," she moves her hands down her body to emphasize her lean curves, "away."

"Stop playing with them," a voice says from a distance, and Queen Synadena emerges between thick green leaves.

"Oh, I won't let this drop," Jeremia whispers, bumping his shoulder into me.

Suddenly, we're confronted by a group of soldiers armed with spears and bows, whose expressions are unfriendly. Their bodies are adorned with feathers, intricate green body paint, and clothes made of roots and leaves.

"The last time I saw you, you were just a kid," Queen Synadena says, moving closer. Her dark brown eyes wander over me, and she reaches out her hand to touch the scar on my cheek. "What happened to you?"

"The place that forces us to meet under such circumstances," I answer, feeling the burning heat of her fingertips on my thin skin. "We need your support."

She pulls her hand back. "I already told her that King Keres isn't our enemy."

"Not yet," I answer, looking over my shoulder at Jeremia. "We're not talking about the self-appointed King here. We're talking about Otyx, the God of the Underworld."

"You know that's not the reason why you're here," Queen Synadena says.

I look at Jeremia again.

I want to tell him the truth about Soulin. I do. But what will stop him from leaving me behind once he knows about the secret she's hiding? Undoubtedly, I would do it if I wasn't so close to our Queen.

"How about you show our new guest around," the Queen says to her daughter. Opaline hooks her arm into Jeremia's and pulls him out of view into the foliage before he can protest.

"Soulin is dying," I say, finally able to speak freely.

"I know."

"You do?"

"I've known for years," the Queen says, closing her eyes. "You think I'm not aware of what's going on?"

"No, of course not. But—"

"But you think I should do more," she says, walking up to my horse. She lays her palm on its neck, and I watch my horse close its eyes. "I can't risk my people's lives to prevent something inevitable. Soulin has chosen her path, which I'm not proud of, and she has angered the Gods."

"I don't understand."

"By turning her back on Lunra, she neglected the most powerful connection keeping her and her kingdom alive. Since the tragedy, she dedicated her life to destroying everything her father and ancestors created. Unfortunately, a choice like that comes with consequences she's unwilling to pay. Defeating King Keres isn't going to change the course of her destiny."

I don't know what I was thinking. Killing the King in the North won't change the fact that she's dying. But, somehow, I told myself, if I can make her desire for revenge come true, it will fix her.

But it won't.

"You and your soldiers are welcome to find refuge in my kingdom. Tenacoro will never turn away people who are seeking peace."

With the situation becoming increasingly clear that the Queen won't be coming to Soulin's aid, I must make a swift decision.

"I can't," I say, backing away slowly. "Please send Jeremia on his way once Opaline returns with him."

"You don't have to do this, Khaos," she says, her eyes softening.

"Her army will reach Terminus in three days. So if you change your mind, that's where you will find me. Otherwise, it was my pleasure to see you one last time. Even though Soulin doesn't say it, you're one of the most important figures in her life."

I didn't mean to use guilt to get what I want, but I need the Queen to hear it because it's true. Soulin would never say it or show what she feels for a person. So it's the least I can do for everything Queen Synadena has done for her.

The Queen's eyes fill with tears as I grab the reins of my horse and pull it back to the bridge.

"You're making a mistake," she whispers under her breath behind me, but I don't halt.

As I walk back across the bridge, my horse trailing me, my heart pounds in my chest. I'm relieved to have avoided any confrontation with Tenacoro but I'm also disappointed that my attempt to establish an ally has failed.

I leave the rainforest behind, the encounter with Queen Synadena etched in my memories.

Despite the knowledge of riding into my certain doom, I can't change my mind. If Soulin is ready to die during the battle, so will I.

THIRTY-NINE

QUEEN SOULIN

It has been two days since I sent my army north, leaving only a few guards behind to watch over the empty kingdom while I devise a plan. In two more days, my soldiers will reach Terminus. By then, I need to possess a Painite.

My new powers give me the ability to strengthen my moths. With the help of Adira, I will be able to fuel the Heiligbaum to fortify my connection to Lunra and have enough magic left to take Keres on.

Maybe then, Lunra will see that I'm strong enough to lead Crymzon without a Soulmate and grant me more time to secure the future of our kingdom.

I just have to make her believe I'm worthy of keeping my magic. And if I can't do that, at least I don't have to sit around doing nothing while waiting for my death.

The palace halls are awfully quiet since the servants were either promoted to soldiers or are now prisoners kept outside the Wall.

I walk through the halls, searching the palace for another soul. I'm so used to being followed by Myra, guards, or servants that the stillness of my home feels terribly wrong. It feels like the calm before the storm, when the wind stands still before it rages, tearing down buildings and hope.

"My Queen," a female voice says behind me, and I grab the handle of my whip, which is tightly curled around my thigh, while I whirl around to face her.

"You know, your pretty head will look stunning on a stake next time you sneak up on me like that again," I say to the girl, who's pressed against the wall, her face full of fear.

"My apologies, Your Majesty. I didn't mean to startle you," she whispers, curtsying.

"What do you want?" I snarl, my eyes scanning her frail body and dirty clothes.

She seems to be one of my kitchen aids. Her nails are cut short, her dress covered in handprints, like she uses it to wipe her hands clean after preparing a meal, and her hair is tightly bound.

"I'm the fastest message carrier and—"

I cut her off, waving my hand. "I don't care who you are. Get to the point."

"Your Majesty," the maiden begins, her voice shaking slightly. "I'm afraid I have bad news. Our trading partner's food delivery has not arrived."

I narrow my eyes in anger. "What do you mean *it hasn't arrived*?" I demand.

The maiden swallows hard, her face going pale. "I'm not sure, Your Majesty," she stammers. "Perhaps there was an issue with the delivery, or it's delayed. But without it, we cannot prepare the feast you requested."

The floor beneath us shakes. The girl falls to her knees, pressing her forehead against the stone floor as if this could save her from my anger.

"Excuses, always excuses," I spit. "I will not stand for this. You will send a messenger to Tenacoro at once to demand an explanation, and if they cannot provide one, I will cut off all trade with them."

The maiden nods quickly. "Of course, Your Majesty," she says. "Right away." The kitchen maid hurries from my view and my heart races.

How can Queen Synadena do this to me? Is it because I insulted her daughter? Or because she thinks I'm already dead?

In return for fruits, vegetables, and meat, I send her the finest silk Escela offers. I even go so far as to dye it emerald green before sending it off.

How can she betray me like that?

I pace through the hall, and the walls around me shake when I think about all the ways I could make her pay.

No one can treat me like this.

"Guards," I yell. It takes another shout for someone to appear.

An older man waddles in my direction, dressed in dented armor. "Yes, my Queen?" he huffs, and my mood plummets even deeper.

"Are you kidding me?" I ask, taking this man in as he seems to be taking his last breath.

"I'm not sure what you're referring to, Your Majesty."

"They left *you* to protect me?" It's so ridiculous that I almost start laughing. "What am I supposed to do with an old fart like you?"

He studies me for a moment, steadying his breath. "I'm not sure any guard can keep you from harm. You're skillful enough to do that yourself," he says, finally coming to a halt before me. "I was recruited because I was there while searching for the last Painite."

The last word catches my attention.

"You're one of my father's best friends," I whisper, inspecting him closer.

King Obsidian never had guards. He didn't need them. While I surround myself with an army, he only had a handful of trustees he relied on to help him run the kingdom. Each of them was assigned a different part of his duties, relieving him almost of all of them.

How do I not remember him? I've known all the people in my father's close circle. But this man, I swear I've never seen him before.

"I wouldn't say his best friend, but trustee comes pretty close," he says, a smile forming. He stretches out his hand, and I stare at it. "Conrad."

I move my shoulder slightly back, but the gesture is enough to signal I won't be taking his hand. He drops it slowly.

I thought all his trustees were in the Throne Room when I burned the place. But, somehow, this man has stayed hidden from me for years. So why present himself now?

As if he could read my mind, he speaks. "I have children and grandchildren out there. If the Heiligbaum runs out of Painite, I will lose everything," he says, his smile dying.

"Meet me in the courtyard in a few minutes," I say, walking past him. "And use your magic to speed up. I won't wait for you if you can't keep up."

As expected, Conrad awaits me outside. His eyes widen when I walk down the steps, Adira and Barin following closely behind me.

"How is that possible?" he asks as he studies Adira with an open mouth.

I'm so used to seeing my oversized moths that the reaction of others surprises me every time.

"Please don't drool on them. Their scales are quite sensitive," I respond, waiting for Adira to lower her body so I can climb on.

Atop Adira, I watch Conrad trying to mount Barin. I'm not sure if Barin is messing with him, giving Conrad a hard time to climb him, or if his bones are so old that he can't make it.

I watch for a few silent moments as Conrad struggles to lift his leg high enough. Then, with a flick of my wrist, he levitates off the ground before I let him down on Barin.

"Thank you," he smiles, holding onto Baron's body.

His happiness makes me nauseous. "This is the first and last time I'm going to help you," I growl, slightly kicking Adira.

Without hesitation, she flaps her wings, taking us higher and higher.

Barin follows her example, and I'm taken aback when he doesn't use any of his tricks to rid himself of Conrad. I picked him over the other females because I was sure he would cause a scene. But he carries Conrad with such a gentleness that my insides boil.

"Even my wildest animal feels pity for you," I mumble.

"What was that?" Conrad yells at me, cupping his ear to hear better.

"Don't fall behind," I say, signaling Adira to move forward.

I thought about flying over Tenacoro to give Queen Synadena a visit. The audacity of breaking our trading agreement is still not sitting right with me.

Either something is going on in Tenacoro I don't know about, or the Queen has played me for years and has just been waiting for me to drop dead to be done with me.

But I have other priorities right now.

Once I have the Painite and enough magic to defeat Keres, I will head straight to Tenacoro to kick her ass.

No one, and I mean *no one* disrespects me this way.

"Are you all right?" Conrad asks, a broad smile plastered on his face.

"If you ask me that question again, I will take your tongue," I growl back, ignoring looking at him.

How could my father stand him? It's only been a few hours since we started our trip, and I'm so close to commanding Barin to buck him off.

His happiness is exhausting. There's not a single person out there who can be this happy despite everything that's going on. He must be ignorant or incredibly naïve.

But neither trait seems to fit Conrad. My father wouldn't have chosen him as a trustee if he didn't inhabit some kind of contribution to Crymzon.

"I never expected to wander outside the Wall again," he says, running his hand over Barin.

"I can't believe it either," I say, rolling my eyes.

Silence stretches between us, but not for long.

"Besides your hair color, you're nothing like your father," Conrad says.

His words ignite my short fuse. "Is that so?" I ask. "My father was always face-deep in some woman's boobs, so it's hard to remember him."

Conrad chuckles. "Oh gosh. I miss those orgies. What a shame that they had to end." He laughs louder. "Or maybe it's a good thing. My house was just big enough to house all my seventeen children and wife."

I choke. "Seventeen?"

"I know, I know. We could have used a contraception spell, but my wife just loved playing with fire. Who would have thought she's so fertile?"

"No wonder Crymzon is running out of space," I mumble, trying to imagine having sixteen siblings.

"It sounds like you know little about your subjects."

"Of course I do."

"Then why did that number catch you off guard? As a ruler, you should know that the birth rate drastically declined once you relinquished public love."

"What does the banning of orgies have to do with all of this?" I ask as heat rises inside of me.

"It's Crymzon's language—love and the moon. Without being able to express those, you take away everything we hold dear."

"I think we're doing just fine with that rule."

"But are we? Fewer Crymzonians find their Soulmate due to a lack of being able to try different partners. At this rate, Crymzon will be underpopulated in a few hundred years."

I will not entertain this conversation any longer. How dare he question my decision to rid my kingdom of the disease my father put into their heads?

"And currently, Crymzon is bursting out of its seams," I say, waving my hand.

As commanded, Barin reacts to my motion and shoots straight into the sky. Of course, Conrad didn't expect that sudden maneuver, and I can't help but smile when I see him falling off his back.

Conrad's face is distorted with fear as his limbs swim through the air, rushing past him. I watch as he gets smaller and smaller, nearing the ground, and satisfaction boils up inside me.

Barin flaps before me, his enormous eyes zigzag between Conrad and me as he waits for a command.

"Shit," I say, frustration taking over. "Go get him."

As if Barin has been waiting for my approval, he pulls his wings and legs close and shoots through the air like a fuzzy arrow.

Even though every fiber in my body enjoys the few seconds of silence, my mind wins. Without Conrad, I have to search Terminus alone. Although this time, I have my full magic, it might not be enough to pinpoint the location of the Painite. And without Painite, Lunra will never see me as worthy.

Barin shows up beside me, carrying a green-faced Conrad.

"If you don't shut up, it will be my pleasure to watch you hit the ground full force, breaking every bone in your body before some wild creature slurps you off the dirt," I warn, keeping my eyes on the dark mountains approaching in the distance.

FORTY

KHAOS

T he early morning sun has barely risen above the horizon, casting a golden hue over the dense forest that lined the banks of the roaring river. To my surprise, I'm waking up to Jeremia feeding the horses.

"It's about time you open your eyes," he says, whistling a sweet melody.

"Please make it stop," Rene says, covering his ears.

"You guys should have been there," Jeremia says between notes. "Tenacoro's hot springs have healing powers."

It takes me a few moments to awaken fully and comprehend what he's referring to.

So far, I've only heard rumors about the healing properties of Tenacoro. It's said that its hot springs are fueled by Emara, Goddess of Vitality.

"You took a fucking bath while we were sweating our butts off, and you bastard didn't think about inviting us?" Blake, the oldest of us, asks in a bitter tone.

Jeremia chuckles as he moves on to my horse. "If I remember correctly, you guys were too chickenshit to cross the bridge."

"We were tired," Kasen says.

He has been quiet the entire ride from Crymzon. To this point, I thought he was deaf or missing his tongue.

"Whatever you have to tell yourself," Jeremia laughs, throwing another pile of grass he found to the ground in front of my horse.

As much as I want to know what happened to Jeremia after Opaline took him away, we must get going. Our detour cost us almost a day's ride. I can't risk missing the Crymzon Army marching north.

"Stop it," I say, picking myself off the hard ground. "We need to hurry if we want to catch up with our men."

My words kill the bickering faster than Soulin's whip finds aim.

Within minutes, we are mounted and trailing the river up north. The closer we get to the second bridge separating Crymzon from Eternitie, the stronger the feeling of magic inside me gets.

How is it possible that Myra's magic still surges through me? Typically, someone else's magic fades slowly when unused. But not hers.

I look at my hand as little sparks sizzle on my skin, and I slam my other hand on top to cover it before looking at my soldiers.

There won't be an issue if they see my magic because, after all, they still think I possess some, even though I ran out years ago. But the thought of having *hers* and riding away with it still makes me uncomfortable.

"You're awfully quiet today," Jeremia says, falling back out of the formation to ride beside me.

I scan the vast landscape and horizon for any threat before facing him. "There's nothing to say."

***

The sound of rushing water mixes with the clatter of the horses' hooves as we follow the riverbank toward Eternitie.

Ahead, a bridge comes into view, and I quicken my pace, eager to reach our destination.

As I approach to examine it closely, I see that the wooden planks are covered with red boot prints, indicating that it has been used as a passage.

"We're too late," I say, scanning the hill-covered area stretching across the bridge.

"Are you sure they already passed through?" Blake asks, searching the ground.

"Who else should have left those prints?" Rene counters and Blake's face goes blank.

There's no way the Crymzon Army is that fast on foot.

Except...

"Remember the magical surge right before we left Crymzon?" I ask, searching their faces for approval.

I have to be wrong. Please let me be wrong.

What if everyone felt it? What if our magic is finally back?

If my small squad felt it, they could have used it to suppress their tiredness yesterday. We could have made it to Tenacoro in a half-day ride.

Maybe they tried to ration the new power, wondering when they will run out eventually. Or they thought nothing of it, and that's why they didn't mention it.

"What about it?" Kasen asks, riding closer to me.

That's precisely the answer I need.

The entire time, I thought I stole Myra's magic, but that isn't the case.

My stomach turns the longer I think about it. If that isn't Myra's power I'm feeling, that can only mean Soulin has gotten her hands on magic. But besides a ceremony to request more from Lunra, there's only one way to receive it.

Through a Soulmate Connection.

Bile rises in my throat when I realize Soulin must have found her Soulmate shortly after she stripped me of my title.

It clearly isn't me because we would have felt the connection in the water chamber if I was.

"Are you okay?" Jeremia asks in a hushed voice. "You look a little pale."

My mind races, rethinking the moment in the water chamber. Everything we did behind that closed door meant nothing to her. I was just another man she tested to regain her magic, and I failed her.

Straightening my shoulders, I tuck on the magic inside me, and I'm disgusted by it. The thought of using Myra's magic was repulsive, but using Soulin's magic created by fucking another man worthy of a connection with her is just sickening.

"I miscalculated," I say, pushing the disgust creeping up my throat aside. "With the help of their new power, the soldiers are faster than usual. We need to catch up to them."

I don't wait for them to answer. Instead, I press my heels into my horse, and it bolts forward over the bridge. I ride hard, my horse straining beneath me as we gallop toward the enemy.

Instead of feeling grateful that Soulin finally regained her magic through her Soulmate Connection, I feel rage. Pure disgusting rage.

Who is a better match for her than me?

I couldn't care less that I dedicated my entire life to her or that she's the Queen. But how can it be that I wasn't enough?

I know her. I mean, the real *her*.

The innocent little girl who used to creep up on me to scare me; the girl who would steal herself away with me; the first girl who ever held my hand to show me she cared for me when my mother died.

After all, Soulin was right.

Love makes you weak and blinds you in the most cruel way.

I won't let that happen again.

Once Keres is gone, I'm not going back to Crymzon. That is, if he doesn't kill me first. The only thing that keeps me going is the thought of my dead body being resurrected to haunt Soulin.

Soulin will remember me, one way or another, and she will realize she made her biggest mistake yet.

FORTY-ONE

CYRUS

I listen to Liza's ragged breathing for hours, grateful she's still alive. Unfortunately, she doesn't have much time after what Monsteress did to her. Liza needs a healer to tend to her open wounds; otherwise, an infection will weaken her even more, maybe even claim her life.

I've seen it countless times in Eternitie. Untreated wounds that turn from bleeding to oozing to death in a matter of days.

Liza stirs once, and I expect her to say something, but my hope gets crushed when she goes still again.

My eyes have adjusted to the room's darkness, but it's still difficult to make out anything. As I'm sitting on the warm, hard ground next to my friend, I can't help but feel helpless and scared as I wait for help to arrive.

Deep down, I know no one will come to rescue us, yet I can't shake holding onto that hope.

Shit, I'm the help. I was supposed to rescue Liza, Devana, and the rest of our village before finding shelter far, far away from Crymzon and Eternitie. I made it out of Crymzon in one piece once, just to return to my inevitable doom.

Suddenly, I hear a faint creaking noise and tense up, my heart racing. The door to the room opens slightly, and a faint sliver of light seeps in. I strain my eyes to make out what's going on and freeze, not knowing what to do. Then I see a hand reach in and toss something onto the ground before quickly slamming the door shut.

I hesitate for a moment, unsure if I should approach the unknown items until my curiosity gets the best of me. I crawl over to the objects and pick them up, one by one, running my fingers over them, trying to figure out what they are.

The pungent smell of herbs burns in my nostrils as I bring one object to my nose. To my relief, I realize it's a small tin of healing balm.

Oh fucking Gods, I hiss out, lifting my head to the ceiling and closing my eyes. *Thank you.*

Maybe it wasn't the Gods after all. Perhaps it was the soldier who apologized to me just before locking Liza and me away.

It doesn't matter.

I continue to explore the floor, feeling my way around until my fingers brush against something hard and cylindrical. I pick it up and feel a wick sticking out of one end.

It's a candle.

Frantically I search the ground for matches, and to my surprise, I find some. I quickly strike a match and light the candle.

The candle, once lit, provides a minor source of light that makes the room feel a little less scary. With shaking hands, I open the tin and apply the healing balm to Liza's wounds, praying it will work.

As I tend to her wounds, her breathing becomes steadier, and her color returns in the faint light. If I listen closely, I hear the herbs sizzling as they work their healing powers.

Huddling Liza in the darkness, the flame casts flickering shadows on the walls. I caress her head, pushing back the short strands of damp hair to see her sweat-coated face.

"I got you," I whisper, pressing her closer to me. "Don't worry. I'll get us out of here."

I can't tell if I would be brave enough to say those words if Liza was awake, but I keep saying them over and over to make myself believe my own words.

FORTY-TWO

KHAOS

I will not use *that* magic; I keep telling myself as we ride through a dense veil of mist, separating Terminus from the rest of the land. The temperature drops abruptly, causing my breath to fog up in the cold air.

I watch my soldiers pull their cloaks out of their saddlebags to wrap them tightly around themselves while using magic to keep warm and toasty.

I will not use that magic.

The frosty air stings on my skin, but I ignore it.

As we ride on, the veil becomes thicker and more impenetrable. I can barely see beyond my horse's nose, and the ground beneath me becomes slippery and treacherous. My horse snorts and paws at the ground nervously, sensing danger beyond the mist.

Finally, I emerge from the veil and see the mountain range looming before us.

Old memories flash through my head. I swore to never revisit this place. It feels like yesterday when King Obsidian sent me out here to find a Painite, the coldness rendering most of my stay to pure misery.

"Can you hear that?" Jeremia asks, leaning over his horse.

I strain my ears. That's when I hear something in the distance.

The air is filled with muted sounds of clashing swords, screams, and whistling.

I urge my horses to the front of our formation, picking my way carefully through the rocky terrain. The black mountains tower above us, their craggy peaks disappearing into the clouds.

My heart beats faster and faster the closer we get, fading the need to use magic to warm myself up.

Finally, I reach the bottom of the mountain range, where I can see the rest of our army already engaged in fierce combat with the enemy.

My soldiers are close behind me, and I whirl around to meet their gazes for the last time. "May Lunra watch over you," I say, drawing my sword.

The battlefield is a chaotic scene of swirling dust, clashing swords, and flying arrows. The sound of metal meeting metal rings in my ears, punctuated by the occasional scream of a wounded soldier. The air is thick with the smell of blood and sweat, and the ground is slick with gore.

At the front of the battle, the two armies clash with a thunderous roar, pushing and shoving against one another in a desperate struggle for dominance.

Amid the melee, a group of archers stands back from the front line, raining arrows down on my army. The whistling of the arrows cuts through the air as they fly towards their targets, finding their mark in the flesh of Crymzonians. The archers move with precision, their shots calculated and efficient as they aim and fire, taking down one after another.

But it isn't just swords and arrows being used in the battle. Magic is also at play as my soldiers fight back, casting spells and incantations that cause devastating effects. Flames erupt from their fingertips, burning through the ranks of Keres' army, while bolts of lightning crackle through the air, striking down enemies in their path.

The ground is littered with fallen bodies, some wearing the signature red Crymzon armor and some wearing dirty, ragged clothes. I step through the carnage to what looks like a line of my soldiers fighting back.

I haven't even reached the outskirts of the battle before arrows rain down on me. Someone behind me uses his magic to shield us from the incoming attack. Finally, I dismount my horse before it spins around to run out of the war zone.

"There's too many!" Jeremia yells behind me, fear clouding his voice.

"Use your fucking magic to survive!" I bark over my shoulder. "Take out the archers first."

Just because I won't use my power doesn't mean he can't.

Something steers before me. I watch as a person submerges from beneath a fallen soldier. Whatever comes walking my way is neither dead nor alive. The man's eyes are black, and something dark drips out of an open wound in his abdomen that should have been fatal.

"What in Lunra's name is that?" Kasen yells from behind me, but before I can answer his question, a magical orb hits the man right in the gut, ripping him in half.

I hear a barfing noise behind me. "Pull yourself together," I bellow, making my way through the dead bodies, scanning the ground for more movement. "And watch the ground. Not all of them are dead yet."

Luckily, I don't encounter another one of Keres' abominations before I reach my soldiers fighting for their lives.

I pull on a man's armor, and his eyes widen when he recognizes me. "Where's Soulin?" I ask him, who's eagerly awaiting to get his turn to cut down one of Keres' soldiers.

"She hasn't arrived yet," he says, freeing himself to break through the row.

He doesn't make it two steps before a blade finds its way into his head, and he crumbles to the ground.

I'm stupid to think that Soulin would be here to watch her soldiers bleed for her. With her newly gained Soulmate *and* magic, she's the most powerful of us and could take down half of Keres' army with a single one-hand movement. But this bloodbath is beneath her, just like the stable boy she vowed to always carry in her heart.

All of us are just pawns in her grand scheme. We're nothing more than the dirt beneath her feet.

This is the moment I change my mind.

Why am I sacrificing myself for her? Why am I allowing all my soldiers to fall to protect a Queen who didn't even show up to her own battle?

"Fall back!" I scream, but my words meet deaf ears. "Fall back!" I yell again, loud enough to reach a few soldiers fighting in line.

They hesitate for a moment but slowly step back, yelling my order out to spread my command.

More and more soldiers drop their weapons and fall back.

This battle isn't worth it. Those poor souls deserve a better fate than what Soulin dealt them.

Jeremia's voice finds its way into my ears. "Khaos!"

I search the crowd of Crymzonians and disfigured males and females until my eyes finally fall on Jeremia. He's sprinting in my direction, his face distorted.

He lifts his hand, and magic pours out of his palm, but it's too late.

A sharp ache erupts in my shoulder blade. The air presses out of my lungs when I hear my ribs crack. I'm frozen in place as the pain moves from my back and ribs through my heart and chest.

My head drops to the ground after the initial terror subsides. That's when I see the blood-coated blade sticking out of my chest.

A wheezing sound erupts in my throat as I gasp for air. I cough, and blood covers my tongue and fills my mouth while my lung feels like bursting into a million little pieces.

Before I can comprehend what's happening, the blade, which holds me in place, disappears out of my view, and my knees buckle under the excruciating pain in my left side.

The noises surrounding me become dull, and all I hear is Jeremia yelling my name repeatedly.

Something slumps into me, pressing me face-first to the ground until the weight suddenly lifts.

"Khaos!"

I feel hands touching me, but before I can answer, I dip into darkness, and everything goes quiet.

FORTY-THREE

Queen Soulin

We've been here for a day already. By now, my army should be only a day's ride away from Terminus, so I must hurry.

Using my magic to keep myself warm without the need to bundle up, I make my way through another pathway between the narrow mountain cliffs, my silky red dress flowing in the wind.

"We've been here before," I snarl, scanning the black rocks.

I've tried everything from using my power to find the location of the Painite to threatening Conrad to kill him to speed things up. But nothing worked.

"I swear on my life that this is the way," Conrad says, a smile lighting up his face.

It didn't take him long to regain his composure after almost falling to his death. While the rest of the flight was quiet, and he didn't talk aloud, he kept mumbling under his breath.

"I hate your smile," I spit out, following the path deeper into Terminus.

"I think I'm quite charming when I'm positive," he counters, stumbling behind me.

Suddenly, I feel a tugging sensation inside me like a wild animal pulling on a leash. With each pull, the pain radiating through my body forces bile up my throat.

I whirl around to face Conrad, who stops in his tracks, his smile fading into a smirk.

"Are you using your magic on me?" I hiss out, holding my chest to ease the pain.

"Why would I do that?"

"Stop playing games with me. Is this why you brought me here? To kill me?"

His eyebrows shoot to the sky, and his smirk vanishes. "I promise you, my Queen, it's not my intention to cause you any harm."

I bolt in his direction and grab him by the throat. "Stop lying to me. I knew something was wrong with you. I've never seen you at my father's side."

"Your Majesty," he mumbles, his face turning red. "Whatever you feel, it's not me."

He raises his hands so I can see them.

An excruciating pain, like a fiery blade being shoved into my chest, forces me to let him go, and I fall to my knees.

What is going on?

I look around, trying to find the source of my pain.

How is this possible? There's no one around to inflect any wound, so why do I feel like dying?

"What's wrong, my Queen?" Conrad asks, his hands resting on my trembling shoulders.

"There's something inside me," I press out between labored breaths.

He shakes his head, kneeling down. "I don't understand."

He scans my body for any signs of foul play, but I can see in his facial expression that he can't find any.

"Something is terribly wrong," I repeat, summoning my magic to ease the pain. But when I reach inside me, I feel the strains of power slipping through my imaginary hands.

I try it again.

And again.

Until I feel my magic dissipating.

The coldness of Terminus hits me like a boulder.

No.

It's too early.

I still have four more nights.

No!

"How can I help?" Conrad asks as I hunch forward, the pain almost swallowing me whole.

"I need...," I mumble, my throat closing up. "I need...you...to take the pain," I say between shallow breaths.

I press my hands to my chest, hoping to find a sliver of remaining magic.

Nothing.

Conrad strengthens his grip on my shoulders, and I feel his magic running through my heart, easing my discomfort.

I try again to grasp my power once the throbbing in my chest is replaced by a dull ache.

No luck.

Has Lunra broken her promise to give me magic for seven nights? Has she decided to end our agreement early?

But why?

I'm so close to finding and feeding the gem to the Heiligbaum.

The Heiligbaum.

Cold sweat forms on my skin.

What if the tree ran out of fuel?

I heave myself off the ground and meet Conrad's eyes. His lips are curled with excitement.

"Lunra have mercy. For a second there, I thought you were dying," he says, wiping sweat off his forehead. "I'm so grateful you're ok."

His smile seems genuine. How does he do it?

I shake my head, still feeling the pain inside my chest, but it's barely noticeable.

Yet, I can't ignore it.

Something is wrong. I need to find out what's causing it. The tug in my heart got stronger the moment the overwhelming pain eased. It feels like it's trying to pull me away from here.

"Listen to me," I say, grabbing Conrad by the arm. "Finish the mission. Find the Painite and return to Crymzon at once."

His eyes widen. "What about you, Your Majesty?"

"There's something I need to do. For the sake of your family, find that damn stone. And if I don't return in time, throw it into the Heiligbaum without me."

This is not the proper way to restore the tree's power, but it must be sufficient. If Crymzon's most ancient soldier can feed the Heiligbaum, the connection to Lunra should be strengthened, and more magic will return to me.

"Barin will carry you safely home," I say, watching the sky for my moths.

I've used a spell to shield them from curious eyes and to keep them warm. When I look up, I see them soaring through the clouds, waiting for my following command.

I whistle and watch as Adira drops out of the sky to reach me. She hovers over the canyon, unable to squeeze through the narrow slit above me.

Without words, I point at a wider opening not far from us, and she flaps away before descending to the ground.

"Your family will die if you don't find the Painite," I say as I walk in her direction, my heart sending a jabbing pain through my body as if I'm going in the wrong direction.

I push the uneasy feeling aside and mount Adira before locking eyes with Conrad again. "Hurry."

It's the last word that slips over my lips before Adira lifts off the ground, and I direct her on the course to follow the strain in my heart.

FORTY-FOUR

QUEEN SOULIN

T he internal tugging leads me to a massacre.

My eyes fleet over the ground covered in unmoving bodies, blood, and a black substance, which I know all too well. I remember the rotten smell of the soldiers I battled before I lost all my magic and Cyrus rescued me. The stench and consistency of the substance force my hair to stand, and the smell of sweat and shit in the air makes me gag.

How is my army already here? I've carefully crafted my plan to include enough time to deliver the Painite to Crymzon and return in time to lead them.

But I haven't calculated the power of the refreshed magic. Every month, my soldiers took longer and longer to return from their missions. I got so used to their speed that I forgot how it is to use magic to fasten their agility.

I scan the battle eagerly, trying to figure out what is causing the pain radiating through my chest.

It must be a connection I have to my men and women dying. Though I've never felt it before, they somehow must be linked to me.

I point at a spot close to the outskirts of the bloodshed. Adira floats down to the ground, but not low enough for me to jump off.

"What's wrong with you?" I ask, pressing into her sides to force her to the ground.

She flaps her wings and gains another foot into the air, sending freezing air to ruffle my dress.

"Stop it," I hiss, bearing down on her again until she caves in and lands.

I lift my leg and jump off, but before my feet can find traction, another wave of pain hits me, and I stumble forward. Then, clutching my chest, I straighten myself.

I'm only fifty feet away from my soldiers fighting back a wall of Undead when I hear my name being called out.

"Queen Soulin, over here," someone yells, but I ignore the request.

My heart feels like it's about to burst into a gazillion pieces while still sending me a direction to go.

Mumbling, I stagger through the dead bodies to follow this excruciating tugging sensation. All this would be much easier if this ache wouldn't drain me of my magic. I can see my soldiers using theirs, so why is mine not working?

"Queen Soulin!" a familiar voice screams. My eyes wander to the soldier calling out to me. His face and beard are covered in blood, and his frantic hand movements tell me to hurry.

I recognize him as one of Khaos' closest guards. I've seen him more than any other soldier guarding my doors when Khaos wasn't available.

As much as I want to disregard him, my internal pull leads to him, and I follow it.

My face scrunches up when I step on a dead man's face and slip. I'm only ten feet from the soldier, and I expect him to close the last steps between us to let me know what's more urgent than joining my soldiers against Keres' army. But he turns around and kneels, forcing me to follow his gaze.

My heart shatters when my eyes land on the black curls coated in blood, and my knees almost cave in. On wobbly legs, I reach the soldier and look over his shoulder to meet Khaos' face, his eyes closed.

"I wasn't fast enough," the soldier says, his voice shaking.

Everything around me goes quiet as I push him out of the way to see the hole in Khaos' armor where his heart used to be. Blood shoots out of the opening in small gushes with each heartbeat.

"He's not dead," I whisper, falling to my knees beside him. "He's still alive."

"Not for long," another voice says beside me. He immediately shuts up when I raise my head, and he realizes who I am.

I memorize his face to punish him for his comment later, but now Khaos needs me. I grab his face softly. "Khaos? Can you hear me?"

He grunts, and even that tiny movement sends a shockwave through my body.

My fear of losing him turns into something else. "I told you to leave! Why didn't you leave? You're not supposed to be here," I bark, pressing my hands against the flesh wound gaping in his chest.

I reach inside me, scraping up the last pieces of magic to force them into his chest, but I come out empty-handed.

"You can't die," I whisper, searching for magic, but it's depleted. Finally, I look up and lock eyes with the snarky soldier close by.

"Come here," I say as he stumbles in my direction, his eyes widened with fear.

When he's in reach, I grab his arm and suck his body dry of energy before bundling it up to send it through my hands into Khaos.

His wounds should be healing. They should close now.

I stare at the blood streaming out of him.

And the bleeding continues.

My chest aches from the wound inflicted on him. I feel his heart pounding in my chest as if we're sharing the same one. Hurt overwhelms me, and a tear escapes my eye as I take the pain in.

He wasn't supposed to be here.

So why is he? Why did he ignore my command again?

Through ragged breaths, I clutch my chest, trying to ease the pain of my invisible wound.

How did my father survive this pain when my mother died? It feels like someone is stabbing me repeatedly, rendering my body and mind senseless.

When my father delivered the news of my mother's passing, his face was emotionless. That was another reason I snapped. His coldness for the woman he said he loved the most went cold the moment she departed. She was his Soulmate, for Lunra's sake!

But this is different.

Khaos isn't my Soulmate—we established that when our connection didn't fall into place when we came together.

"What is she doing?" a voice whispers behind me, forcing the outside noises to return to my hearing.

Yes, what the fuck am I doing?

I've tried to save him from this fate. I've sent him away, and he still disobeyed me. If he had listened to me for once, he would be miserable trying to start a new life outside Crymzon, but he would be unharmed.

The state he's in right now, somewhere between life and death, I can't leave him there. I can't wait for him to take his last breath, suffering like a slain pig, waiting to bleed out while unable to move.

"Is she crying?" a woman asks in the distance.

When I gaze over my shoulder to see her face to add her to my death list, I see a dagger lying on the ground.

Khaos deserves better than this blood-crusted dagger, but without my magic, I can't give him the death he deserves—silent and painless.

I snatch it and raise my trembling hands, the blade pointing at Khaos in the air to deliver the fatal blow.

"Don't," a female voice echoes from the distance when I bring the blade down on his chest, aiming for his heart.

I already feel the blade penetrating his armor and flesh before it ever makes contact—but I freeze just an inch away from his chest.

I can pick that powerful voice out of a million.

As I rise from the ground, my eyes meet Princess Opaline riding on something that looks like a grass-covered lion over the field of dead. Behind her, an army of ruthless soldiers trails her, all covered in furs, bark, and leather to withstand the brutal cold.

"What an unpleasant surprise," I say, still holding the blade close to Khaos as she approaches into earshot. "Coming to watch my downfall?"

Opaline's animal sprints in my direction. "On the contrary. Khaos visited my mother to persuade her to aid Crymzon against Keres."

My thoughts go back to the missing trade delivery.

So it was Queen Synadena's command to stop sending her goods to me, after all. She must have sensed that this battle would end in Keres' favor and didn't want to waste any of her resources on a dying kingdom.

But that makes little sense.

Tenacoro's Queen would never send her firstborn to her death.

"Why are you here?" I ask, relaxing my hand.

Her gaze wanders over Khaos, tears forming in her eyes, but she doesn't move any closer.

"Did you kill him?" she asks in return, watching me tentatively.

"That's none of your business."

Her army closes in on us, awaiting her command. "Soulin. Did you kill him?"

I watch his chest slowly move up and down.

In a few breaths, he will be dead.

In a few breaths, I will never see Khaos again.

Just a few more, and whatever spiral we caught ourselves in over the last years will be gone.

All my memories return, including Khaos. From my first experience outside the palace walls to seeing him daily in the halls or going on special missions with him at my side.

"No. But I can't save him," I whisper as a tear rolls down my cheek.

I raise my hand again, but Opaline is faster. Her lion jumps over us as she rips the dagger out of my hand.

She lands behind me. "It wasn't my mother's order to come to your aid. I took matters into my own hand as the future Queen to support my most loyal kingdom and friend," Opaline says, throwing the dagger to the ground. "I'm here to help *you*."

Opaline slowly slides off her lion creature and steps forward, her hands raised as if approaching a frightful animal. "Please, let me help him."

I look at her and then at Khaos, his curls now clinging to his face. "You know I can't do that. He's a Crymzonian."

"And my friend," she says, taking another careful step closer. "I can help."

Jealousy bubbles up in my chest, and I jump to my feet to go face-to-face with her.

Why does she think she can save him if I'm not able to do it even if I was at my full potential? Her herbs and greens are nothing compared to my magic.

"What do you really want to do to him?"

"He doesn't have much time, Soulin. I'm begging you. Let me help him, and I will return him to Crymzon," Opaline pleads, folding her hands together.

If she touches him, I will burn everything to the ground!

He's mine.

Even though the three of us share a history, Opaline has no right to lay a hand on him. But if there is a chance of his survival, I need to take it.

I nod and step out of the way, watching Opaline carefully as she pulls out a little wooden flask hidden beneath her fur coat. She storms past me and uncorks it...

And that's when hell breaks loose.

Something hard rams into my shoulder, making me stumble closer to Opaline. Then, screams erupt around us, mixed with metal boots getting closer and closer.

I lost sight of the battle unfolding just hundreds of feet away from us and didn't notice the shift in the air.

Crymzon soldiers stream past us, retreating from the mountain cliffs like prey, trying to escape a predator.

I spin around to see what's causing them to run—and my air supply cuts off.

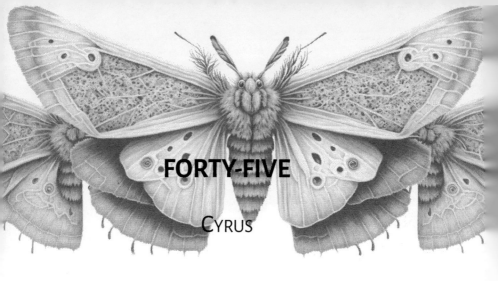

FORTY-FIVE

CYRUS

A faint noise rings in my ears, and I look at her mouth, leaning in closer, hoping to hear Liza's voice again.

Instead, my ears fill with a rattling sound. The walls creak and groan with strain as the ground vibrates beneath us. The earthquake strikes suddenly, violently shaking the room and causing debris to rain from the ceiling.

I cling tightly to Liza, her weight making my arms ache as I strain to keep her upright, hoping the walls will hold. She's still pale and deathlike, her breathing shallow and labored.

As the rumbling continues, the walls begin to crack and buckle. Then, with a deafening crash, a section of it gives way, creating a gaping hole that reveals an unworldly scene outside.

My eyes burn from the sunlight streaming in and then widen in shock as the red streets beyond, littered with rubble and panicked Crymzonians, come into focus.

But I have no time to dwell on the outside world. Instead, my focus is solely on the unconscious woman in my arms. Even though I carefully covered Liza's wounds with the balm to stop them from oozing, without immediate medical attention, she will die before the quake can kill us.

Despair and helplessness wash over me. We're trapped in a cell, unable to call for help, with no way out except through the ragged hole in the wall with a hundred-foot drop.

My eyes wander back to the hole. It's my last and only way out. Somehow, I could find a way to climb down the palace wall to escape this place.

But I have to keep Liza safe, no matter what.

It's my fault she ended up here. I knew the risk I would put her in when I accepted her invitation to stay with her in the village.

Back then, I didn't care what happened to any of those villagers if my father or Monsteress found me, including Liza.

I was taught that the Ordinaries living in the Confines were traitors, smugglers, and outcasts, and I questioned none of it.

Not until I became an Ordinary, and the more time I spent in the village, the more it grew on me.

Liza showed me what it's like to live a primitive life without forced staff and a fortune to spend whenever I pleased. Learning to do everything myself was hard, but I fell in love with the hard work that comes with living.

I shift her weight and adjust my grip, trying to find a more comfortable position as I brace myself for the aftershocks that are sure to come.

I'm not going anywhere.

Liza saved me without ever asking a question of who I was and why I ended up in the Confines. I owe her my life.

As I look out into an unrecognizable world, I hear fear and panic echoing through the air as buildings crumble and the ground shakes with terrifying force. People run and scream in terror, trying to find safety amid the chaos.

Ice shivers down my spine when I realize what's going on: Monsteress is dying, and her kingdom reacts to her pain.

FORTY-SIX

Queen Soulin

An enormous fist grabs me by the neck and lifts me off the ground without effort. I try to gasp for air, but the metal glove-covered fingers press harder into my skin, cutting my air supply off.

Panic flashes through me as I try to wiggle my way out of the grip as sweat begins to pour out of my pores. My vision becomes blurry as tears stream down my face uncontrollably.

I try to breathe desperately, again and again, but it feels like I'm underwater, unable to make my way to the surface.

"And we finally meet again," a voice bellows out underneath the black visor. "I knew the little gift I sent you would bring you right back into my arms."

My eyes roll back as I try to get just the smallest amount of oxygen. My face is getting hotter and hotter with every passing second.

While every fiber in my body tells me to fight for my life, I close my eyes and relax my tensed muscles. It goes against everything I know, but I don't see another way.

I lost everything.

My parents, my brother, and now Khaos.

Whatever Opaline thinks she can do to heal Khaos, it won't work. Without him, the life I know won't be the same, and it's a life I don't want to live.

I concentrate on my wild, pounding heartbeats to slow them down. In the distance, I hear water splashing onto metal, followed by a gasp for air.

"Aren't you happy to return home?" the male choking me asks, and I try to answer.

I don't have to be a genius to know that the man before me has to be Keres. Who else would send my Crymzonians running for their lives after battling an army of Undead for hours?

But I don't understand what he's referring to. I've never met this cruel creation Otyx sent to torture our land.

Yet, his words sound so familiar.

Home. He said h*ome.*

The dead version of Felix used the same word when he talked to me.

It's time for you to come home; those were the words he used just before he tried to kill me when I rejected him.

With every beat, my heart pumps weaker.

Another gasp sounds behind me, and just as I make my peace with dying, I hear *his* frail voice. "Soulin!"

Hearing Khaos call out my name sends sparks through my veins. Even though it was quiet, it sounded like a barking order.

It's impossible. Nothing is strong enough to bring someone back so close to death.

Yet, he keeps saying my name, his voice getting stronger with each try, and somehow, it changes from anger to something else.

"Soulin? Soulin. Soulin!"

That's when I feel our connection snap in place, and the magic reaching me.

I felt it before—the tingling inside my veins. A rush of power surges through me uncontrollably, strengthening me from within. It's the same sensation I felt when Lunra granted me more magic for seven nights, but somehow, it's stronger.

My heart starts to pump harder. Whatever broke inside it when I watched Khaos taking what I thought were his final breaths, now fills with warmth.

But I don't have time to think about what all of this means.

My body hums with power, and instantly, I use a sliver of my magic to force oxygen through my bloodstream.

With fresh energy, I open my eyes and stare at the self-made King before me.

Still unable to speak, I hold on to his fist clutching my throat, and lift my leg to kick his visor up, and to my surprise, I succeed.

I had years to prepare myself for this moment. This is not exactly how I imagined coming face to face with Keres—him holding me in a chokehold—but I envisioned all the ways I could kill him when we met.

After battling his Undead, I got a good idea of what he might look like and imagined him with soulless black eyes, pale skin, and disgusting teeth. But when my eyes fall on the red curls forming beneath his helmet, my newly mended heart skips a beat.

Another wave of panic forms inside me.

I can't do this again.

It can't be him.

I can't kill everyone around me with my magic because he's forcing me to.

Shaking, I use my magic to summon a glass blade in my hand and cut off the arm of...

My father.

I drop to the ground, his hand still attached to my throat. I rip on the limb and throw it to the floor in disgust.

"Get out of here," I bark over my shoulder at Opaline, not taking my eyes off the undead version of my father. "You have about ten seconds to reach the veil before it gets ugly."

Seeing the smirk forming on my father's face brings back the same feeling I had staring into his eyes while he told me my mother and baby brother had died. Again, I feel my magic bubbling to the surface, but this time, I'm prepared.

I suppress the urge to explode. It would be a waste if not every single ounce of my rage would go to the person I hate the most.

"Your God really has some sense of humor," I say, studying him. "And all this time, I thought Keres was an unknown danger plucked from the dead. And here you are. A man I already defeated once."

His face has fallen in just like my brothers, but he's taller than I remember. He towers above me like I'm six again.

Why did Otyx bring my father back? From all the people he could have used to bring his terror to Escela, why *my* father?

"Tell me you haven't thought about me daily since killing me?" He smiles, black slime oozing out of his mouth. "The urge to see your father again to apologize was strong enough to grant you your wish."

I scoff, listening to the retreating footsteps behind me. I must stall him a little longer until I can tear him and this place apart.

"To be honest, you were a lot on my mind. But not to tell you what you want to hear."

"I see you're still cross with me for what happened to your mother."

The mention of my mother almost breaks my concentration to keep my magic at bay. "How fucking dare you talk about her?"

"That's why we're here, isn't it? Because little Soulin can't get over the loss of her beloved mother."

My breath quickens. I can still hear distant movement behind me. It's too early. If I use my magic now, I will kill them too.

I swallow hard.

"Did you know she asked for a Starstrandian lover for decades, and I turned her request down?" he asks, his black eyes swirling in darkness with amusement.

The blood in my veins freezes.

He continues, taking a step closer. "Did she ever tell you I wasn't her only Soulmate?"

I ball my hands into fists. "Whatever you're trying to do, I won't bite. It was *you* who doomed her."

"That's what you keep telling yourself, but it's not true. She found another Soulmate when I took her to Starstrand to meet the Queen. Their connection was so strong she felt it when he entered the room. After that, she begged me year after year to let her complete the Connection Ceremony with him. But how could I say *yes*, knowing it could kill her?"

"You're so full of shit."

"My child, your mother fucked him behind my back to fulfill the ceremony. Afterward, she told me she found a way to bear his winged child and beseeched me to let her carry on their relationship while promising me I would always be her first choice. And I was. But love made me blind, and I should've known she would lie about her survival rate. She really thought she would be the first Crymzonian to carry out a babe with wings successfully despite all the evidence that it was never done before. She tricked me and herself into believing her lie. A Soulmate Connection can make you do horrific things."

My thoughts wander to Khaos. Deep down, I always knew he was my Soulmate. That's why I used my magic to suppress my feelings for him and shield myself from the truth I knew all along.

There was no way I could let a connection get in my way of taming the rage inside me. I needed that feeling to keep going; to find someone to hold accountable for my mother; to feel invincible.

But just seconds before our connection snapped into place, I wanted to give up because the feeling of continuing a life without Khaos was too much to bear. I accepted death.

I step closer. "Why you? From all the people Otyx could have chosen, why *you*?"

His black liquid-covered teeth show when his smile widens. "*You* tell *me*. You still haven't moved on from the past and enjoy being punished."

A spark rushes through my heart into my hands, but I hold it back just a second before it can escape through my palms.

"Otyx scheme has nothing to do with me. I'm just here to ban you back to the underworld where you belong, finally."

"Such harsh words from a woman who killed hundreds of innocents. You can't be the judge and executioner without answering for your own actions."

Slowly, I twist my head to the side to listen for the retreating footsteps. I can't hear a thing.

The moment has finally arrived. I twist my palms upwards and dig into the power radiating through me...

And I watch as Keres raises his arms faster than I can release the tension in my body.

Grunts erupt behind me.

"It was nice of you to bring new soldiers to my doorstep," he laughs as I turn my head to watch the fallen return from their death.

He wanted this, and I delivered it right to him without even thinking. All those dead soldiers belong to him now. With one action, I've allowed him to add hundreds of undead souls to his ranks.

When I press my magic down again, my jaw hurts from grinding my teeth. "What do you actually want from me?"

"Only you can answer that question."

I stand with my back straight and shoulders squared, staring my biggest enemy in the eyes. The sound of my heartbeat fills my ears, drowning out the noise of the world around me momentarily.

I've waited years for this moment, and it's finally here. I'm so close to taking revenge for my mother's death.

But then, in the distance, I hear the unmistakable sound of boots hitting the ground. His army has risen.

My heart quickens as I realize his soldiers are closing in on me from behind. Of course, I'm outnumbered, but the magic from my new Soulmate Connection with Khaos hums in my body, signaling me to use it.

The sound of boots grows louder and more frenzy as the Undead pick up their pace.

I take a deep breath, steeling myself for what's coming, and stand my ground, my eyes fixed on their leader.

For a moment, everything is silent. The only sound comes from the wind whistling through the black cliffs.

Then, with a roar, the soldiers charge...

And I close my eyes.

I feel the magic inside me pulsing like a living thing. It's like an impulse radiating through me, a force so strong that it threatens to overwhelm me. But I refuse to let it consume me again; instead, I harness it to do my bidding.

With a deafening scream, I unleash the magical blast. A shockwave of pure energy ripples through the air and outwards in all directions, vaporizing everything in its path.

My power hits Keres' army head-on. The soldiers scream as they disintegrate into dust, their bodies melting into nothingness. The ground shakes with the force of the blast, and more and more power courses through my veins.

Then, everything around me falls still.

The only sound is my breath, deep and heavy. I don't even bother looking at the outcome of my doing. I know for a fact that there's nothing left but a smoldering crater where Keres and his army once stood because I've done this before.

I was told my power would be immense after finding my Soulmate, but I also know that everything comes at a cost.

I wait for the usual exhaustion to creep over me and the magic to drain from my body, and I'm taken aback when I feel rejuvenated.

A clapping sound forces me to open my eyes.

"Bravo. You've done it again."

For crying out loud!

Before me stands the ugly version of my father—unscathed.

Ash particles of burned soldiers rain down on us, and the air is heavy. I try not to think that the burned flesh smell reminds me of a cooked meal, but my mouth waters, and I push the thought aside.

Why didn't it work? How is he still here?

As if he can read my thoughts, he squares his shoulders, and a wicked smile forms on his lips. "Your magic won't work on me this time," he snickers. "I'm made of dead cells, shadows, and a God's power. You really think your little parlor trick is enough to kill me again?"

If my magic isn't enough, then what *can* kill him?

My throat goes dry, and I open my mouth to say something, but Keres interrupts me. "Spare me with your excuses. You've learned nothing since your mother died."

And with those words, he turns into thick, black smoke, and I watch as the bone-chilling wind carries him away.

FORTY-SEVEN

QUEEN SOULIN

How could I let him go? He was right there, just an arm's length away, and I let him slip through my fingers.

"Come back!" I yell, my nails cutting into my palms as I storm forward. "I'm not done with you!"

A loud laugh rumbles through the onyx-colored mountains.

"You fucking coward!"

Raising my hands, I summon my magic and unleash an orb on the rock formation before me. The cliff shakes and splinters into a million pieces before it crumbles to the ground, coming to a halt just feet away. I aim for another ridge, and it shatters to the ground.

When I focus on another, the quiet fluttering sound of wings makes me halt. Adira appears before me, and her black eyes study me wearily.

If Adira feels safe enough to land, my undead father must be out of reach. Therefore, every attempt to lure him back onto the battlefield is useless.

My breath is unsteady as I think about what to do next.

I can't let him win.

He can't just turn his back on me and expect me to let him go. He's the one who backed out of this fight, and a retreat can only mean one thing: he knows I would've kicked his ass if he stayed. He knew it the second I cut his disgusting arm off, the exact moment my magic returned.

Right now, it would be the best time to search for him and end this once and for all.

I look at the remaining mountains before me. Adira jumps into my face as I step forward and opens her wings to block my view.

"Get out of my way," I bark, pushing her, and to my surprise, she backs away, folding her wings tightly against her body—beside one.

It won't take long to turn this place upside down to uncover where he's hiding, but my thoughts drift to Adira.

Why isn't she folding all her wings?

Inspecting her closely, I see two arrowheads sticking out of the thin layers of chitin and scales.

"Oh no," I say in a hushed voice, gently caressing her wing. "Those bastards!"

When my fingers curl around the first arrow to snap it, Adira moves, causing an even bigger rip.

"You have to stay still," I whisper, trying to reach for the arrow again, but she backs away.

I'm so accustomed to handling everything without magic to save it for emergencies that it takes me a moment to realize that I don't have to ration it anymore.

Rubbing my fingers together, I send my power with a delicate touch over her thin wing until it reaches the first arrow. With a slight twist of my hand, the arrow pulverizes, leaving a gaping hole in its wake. I repeat the motion for the other one before placing my palm flat on Adira's body to send my magic through her. Not only do I heal the puncture wounds, but I also renew her energy without even tapping into my magical source.

"Better?" I ask, observing her body's movements. Adira spreads her wings and folds them repeatedly as if she can't believe she's restored.

A weird sensation pulses through my heart the longer I watch her. At first, I thought it was my desire to finish what I started, but with every beat, another longing becomes stronger, and an image forms in my head.

Khaos' eyes appear before me, the warm dark brown color soothing my nerves. Where is he now? Is he still alive? Was Opaline able to save him, or did the deprivation of oxygen play tricks on me, and I imagined his voice?

No. He called my name. I'm sure of it.

I scan our surroundings for movement until I remember vaporizing everything and everyone within a 1-mile radius. I had no other choice. It was them or me, and I always choose *me*.

More images form in my head, and the feeling growing inside my heart gets stronger.

I can't do this.

I can't let the Soulmate Connection win.

With every heartbeat, my connection to Khaos will get stronger. Everything I feel, he can feel. We practically share the same heart now without ever agreeing to it.

I told him what would happen if I found my Soulmate. I warned him I wouldn't let someone else control me because of a stupid feeling.

Killing a stranger is a breeze. One blade swipe at the right place, and that person is history without ever seeing me coming.

But that won't be so simple with Khaos. He knows me. He knows my way of thinking and how I handle my weapons. He will see my attack coming from miles away.

But I can't risk it. I can't let a man ruin my life, even though it's Khaos. Fuck, especially because it's Khaos.

If I let the connection grow, it will consume me. It will weaken me.

Killing Khaos is a small price to pay if that means I can rule without an attachment and without the fear of losing him to someone else's blade. All of this will only get harder the longer I wait.

As I climb Adira, another thought plagues me. I've left Conrad behind on my vital mission. Even though my magic has returned—stronger than ever—I can't let the fire of the Heiligbaum extinguish. Without it, my connection to Lunra will be cut off, and I need her for what's to come.

Killing my father; no, that creature wasn't my father, Obsidian. It's a meat husk with the memories of my father, Otyx used to manipulate me and force me to my knees. The new name of that abomination fits him just right: Keres.

Killing Keres, Khaos, and finding the Painite are all critical tasks that I need to get out of the way as soon as possible, yet I have to decide which is the most time-sensitive.

Of course, the Heiligbaum wins. Without Lunra, I might have enough power to finally take Keres on with the Soulmate Connection, but I still need her. Only she can open a path for me to meet the God of the Underworld himself.

Why stop after Keres when I can bring a God to his knees?

"Let's find Barin," I say to Adira, and she softly lifts off the ground with her healed wing.

FORTY-EIGHT

KHAOS

My eyelids feel heavy as if weights are attached to them, when I try to open them. The world around me is hazy and unreal, my mind in a fog as I'm jostled by a creature carrying me. I struggle to make sense of my surroundings as a cool breeze touches my face and the rough texture of the creature's fur rubs against my back. Even though I can't quite identify my savior, it has a comforting warmth that makes me feel safe.

Somehow, this thing holds me securely in place as it moves swiftly through a dense rocky area, the stones blurring past us in a dizzying rush. The world around me sways and blurs, and I feel like I'm floating in a dream-like state.

As my consciousness wavers, I try to recall what happened to me.

Slowly, I begin to remember the last images I saw before my current state. They're distorted, but I know it has something to do with Soulin.

I remember a fierce battle with swords clashing and arrows flying.

Rage grabs me as a clear image of Soulin appears before my eyes. She betrayed me. She fucked another man for power mere moments after she sent me away.

But then I saw her in Terminus again. She was there. I yelled her name to tell her I knew what she did. I wanted to scream and hurt her, just like she hurt me.

Then, my brain processes the words she said while she thought I was dying.

"I told you to leave! Why didn't you leave? You're not supposed to be here."

"You can't die!"

"I can't save him."

I remember hearing her fighting with Opaline, not because Soulin wanted to kill me, but because she had difficulty accepting help.

I feel her hands touching me as if she's here right now. She tried to heal my wound with magic over and over again.

More images appear before my eyes.

Her back is turned to me, and I watch her red curls sway in the wind as she's lifted off the ground. The image of the black armored soldier holding her into the air makes me flinch. He grabbed her by the neck and was so close to crushing her bones when I felt it—the connection between us falling into place.

I tried to call out for her again, but the overwhelming pain of uncontrollable magic rushed through me, knocking me unconscious after a few tries.

I try to focus on the memory, to hold on to it, but it's slipping away from me as I drift in and out of consciousness. The world around me fades again, and the creature's movements become slower and more gentle.

The memories feel like a distant echo, but it's the only thing I can cling onto to stop myself from passing out again.

I was wrong.

The entire ride from the bridge to the battlefield, where I got stabbed by one of Keres' soldiers, I thought Soulin had used me. I even went so far that I devised ways to make her pay.

Looking back, I feel like an idiot.

I'm still unsure how she mastered getting her hands on more magic without dipping into a Soulmate Connection, but she did it.

For a moment, I thought she was the villain—Monsteress—so I didn't hesitate to want to harm her after she broke my heart.

I slip away again, losing my grip on consciousness, as a pang of regret washes over me. I wasn't there for the woman I love—my Soulmate. If I hadn't been such an enormous foul, I could have helped her. But instead, I let rage consume me, leading me close to my own death.

My heart aches, and I have trouble figuring out if it's still from the sword that pierced my heart or if this is the unbearable longing to see my Soulmate.

With each heartbeat, the sensation gets stronger.

I need to find her.

With that thought, I surrender to the darkness, hoping to wake up in a place where I can be with her once more.

As I drift away, the last thing I see is the face of the man holding Soulin in the air. I would have missed it if she didn't kick his visor up just before my vision went dark.

My heart skips a beat when I realize who Soulin actually went up against.

Otyx hasn't just sent anyone to mess with my Queen, my Soulmate.

He sent her father.

FORTY-NINE

QUEEN SOULIN

My search for Conrad and Barin is fruitless. It's either a great sign because somehow Conrad isn't a liar as I suspected, and he actually found a Painite, or both, my fighter moth and the old man are dead.

But my gut feeling tells me I will see that unbearable human again because luck loves fucking me over, and watching Conrad's lips widen into a smile is the last thing I want to witness again.

With the kick of my heel, I turn Adira around, and with the help of my magic, she practically shoots through the air toward home.

Not long after leaving Terminus behind, we soar over the mountains surrounding Eternitie, where I spot my remaining soldiers. They look like little ants making their way through the hill-covered landscape, only a few minutes away from the bridge that separates my kingdom from King Citeus.

I'm relieved to see that more than half of my army is still intact as I guide Adira to leave them behind.

My heart aches when I see Tenacoro in the distance. The rich green colors of the jungle seem out of this world, but that's not why I'm hurting.

I feel *him*.

I feel *his* heartbeat getting stronger with every wing flap.

Somehow, Opaline kept true to her word and brought him back from the edge of death.

My eyes widen when I realize I'm heading for Tenacoro.

I'm unsure if Adira went off course because she could feel my desire to see Khaos or if I spaced out and redirected her myself.

"Home, girl," I say, kicking her with my left heel, and without hesitation, she steers to the right.

This can't happen again. I can't let my feelings take over whenever I feel Khaos close to me.

I reach inside me and strengthen the magical barrier around my heart, where I keep all my emotions in check. But even with doubling down on the suppressant, I can still feel the longing to give Adira the command to head back to Tenacoro.

Now I wish I had finished him.

Nothing, and I mean *nothing,* can stand between me and my kingdom.

Not Keres, no God, and for sure not Khaos.

Soaring through the sky on Adira's back away from Tenacoro makes my heart heavy with grief and exhaustion. The battle was short but grueling, and I barely emerged victorious if I can call it that.

While I haven't been able to kill my father *again*—at least not yet—I hold on to the only silver lining on the horizon. If Conrad did indeed return with the Painite, all of this was worth it.

After refueling the Heiligbaum, Keres and Khaos are the least of my problems after my kingdom is restored to its former glory. Then, I can face Otyx himself.

As I approach Crymzon, my eyes widen at the sight that greets me.

What in Lunra's name happened to my kingdom?

The once-beautiful city lies in ruins, its buildings charred and broken, its streets littered with rubble and debris, and the wall is half torn down. The air is thick with smoke and the stench of death.

My hands tremble as I realize that my worst fear has come true. I'm too late.

While I was busy facing the man I thought was dead for almost fifteen years, the ruin of the Heiligbaum has laid waste to my kingdom in its wake.

I land Adira in what was once the center of Crymzon. Taking a deep breath, I look around, surveying the damage. The once-beautiful kingdom is now nothing more than a wasteland.

A surge of anger rushes through me as I realize the extent of the damage. If my subjects were in their houses while the Painite inside the tree burned out, there won't be any survivors.

My eyes land on the prison, and to my surprise, the building is still intact beside a hole in the wall where the bridge used to connect to the Crymzon Wall.

I dismount, my legs shaky from disbelief, and set off through the ruins, determined to find out where the stench is coming from. After my command to incarcerate every person left behind, and with the prison still intact, there shouldn't be any signs of death.

As I stroll through the shattered streets, my eyes take in the destruction, and I draw up short when a red stain on the ground appears.

If there is blood, there must be a body. But as I search the rubbles, I can't find a single body part belonging to the stain.

A sound behind me makes me stop in my tracks. I turn to see a group of survivors emerging from a nearby building, their faces dirty and tired, and their eyes filled with rage.

With a deep breath, I straighten my shoulders and turn to face my people. I raise my voice and speak to them, my words ringing across the ruined city.

"We will rebuild," I say. "We will rise from the ashes of this defeat, and I will make our kingdom stronger than ever before. We will not be defeated, for we are a people of Lunra, Goddess of Love and the Moon."

I've expected them to cheer and be humble to see me, but their faces harden even more.

"What did you do to our families?" a woman shouts, picking up a rock off the ground.

"They have fought bravely against the danger in the North and are only a day's march away from Crymzon," I answer, my eyes focused on her fingers curled around the stone. "If I were you, I would reconsider my next move wisely."

"Or you do what? Imprison the last of your subjects, so you can rule a Kingdom of Nothing?" She looks around, her eyes wandering over the surrounding chaos. "I wish you would've died instead of your father."

With a quick hand movement, I summon my magic to constrict her throat, but a loud crack sounds in my ears, and I watch as life leaves the woman's eyes.

The mention of my father on top of my new powers was too much. Releasing the tension of my fist, the woman collapses to the ground, leaving her neck bent at an unnatural angle.

"Monsteress!" the man beside her yells, falling to his knees to help the woman, but she was dead before she even touched the ground.

"Let this be a lesson. Never question me again," I say through clenched teeth.

Another woman steps forward. "This is not a lesson. It's murder. What gives you the right to treat us less than trash?"

"I have enough of this," the man says, pulling a knife out of this boot and pointing it at me. "This needs to end. Your reign needs to end."

"And then you're going to do what? Live here in the rubble? That's exactly what Crymzon is going to be if I die."

"I would rather be an Ordinary than a Crymzonian. I have nothing left here. You took my sons and daughter, and imprisoned my wife."

I smirk at him. "Then leave," I say, pointing my finger at the spot where the gate used to stand. "No one is going to hold you back."

The silent stare between us is almost deadly, but I won't back down.

Does he even know what I have done to save them? I braced the freezing north twice just to get my hands on a damn Painite. As a result, I've lost half of my men trying to take Keres down, and I got sucked into a connection I don't want.

And this is how they repay me?

"Monsteress, Queen of Nihility," the man says, clapping the other man on the shoulder. "Let's go."

There's a silent exchange between the handful of men and women before they walk away from me.

Even though I allowed them to leave, no one turns their back on me.

My eyes are fixed on the horizon, where the sun has just begun to lower, casting a warm glow over the desolate land below.

With a wave of my hand, I call forth my magic, a shimmering red light emanating from my fingertips. My power flows out from me, spreading across the kingdom like a gentle breeze, revitalizing the caved-in houses, rebuilding the shattered wall, and repairing the broken roads.

The fallen stones mend themselves, the broken wall rising to its former height. The dirt and rubble covering the streets move and shift, sweeping away to reveal the clean sandstone beneath.

As the magic works its wonders, I watch my subjects halt. I want them to observe how I bring my kingdom back to life. But as I study them, I notice they continue walking away from me, their faces cold and impassive.

My heart rages, and the stone slaps fly past them to their original position, missing them by a hair.

My people have lost faith in me. They have grown tired of the war and the endless struggles without magic, and they no longer believe I can lead them to a better future. The magic that has once awed them is now nothing more than a mere parlor trick, a hollow gesture that does little to address the underlying problems.

My magic alone isn't enough to restore their trust in me.

I watch with trembling hands as they walk away, their footsteps echoing in the emptiness of the once-great kingdom. And as the sun dips lower in the sky, I realize I don't need them.

This life—my life—was never about them. I don't need people cheering for me to do the right thing. Without me, they are nothing, but without them, I'm still the most powerful individual in Escela, right beneath the Gods.

I no longer pay attention to their departure, focusing solely on the task at hand. My power surges through me, repairing everything in its path. The palace is now a grand fortress again, its towers reaching towards the sky.

I stand amidst the grandeur of my restored Crymzon and look at the beauty I created. With the snap of my fingers, the woman before me catches fire. I follow the ashes being carried away by the wind.

All I have to do now is wait for my army to return and fill the empty streets.

I hear wings rustling behind me, and when I turn, I see Barin coming in for a landing with Conrad on his back.

"I'm not sure what sign I have been waiting for to know about your return, but this wasn't it," Conrad says with a bright smile, looking over the restored houses.

"And I hoped to find you crushed beneath rubble to be finally done with you," I hiss, rolling my eyes. As irritating as Conrad is, I can't shove down the grateful feeling inside me to see him. "Did you find it?"

"You mean this?" he asks, drawing something from his uniform pocket and holding it up for me to see.

He jumps off Barin and approaches me, his hand outstretched, holding a small but stunning gemstone.

I snatch it from him and hold it up to the light. As I turn it around in my hand, I marvel at its beauty. The Painite is translucent and has a polished surface free from blemishes or flaws. Its shape is a long, thin crystal with pointed ends that narrow as they reach the center of the stone. Under even closer inspection, I notice its unique features. One of the most distinctive ones is its pleochroism—it appears to change colors when viewed from different angles. As I tumble the stone in my hand, it shifts from a deep red to a warm orange and then to a rich brown.

"This, Your Majesty," Conrad says, his face beaming, "is a Painite."

"I know what a Painite is," I snarl back, facing him.

Conrad keeps smiling, and a hint of satisfaction fills his voice. "I stumbled upon a mine deep in Terminus where it was waiting to be discovered. It was exactly where we found the last one. It's as rare and precious as you, Your Majesty."

"I'll take it from here," I say, looking past Conrad to check Barin for any injuries. Both males seemed to have stayed out of trouble while I was gone.

Barin bolts in my direction, his wings almost taking me out as he jumps around me like a puppy.

"Has my father ever used you as a messenger?" I ask, scratching Barin's body to stop him from running me over.

"All the time," Conrad answers enthusiastically. "But whatever you have in mind needs to wait. I need to check on my family first. Out of precaution, I sent them out of Crymzon until my safe return. It's time for them to come home."

My nostrils flare. "They can wait until you've fulfilled your duty. I need you to deliver a message to Queen Synadena."

Conrad perks up at the Queen's name, and his smile fades when I recite the message I have been working on since leaving Terminus.

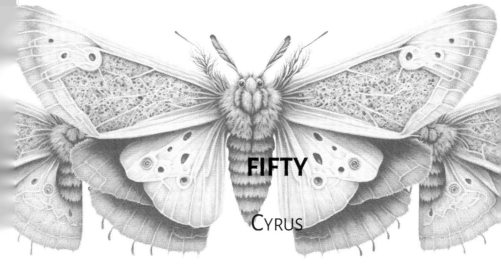

FIFTY

CYRUS

I'm not sure anymore what's going on. One minute, a horrific earth-quake that makes me fear for our lives strikes the entire kingdom. And the next, it stops as fast as it started like nothing ever happened.

Does that mean Monsteress survived? Or is this the calm before Crymzon gets sucked into the underworld, leaving no trace of us behind?

The screams outside die down just like the rumbling shakes. Most buildings are scattered on the streets, and I see people lying on the ground unmoving while others rush to aid them.

How many lives has Monsteress claimed this time? Is she even aware of what she has done?

There is no doubt in my mind that she's responsible for this.

After scanning the calamity outside again, I kneel beside Liza, my hand gently shaking her shoulder as I urge her to wake up.

How am I supposed to reach her if not even a destructive quake could get her to open her eyes?

I can't give up now. Determined to get her out of here, I keep nudging her delicately.

As Liza's eyelids flutter open, she groans softly and winces in pain.

I take a deep breath and steady my voice. "Hey, can you hear me? We need to get out of here. Can you stand?"

I'm confident she can't, and I don't want to rush her, but we must get out of here fast.

Liza blinks a few times, trying to focus her eyes on my face. She nods weakly but winces again as she tries to move.

I assess our situation again, noting her injuries and the fact that we're still locked in a small room.

I lean closer to her and whisper urgently. "We have little time. Monsteress could be back any minute."

She nods again but still looks disoriented. I put a hand under her arm and help her sit up, supporting her weight as she tries to get on her feet. She stumbles slightly and leans on me for support as I catch her and help her regain her balance.

"We need to leave," I whisper, pulling her closer. "Okay, we're going to take this slow. Just put your weight on me, and we'll get out of here together."

Step by step, I lead Liza to the door, trying to push my shoulder against it to open it. Swearing under my breath when I realize it won't budge, I look around the room for something to use as a makeshift tool and spot a piece of rock lying on the floor. I pick it up and wedge it into a crack between the wall and the door to pry it open.

"Come on. We have to move quickly now."

I take Liza's arm again and carry her out of the cell down a dark hallway that seems to stretch endlessly. She exhales sharply with each step, but I keep encouraging her, telling her we're almost there.

We move slowly, trying not to make too much noise or draw any attention to ourselves.

Wherever I look, I see overturned furniture, ripped paintings hanging from the walls, and debris littering the floor. I check each room as we go. But it's the same story - abandoned and in shambles.

As we make our way through the empty corridor, Liza's wounds begin to bleed again, causing her to gasp in pain as my hands get covered in her blood.

I pause to help her, leaning her against the wall and tearing a strip of cloth from my shirt to use as a makeshift bandage.

"Almost there," I grunt under her weight as we continue.

Liza takes a deep breath before exhaling shakily.

We're not safe yet, but we're out of my cell, and that's a start.

Finally, we reach the end of the hallway, and my eyes fall on a staircase leading to the entrance hall. Bright light floods through the broken walls and Liza squints against it, her eyes adjusting slowly.

I tug her arm gently, urging her to move faster. "I know you're hurting, but we're running out of time."

I can't tell if Monsteress is near Crymzon, and I don't want to find out.

We pick up the pace, dodging broken wall pieces scattered across the stairs.

"Be careful," I instruct, gesturing towards the missing steps below us. "I'll follow behind you."

Somehow Liza finds the strength to make it down the steps. As we enter the entrance hall, I stop in my tracks. Before us lays the grand hall where I woke up after being captured in our village. This room once symbolized power and opulence, but now it's lying in ruins. The walls are crumbling, the windows shattered, and the grand entrance door lies open and inviting.

Right here, I've seen Devana and the other villagers for the last time. I was so occupied with returning to Crymzon to save Liza and take care of her that they slipped my mind.

Devana.

My heart aches when I think of her.

"We need to find a way to free our friends," I whisper as we approach the door, and I notice something strange - no soldiers are patrolling any part of the palace we've walked through or the grounds. It's as if everyone vanished.

We exchange a look, both equally confused and hesitant. But we can't stay out in the open for long. Liza's wounds need proper attention, and we must find shelter before the sun sets.

With no other options, we cautiously make our way into the courtyard, and I keep my guard up and my senses sharp.

The outside of the palace looks no better than the inside. However, it's clear the quake was more potent than the ones in the past.

So what happened to Monsteress? And where is everyone?

Beyond to broken fountain, I spot a group of people walking in our direction, some injured, others upset. Unfortunately, I don't recognize them as members of my former royal court, meaning they must be Monsteress' subjects.

Just as I decide to sprint over to them to ask for help, I halt when the broken courtyard pieces shake before they scramble over the ground to their rightful places.

"What's happening?" Liza asks, her voice rough and broken.

"Stay here," I answer in a hushed voice and press her against the last remaining piece of the entrance wall.

I watch the strangers pause for a moment before they continue their way to where the gate used to be.

More pieces move below our feet as the kingdom rebuilds itself as if an invisible force is stitching it back together.

Fuck!

"We need to move. Now!" I hiss at Liza, prepping her arm around my shoulders to take most of her weight. "Monsteress has returned."

FIFTY-ONE

KHAOS

I touch the throbbing bump on my head. How have I not noticed this aching pain before?

"I'm sorry. I had to knock you out to bring you to safety," a sweet voice says, and my eyes flicker open to see Opaline hovering over me.

My mind whirls through all the images again, putting all the pieces in the right places just as before.

My anger. Getting stabbed. Soulin. Our connection. Her father.

"I guess congratulations are in order. You finally got the girl," Opaline smiles as my eyes focus on her. "You don't know how long I've been waiting for the day you two finally release the tension between you guys."

"Where is she?" I ask, my throat drier than the Crymzon desert.

"You know, I don't get you Crymzonians. Your law allows you to bed anyone you want, no matter gender or status, and then you act like lunatics when you find your Soulmate. Do you guys stop your entanglements with other people once you find *the one,* or do you continue just messing around with others?"

It's hard to concentrate on her words. My heart aches like a piece is missing, and I know precisely what it longs for—Soulin.

I try to straighten myself, and I'm caught off guard when I find myself sitting inside a pool of water.

"I have to get to her. Where is she?"

Opaline scoffs, and I notice she's sharing the water with me. "A *thank you for saving my life* would have been a great conversation starter," she says as she presses herself off the ground and swims into the deeper part of the circular crater we are in.

I shake my head to clear it. "I'm sorry, Opaline. I can barely remember the last events. I can't even recall how I got here. Thank you for saving my life."

If those words are enough to bring me closer to Soulin, I will say them. She's all I can think about.

I clear my throat. "Is she okay? Did she kill—"

"Her father? Again?"

So she saw him too.

Opaline shakes her head slowly. "I'm not sure. She forced us to leave. But I can tell you that my family and I felt your connection. I've experienced nothing like it before. I've tried to heal your wound with the water of this lagoon. It helped close the external damage, but the power you two set off after you connected saved your life."

I didn't imagine it.

Soulin is my Soulmate after all.

But why did it take so long to show? Why hasn't it snapped into place in the water chamber? Isn't that how it's supposed to work? You complete the most intimate task, and that's when you find out who your Soulmate is.

"I need to check on her now," I say, but my head still aches like I fell from a tower.

Opaline grins, her feline eyes shining as she studies my face. "About that. I don't think it's a good idea for you to travel in this state."

Looking down at me, I first notice a fresh scar. It's located just above my heart, and the memory of the sword sticking out of my chest makes the world spin around me.

As I examine the wound, I observe something strange. The scar is black instead of the typical red color of a fresh injury. I run my finger over it, feeling the bumpy surface.

What can cause such a strange occurrence?

I know wounds can sometimes turn a dark red or purple as they heal, but I have never seen a wound turn completely black. Is it some kind of infection, or perhaps a result of the sword that caused the wound?

My eyes drift past my chest, and that's when I register I'm entirely naked.

I overlook the water surface for something to cover me, but nothing is within reach. Scrambling, I press my hands against my dick and stare at Opaline, who's smiling right back at me.

"Don't worry. I saw nothing," she says, making another circle in the lagoon. "Soulin already hates me for saving your ass, and if she finds out I saw you undressed, I think she will burn my kingdom to the ground."

I have so many questions. Why am I here? How did I get here? And who undressed me and brought me into the lagoon?

But my biggest question that I can't shake is: where is Soulin?

"I need to talk to your mother," I say, pushing all my questions aside.

I know Opaline. She means well, and I'm aware of it, but I need answers, and she won't give them to me freely.

"She's still not on speaking terms with me. You see, she didn't know about me sneaking out of Tenacoro to support Soulin, and she's still furious about that. I guess I can't blame her. But nothing happened. I'm well."

"Many of my soldiers died. I'm not even sure if Soulin is alive," I say, my eyes searching for an escape.

"You would know if she's dead," Opaline answers, swimming away from me. "I know little about your Soulmate Connections, but I do know that you will feel her pain as if it's yours. Maybe not with the same severity, but you would know if she's hurt."

I never really spent time thinking about what a connection would feel like. Even though my heart was always set on Soulin, I knew I would never be lucky enough to call her mine. Therefore, I didn't want to waste my time thinking about what it might feel like to desire another woman.

Thinking of Soulin sends warmth between my legs. I scoot my butt closer to the rock wall behind me to hide the erection under my hands.

I need to get to her. *I need her now!*

"Whatever you're thinking about, it's not going to happen," Opaline says, her eyes fixated on mine.

How does she know what I'm thinking?

"Your eyes darkened like you're ready to mate," Opaline answers with a smile, and instantly, I relax my facial muscles to release the tension around my eyes.

After a few breaths to calm my heart, I stand up, still covering my private parts. "You don't understand. All I can think about is her."

Opaline's smile washes away. "And all she can think about is to kill you."

Confusion clouds my mind. "Why would you say that?"

"Because she sent a messenger, and her message was clear. If you cross the Crymzon Wall, she will *not* hesitate to eliminate you."

I exhale sharply through my nose. "But that makes little sense. She's my Soulmate."

And I'm her only weakness, I think to myself as I connect the dots.

Soulin wouldn't react this way if she didn't feel the same about me. She wouldn't spare her resources to warn me if I wasn't a genuine threat.

"That's exactly why I need to go to her," I say, making my way to some thick roots reaching into the water from the higher ground.

"Did you not hear me?" Opaline asks slowly. "She *will* kill you if you enter Crymzon."

"And I can't wait for her to try," I say, tapping into the new magic inside me.

Soulin might be the strongest Crymzonian because of our Soulmate Connection, but I'm a close second, which finally puts me in the position to fight back.

FIFTY-TWO

QUEEN SOULIN

E ven though my chambers are restored, it feels different.

The usual tumult around me is gone, and my heart aches momentarily when I think about Myra. I wait for her to appear on my doorstep or burst into my chambers, but as long as I stare at my door, it stays empty.

No, I don't need her.

Reminding myself why I sent her away eases the pain in my chest a little.

Still, something is missing.

I feel it burning a hole in my heart without leaving a trace of an actual wound.

I stare at my reflection, noticing the white strand of hair. It shouldn't be there. My power should have taken care of the discoloration, returning it to its red color the second the Soulmate Connection hit me. Huffing, I push it under my curls to hide it again.

In a few hours, my army will be home. They will arrive, unknowing that Crymzon fell while they were in the middle of the battle and that I restored it for their return.

I contemplated creating a feast for them to show my gratitude, but to be honest, while they fought well in my absence, they ran like cowards when the actual threat arrived.

In return for their bravery in facing Keres' army without me, I'm giving them a day's sleep. And then, I will hold the grandest ceremony Crymzon has seen in centuries. I will present the Painite to my subjects and offer it to Lunra for everyone to see.

This gesture will help strengthen their belief in me so they don't turn on me as the cowards on the streets did.

I still wonder how they slipped through my guards' hands. My order was clear: all subjects unwilling to fight would be captured and imprisoned until my return. Someone didn't do their job, and I need to find out who.

Pushing that thought to the back of my mind to revisit later, I think about the next few hours until receiving my army. It will be enough time to call for a Council meeting after the Heiligbaum is restored. Then, I can finally use my secret weapon, Cyrus, to get at least Eternitie on my side.

My time is limited to hit Keres again before he can rebuild his army. The number of soldiers we were up against in Terminus couldn't have been his entire force. He has been collecting Undead for years and this time I'm estimating to face a few hundred, maybe even thousands of them.

Without having control over it, I keep repeating the words Keres said to me.

Your magic won't work on me this time. I'm made of dead cells, shadows, and a God's power.

That's why I need King Citeus. Maybe the gadgeteers know how to trap and kill Otyx's worst creation because my magic seemed to leave Keres unfazed.

You've learned nothing since your mother died.

What lesson did I miss?

How horrible life is without a family? I got that one down.

How hard it is to lead a kingdom without magic? I also did that.

Nothing comes to my mind that could indicate that all of this is my fault. On the contrary, he forced me to raise an army. Because of him, I had to learn how to shield my heart.

Then my mind wanders to the only person who can help me now; the only person still inside the palace.

Cyrus.

Since my return, I haven't checked on my prisoners. But I didn't need to. Even though the outside walls of the palace saw the most damage, there was no way he jumped hundreds of feet and survived. Plus, he would never leave that girl behind, the Starstrandian.

As I leave my chair and look outside the open window, I see little dots appear in the distance. My army is faster than expected, so I need to get going if I want to send out the invitations to the other kingdoms and check on Cyrus.

As I stroll through the grand halls of my palace, I take in the sights and sounds of my home before it fills with the noises of returning staff and guards.

Conrad, who has been standing outside my door, follows a few steps behind, but I hardly notice him, lost in thought as I walk.

He was fast delivering my message to Tenacoro, and even quicker returning home with his family. I'm still clueless about how he managed to do all that within a few hours, but I'm still trying to wrap my head around how the world used to work with magic again.

I must get to the throne room to send my moths to the other Kings and Queens. As I approach a familiar corridor, I pause, my instincts suddenly pulling me in a new direction. Without a second thought, I turn and follow the feeling toward a door that seems to lure me in.

My heart races as I reach out to touch the doorknob, and I feel a mix of excitement and fear, even though I use my magic to suppress any emotions. I wonder what's behind the door and why I'm suddenly drawn to it so strongly.

With a deep breath, I push it open and gasp as I step into a room I know too well. In a panic, I slam the door shut behind me to keep Conrad out.

The morning sun fills the space, showing off ripped fabrics and furniture pieces scattered across the floor. A large, ornate mirror stands in the room's corner, and when I look into it, I notice that my reflection is not alone. Standing next to me is a figure I don't recognize, a man who looks just like Khaos, but he's somehow different.

I stumble back in shock, unsure of what to make of the strange figure in the mirror.

Is it some kind of illusion or a trick of the light?

I look around the room, but I'm still alone. Khaos can't be here. He's hundreds of miles away in Tenacoro.

Slowly, I step closer, studying the reflection more closely. His hair is styled differently. It's sleek and pulled back, his clothing more elaborate, and his expression more confident and assured.

Thinking about his critical state when I yelled at Opaline to leave, turns my stomach around. I'm not brainless. I know why he was in Terminus. He was there for me.

The memories almost force my knees to buckle. This weakness, whenever I think about him, will kill me.

Get out of my head, I think as I close my eyes and triple down on the magic to shove my feelings aside.

Get out!

He's still there when I open my eyes again, and this time he's grinning at me.

Why won't my magic work? Why can't I suppress this horrible feeling inside my heart?

His smile sends a shiver down my spine, making the power boil in my veins.

All I want is for him to wrap his arms around me and hold me before pulling my head back on my hair to kiss me.

Leave me alone, I think over and over again, pressing my fingernails into my palms.

My connection to him is already stronger than I expected. Every cell in my brain is filled with him.

Furious, my face twisted into a scowl, I pace back and forth in his private chambers. I bend down, pick up a wooden piece that used to be a vital part of his bed, and slam it against the stone floor.

Why him?

Why?

As I approach a pile of tarnished fabric, I raise another wooden board high and bring it down with a forceful slam. But as the wood makes contact with the ground, there's a sudden, sharp crack. My eyes widen in surprise as shattering glass fills the chamber, causing me to pause mid-strike.

A quiet hissing noise fills the room, growing louder and louder.

Suddenly, there's movement from within the pile of fabric. With a rustle and a hiss, a creature emerges, its form slithering and writhing. It's a strange, otherworldly abomination with a body made of twisted vines that forms an enormous feline with glowing, pulsating orbs as eyes. As it rises to its full height, it lets out an ear-piercing screech—something human yet animalistic.

I step back, my anger forgotten, as I gaze upon the strange creature.

With a sudden movement, it launches at me, its vines snaking out to wrap around me before they turn into long talons.

My eyes fall on a shattered gadget beneath its feet, and I see another beast crawling out of it.

Sharp nails bury into my chest before I can summon my magic, and this is when I realize that I've unleashed something beyond my understanding.

Its intention becomes apparent as its talons dig into my skin: it's here to kill me.

ABOUT THE AUTHOR

C.K. Franziska is the author of the finished A *Speck of Darkness* series, and her second series, The Crymzon Chronicles. She is the wife of a traveler, as well as the mother of two mini versions of herself and way too many pets. In her spare time, she is also a photographer, traveler, full-time entertainer, and animal lover. She does her best writing at night, at the beach listening to the waves, or while camping. C.K. loves to play make-believe, transporting readers to a place where the heroes have to step out of the seemingly endless cycle of family curses, where the magic is as beautiful and untamable as we think, and where every person deserves to be celebrated.